I0699434

When Jesus Leads

MARTHA GAYLE

Hardback ISBN: 979-8-9915560-4-0s

Paperback ISBN: 979-8-9915560-3-3

eBook ISBN: 979-8-9915560-5-7

Contents

ACKNOWLEDGMENTS

As the Lord led me to write the sequel, When Jesus Leads, of my first book, When Jesus Calls, I want to thank Him for this journey. As I reflected on my personal life, from the first words on the page until the end, I cried, laughed, and prayed often. My heart found healing on many occasions.

This journey of my life has been one that could only be given by Jesus as He has allowed me to share my story with the world. He encouraged me, held me up, comforted me and showed me His overwhelming love.

I want to dedicate this book to my daughter who shared this journey of faith with me. She has been a beautiful light in my life and a treasured gift from the Lord. The bond that we have as mother and daughter, regardless of the trials we face, will never be broken. God is with us!

I would also like to dedicate my writings to my daddy, who has passed from this earth to be with Jesus. My daddy was, without a doubt, one of my most incredible supporters. He was an amazing dad and one of the most selfless people I have ever met. He never had the opportunity to read my published books, but I know he is with Jesus, which gives me much peace.

Daddy, I will miss you, and until I see you again, I will keep doing what you taught me, which is to love as Jesus does, sometimes even when it hurts.

Most importantly, I would like to give God all the glory for this book. He gave me the courage to pursue my dream of writing and the words to write, and I pray that the truth of the gospel changes lives.

Many have been deceived into believing they are not worthy of His love. Do not believe the lie of the enemy. You are worthy in Jesus' name. He loves you deeply!

In *John 11:40, Jesus said, "Did I not tell you that if you believed, you would see the glory of God?"*

Always believe and never give up!

Martha Gayle

1

SECOND THOUGHTS

Mary sat at her office desk and stared out of the window. She could see the bench in the garden. The garden was beautiful and no matter what the season the colors were always spectacular. As she watched a couple of rabbits playing in the distance, Mary remembered how she used to love to sit there during her lunch breaks. She realized she had not been there in a while and began to think about her life. She had many questions: "Why is my life changing so drastically? What does this all mean, Lord?"

Mary had dreamed of a perfect life, but after her divorce from Edward due to his infidelity, she had learned that, in a fallen world, perfection wasn't possible.

Mary had beautiful, long blonde hair and a heart bigger than the world—at least, this is what her friends always insisted.

She sat there for what felt like just a short time, but when she looked at the time on her phone, she saw it had been over fifteen minutes. She realized how confused she had been and continued to hear the words from her friends and family, "What are you doing?" and "Why are you doing this?" She began to realize there was a war raging in her mind, but she desired to follow Jesus above all else. She felt broken, confused, and even scared at times, unsure of the path she was on and the decisions she was making.

Meeting Jimmy had felt almost like a dream, but now it was becoming increasingly real to Mary. While sitting there, Mary reflected on the day they met. Jimmy came into the Inn where she worked as sales and marketing director, and as he sat across from her at her desk, he asked for a donation for a woman in need, Ms. Lizzy.

The Mercy Center, where Jimmy was staying, helped the needy in the community, and donations from local businesses helped them to meet the needs of others.

Mary agreed to donate a room for Ms. Lizzy and a twenty-dollar per day food allowance while her condemned home was being replaced. One of their business mission statements was to focus on the needs in the community.

This was long ago, and the memory of how God spoke to Mary before Jimmy left, saying, "Mary, love him and keep this relationship pure," was a profound memory for her, one that would never leave her memory.

God gave Mary a vision of Jimmy being a humble man and maybe a preacher of some kind.

Three days later, Jimmy told her that God spoke to him and said, "Jimmy, be honest with Mary. She is one of mine." Jimmy had never heard God speak to him, and feeling he would never see her again, he told her the truth. The truth was that he was not at the Mercy Center donating his time. He was there because of his addiction, and they took him in.

After months of Mary trying to understand what God had asked of her and desiring to follow God's will, they dated—mostly with another couple, as Mary was afraid.

Mary sat at her desk and reflected on that day in her mind.

Thinking back, the profound sovereignty of God brought tears to her eyes.

Jimmy was a tall, handsome man with a great personality, but because of his addiction in the past, he had lost everything. He prayed God would save his life and restore his family, and while seeking help, the Mercy Center helped him to start over.

This was the time when Jimmy met Mary.

Mary had never used drugs, and although being in church her entire life, she didn't like addicts. She was frightened of drugs as she had heard too many stories of how they destroyed so many lives. Not only the addict's life but their families too.

Jimmy had a marketing background and had worked tirelessly in the past doing sponsorships. He was very good at his career until he took the wrong path that led to his addiction.

Mary had second thoughts. "I can't do this," she thought to herself. "This is too hard." She was afraid.

Mary thought about Jimmy's phone call when he'd told her about the time he had met with Pastor Butch's friend, Brian. Brian had a similar past to Jimmy's, and God had called him into ministry years ago. He was a profound testimony of God's mercy and goodness.

God had led Jimmy to Brian, a new friend, and while he was praying with Jimmy, a miracle happened.

Mary remembered the sound of Jimmy's voice trembling as he called her to share the experience of what felt like a violent wind going through his body and how unworthy he felt that God would touch him in such a powerful way.

Mary remembered the phone call, and while raising her arms toward Heaven, she said, "Thank you, Lord; you have Jimmy now."

Mary thought about God's power and sovereignty and remembered once more the words God had given her: "Mary, love him and keep this relationship pure."

Mary was reminded of the scripture in *John 3:8 – "The wind blows wherever it pleases. You hear its sound, but you cannot tell where it comes from or where it is going. So it is with everyone born of the Spirit."*

This happened to Jimmy, Lord; He was born in your Spirit. Mary thought.

Mary couldn't wrap her mind around what had happened back then, and was still now trying to understand it all. She knew God was calling her to do something which she didn't know how to do. She was afraid of his past, but He kept reminding her not to be afraid. Almost everyone who she knew attempted to talk her out of it and told her to run; but Mary couldn't run. She wanted to, but something kept her walking forward, and she knew that it must be God.

While shrugging her shoulders and her mind spinning in thoughts of doubt, Mary looked to Heaven and sought peace from God. At that moment, the Lord's words from *Matthew 8:26* resounded in her mind, *"You of little faith, why are you so afraid?"* This was a gentle reminder of the power of faith.

After months of dating and Mary trying to trust God in His will for her life, at times, she felt like she was on a rollercoaster of emotions.

However, Jimmy had asked Mary to marry him, and because she wanted to follow Jesus' will in her life, she had agreed.

Mary's thoughts turned to Elizabeth and the impact of Mary's decision on their lives. Their time together was precious, and Mary cherished their bond. She knew a father figure would benefit Elizabeth, but was Jimmy the right one? She could see God's work in Jimmy's life, which gave her hope. But above all, she was a mother, and her primary concern was Elizabeth's well-being.

Mary had second thoughts about Jimmy and especially about marrying him. She desperately wanted to run the other way and had no idea how she would follow God's calling in her life. *This was not my plan,* she thought. "This was not what I prayed for," Mary spoke out loud.

As Mary sat at her desk, daydreaming about her life, the sound of thunder boomed outside, making Mary jump. A few seconds later, she saw lightning flash through the window. The storm came quickly, and as she stood to look out of the window, she could see the trees swaying in the strong winds. The flashes of lightning were powerful, and the sound of thunder rumbled across the dark sky.

This frightened Mary as she didn't like storms.

Mary was always reminded of times when she had read about how devastating storms could be. They could change a family's life in an instant.

As the wind blew harder and lightning flashed, Mary was reminded of how suddenly life can change. "This storm caught me off guard," Mary said.

In a panic, Mary picked up her phone to check the weather radar and was thankful to see that the storm was almost over. The sky would be clear for the rest of the week.

In this stage of her life, Mary felt as if she was battling a twenty-foot wave, and as it was pushing her back, Jesus was saying, "Keep walking forward, Mary. Stay with me."

Mary realized that following Jesus sometimes meant doing hard things, but she quickly realized He knew what was best for her. After all, this world was about making disciples and being a light in a dark world. She knew she didn't have the strength to do what God had called her to do, and she needed to receive her strength from Jesus to go on with the journey He had set before her. She also knew that struggles would come, but He would get her through whatever came.

As the storm passed, Mary felt grateful. She thought of the rain, how important it was for the flowers to grow, and all the beautiful things God provided us with. It's like our life as we walk with Jesus and how our seasons change. She thought of the scripture *Ecclesiastes 3: 1-2, "There is a time for everything, a season for every activity under the heavens: a time to be born and a time to die, a time to plant and a time to uproot."*

Mary knew her season in life was changing, and she would embrace it as she allowed Jesus to lead.

2

A NEW SCHOOL YEAR

The summer was almost over and had been jam-packed with book signings. Patricia had taken care of Elizabeth during the days that Mary had to work at the Inn. Mary's daughter and Faith had become inseparable. Elizabeth loved to travel with Mary to the book signings. Faith and Patricia would often also come along. They all enjoyed being together as frequently as they could.

Patricia was a beautiful girl and a loyal friend to Mary. She had married her high school sweetheart, Paul. Paul was a youth leader at their church, and he always strived to be a great husband to Patricia.

Faith was Patricia and Paul's daughter and Elizabeth's best friend. Elizabeth was born shortly after Faith, and they spent a lot of time together.

Patricia was blessed to have Paul as her husband. He was a great man. He loved Jesus and his character showed it. She was a great baker too and always made homemade bread. Mary loved her bread and occasionally had her make it for her family when they came into town.

Patricia's dad became a deacon in the church when she was in her teens and the family life became more stable as he began to lead as Jesus would have him lead. Her life as a child was not what she had hoped it would be.

School was starting the following Monday, but Mary and Elizabeth were not looking forward to it. Mary had often wished she could homeschool but knew that, as the only provider, she couldn't.

The phone rang, and as Mary looked down at her phone, she realized it was Jimmy. As she answered the call, the tone of his voice sounded happy.

Jimmy asked if they could spend some time together over the weekend. Mary agreed they could. They made plans to spend the day together on Saturday with Elizabeth.

Mary told Jimmy she had to go as her phone was ringing. This time it was Karen.

Karen was a loyal and fantastic friend who had always been there for Mary when she needed her. She was known to drop everything she was doing to run to Mary's side, and she was a great support to Mary when Elizabeth was born.

Karen had been an advertising agent for over five years when her husband Sam thought she should leave her career to be a stay-at-home wife. They were trying to have a baby, and it had been very difficult for them. Karen prayed often about it and hoped that one day that would be His plan for them.

Karen had concerns about Jimmy and had called to remind Mary that she needed to be careful.

Mary understood what Karen was saying and answered, "I know Karen, and I have almost decided to back out. I can't do this!" I can't marry Jimmy, she thought to herself. What in the world would our life be like? "Karen, I must make the right decision here," Mary said.

Karen was relieved as she hung up, knowing that Mary was thinking more clearly and understood her concerns.

When Karen's call disconnected, Mary picked up the phone and called Jimmy. She told him that her plans for the weekend had changed and that she and Elizabeth would not be available. She also realized that she and Patricia were going shopping to pick up some things the girls needed for their new school year.

Jimmy was disappointed and did not seem to understand. Mary was perplexed but knew she needed time to think about her and Elizabeth's future and would not rush into anything.

Mary's emotions were up and down, but one thing kept coming back to her: She wanted to follow Jesus above all else. She prayed continuously and felt peace knowing that He was with her. She began to speak *Psalm 17:8, "Keep me as the apple of your eye; hide me in the shadow of your wings, Lord."*

Mary decided to change her focus as she realized she needed to check her emails and get some work done. Mr. Henry then walked in with a big grin on his face. Mary was surprised to see him and asked why he was so happy. He began to tell her that the Inn had won an award for the "Most Charming Resort." He told her she was mentioned in the article, and her service had been fantastic for everyone working with her.

"Wow!" said Mary. "This is wonderful news."

Mr. Henry handed her the article to read. "Congratulations, Mary. We should celebrate with a chocolate cupcake." They both began to laugh.

The sparkler-topped cupcake Mr. Henry had given Mary to celebrate her buying the cottage would always be a fun memory for Mary. She remembered the feeling of love and encouragement that he had shown her that day. She loved Mr. Henry, and he knew it.

As Mary sat there reading the article, she whispered a prayer, "Lord, thank you!"

Mr. Henry had been Mary's boss for many years. He was a short man and always wore expensive suits. He was charming, and everyone that met him loved him. He seemed to light up any room he walked in with his smile.

Mr. Henry had an unexpected diagnosis of cancer a couple of years back and had discussed Mary taking his position at the Inn.

Mary prayed about this decision and decided she couldn't take on the responsibility. After God healed him of his cancer, both Mr. Henry and Mary were happy about their choices. They both couldn't thank God enough for His healing power. This humbled Mr. Henry.

Mr. Henry was a friend to everyone, and everyone knew it. They often came to him for advice.

Mary opened her emails and could not believe the number she had about her book. She found one that was very uplifting to her.

"Thank you for your book, "When Jesus Calls!" I bought it and began reading it the same day. I could not put it down. You have encouraged me so much, as I haven't felt worthy of the love of Jesus so many times. You have inspired me to understand that Jesus does love me, even in all my mess. I have felt the weight of the world lift from me. I have repented my sins and know that He has forgiven me. The closeness I feel to Him is beautiful, and I am so happy that I no longer feel condemnation. I will seek to be more like Him and allow Him to work in my heart."

Pam

Mary sat back in her chair and began to cry. She was so happy that God was using her to give peace to the weary, particularly as she sometimes didn't feel worthy herself.

God always encouraged Mary through His word. She could not even begin to imagine her life without Him.

The rest of the day seemed to go by quickly, and it was soon time for her to pick up Elizabeth from Patricia's. She closed her laptop, grabbed her purse, and walked out the door.

As she arrived, Elizabeth was happy to see her mom. Mary and Patricia talked for a few minutes about their days. They both had had a great day, and Mary was excited about getting home.

Elizabeth hugged Faith and said goodbye.

As they walked in the cottage door, JJ was waiting for them. Sunshine ran through the house, and they laughed as the bell on her collar jingled. Elizabeth sat down on the floor and JJ came running to her. She was happy to see them both.

Mary had bought the cottage while living in an apartment before Elizabeth was born.

The cottage was perfect. The yellow paint and white trim were precisely as Mary had hoped for when she found it. The ocean was close, with a private walkway. It had two bedrooms and two full baths. One looked out over the ocean and the other one was at the back of the house. The living room was charming, with beams in the ceiling and shiplap on the walls. The kitchen opened into the living room and was always wonderful when she had gatherings with her friends.

Mary hoped she never had to leave the cottage as it was the only home Elizabeth knew, and she loved it there. She loved the walks on the beach and JJ loved it too.

Elizabeth asked her mom if she could walk JJ on the beach for a few minutes. Mary agreed. JJ loved walking on the beach, and Mary was always reluctant to let Elizabeth go alone. She knew the rules for staying close to the cottage and could see her through the kitchen window.

Mary began to prepare dinner and decided she would make Elizabeth's favorite. She loved spaghetti, and Mary thought it would be quick and easy. She was tired from her day.

After cooking the ground beef and filling her pot with water to boil, she peeked out the window to check on Elizabeth. She didn't see her and JJ anywhere. She immediately turned down the burners on the stove and walked out onto the deck. She began calling for Elizabeth and received no answer. This frightened Mary! She walked down the dock toward the ocean in a panic and saw Elizabeth and JJ walking back toward the cottage.

Mary was relieved. As Elizabeth got closer to her, Mary, in a panicked voice, said, "Where were you? You scared, Mom!"

In her innocence, Elizabeth had not thought about how far away from the cottage she had walked and told Mary she was sorry.

Mary hugged her and said, "It's okay, but you know the rules. Mom would be so miserable if I lost you."

Elizabeth hugged her mom and said, "Mom, I'm sorry, I love you."

Mary realized she was overreacting, but the world had become a little scary, and she felt she couldn't be protective enough of her daughter.

When they got inside, Elizabeth pulled out the paper to review the school supplies she needed and discussed them with her mom.

Mary finished preparing dinner, and while draining the pasta, she looked at Elizabeth with a proud smile. Elizabeth smiled back with a giggle. Elizabeth's giggle was always a joyful sound to Mary. Elizabeth knew how blessed she was, and Mary loved her with all her heart.

Mary was proud of Elizabeth and knew that life was different for her because she did not have a father figure. They never talked about it, though, as Mary knew she couldn't change anything and saw her life as a blessing.

Dinner was ready, and they sat down together to eat. Mary began to say the blessing to thank Jesus for their food.

Mary attempted to always remember to ask Elizabeth how her day went. Sometimes, she had a lot on her mind, and forgot, but Mary wanted her daughter to always know that how she felt was important to her.

Elizabeth began to tell her about a new kid in her gymnastics class. Her name was Morgan. Morgan had moved from the west coast and had no friends yet. Her dad had taken a new position they couldn't turn down, so he moved his family there. The move was hard for Morgan as she had many friends in the town they lived in and had to say goodbye to all of them. Elizabeth told Mary how she introduced Morgan to her friends.

Mary could feel Elizabeth's joy. Mary had always tried to set an example for Elizabeth to be kind to others and never judge them.

Mary asked Elizabeth if she wanted Morgan to come to spend the night soon. With another childlike giggle, she quickly answered with a yes!

"I will ask her next time I'm at Gymnastics," Elizabeth said.

Mary was pleased that Elizabeth had met a new friend and was so encouraged about how she had treated her.

As they sat down to eat, Mary began to pray. *"Lord, thank you for your protection today and all the blessings you continue giving us daily. Thank you for the heart you have given my daughter to love people and make them feel special. Please use this food to nourish our bodies. In Jesus' name, we pray, Amen."*

The spaghetti was delicious, and their time together talking was always precious to Mary.

Elizabeth looked at Mary and said, "Mom, you're the best!"

Mary smiled and said, "Ditto, my sweet girl."

The phone rang, and it was Patricia. "Hi, Patricia," Mary said as she picked up the phone.

Patricia began the call by asking Mary if she could keep Faith after their shopping trip and that she would pick her up on Sunday.

Elizabeth heard the conversation and ran into the room excitedly, saying, "Mom, yes!"

Mary smiled at Elizabeth and said to Patricia, "Of course we will, Patricia." Mary agreed the time was great and thought they might go to the town pizza restaurant for dinner.

Night had come, and it was time for Elizabeth to shower and get ready for bed. When she had finished, she entered the living room in her pajamas. She had a real style for pajamas, as most had patterns that always reminded Mary of her sassy personality. Organic cotton was her favorite fabric, but the pattern was just as important to her.

Mary was sitting on the couch with JJ and had her laptop open. She was reading her emails. Elizabeth enjoyed hearing how readers responded to Mary's book, so Mary often read one or two to her when she could.

This was the perfect time, she thought. "Hey, baby," Mary said. "Come sit with me and JJ." They snuggled together on the couch, and Mary asked if she wanted to hear one of the emails she had received.

Elizabeth shrugged her shoulders and nodded her head, yes, with excitement.

Mary began to read:

"Mary, thank you so much for the inspiration you gave me through your book, "When Jesus Calls." I needed to tell you that.

You have inspired me more than you can imagine. I am young, and as you know, peer pressure is very real today. You have helped me understand the importance of looking to Jesus and protecting my heart. You have saved me from pain. I am learning to stay closer to Jesus, and I thank you!"

Samantha

Elizabeth looked at Mary and smiled. She loved snuggling up with Mary, so she put her arms around her and hugged her. JJ was still sitting next to them, and the thought of her life now comforted Mary.

Mary told Elizabeth it was time to get into bed, and they both got up from the couch and walked to her bedroom. She climbed into bed. Mary tucked her in tight, listened to her say her prayers, and kissed her goodnight.

Mary returned to the living room with JJ and reopened her laptop. She wanted to reply to any emails she had received before bed, but she was tired and needed to get into bed as well.

After answering them all, Mary entered her room, changed into her pajamas, grabbed her journal, and crawled into bed. JJ came right behind her.

Mary journaled, read her bible for a few minutes, then decided to write for a while.

Mary wrote for about an hour until she couldn't stay awake any longer. She put her laptop down and closed it. She got up to check on Elizabeth, went back to bed, and fell asleep.

At the sound of her alarm clock, Mary reached over to turn it off. She stretched, and as she put her feet on the floor, she heard Elizabeth calling her. She ran into her room to see if she was okay. Elizabeth had had a bad dream.

Mary comforted her, sat on the bed beside her, and asked her to tell her about it.

Elizabeth explained that they had moved to a strange town in her dream, and she was attending a new school.

Mary hugged her tightly and told her they were not moving and that she would not be going to a new school. She explained that she may have had the dream because her new friend Morgan had moved and reminded her of the story she had told her at dinner.

Elizabeth looked at Mary and smiled. She prayed, reassured her that all would be okay, and said, "Now, we better get dressed for our shopping trip. We need to meet Patricia and Faith soon."

Mary went into her room and jumped in the shower. She decided to be a little more casually dressed, as it was Saturday. She enjoyed dressing down on the weekends.

They sat down and read their bibles together before leaving. Mary prayed for protection and a joyful day in Jesus.

Finally, they were all together at the Galleria. They were late getting Elizabeth's school supplies as their weekends had been so busy. "This will be a great day. It looks as if there are many sales. Maybe we picked the best time," Mary said.

Elizabeth and Faith had similar tastes in clothing, so together, they all looked around and found some adorable pieces they loved for their new school year. They could also find all the necessary supplies, such as pencils, notebooks, etc., on their list. All boxes were checked. Elizabeth and Faith were ready for a new school year.

Mary said, "Hey, let's go grab some lunch. How does a hot sub sound?" The Galleria had a great sub shop, and everyone could choose whatever they wanted on them.

As they ate lunch, they talked about their new school year. Mary asked if they were excited.

Elizabeth and Faith both looked at each other, then Elizabeth spoke up, "Not really, because we will miss each other during the days. But hopefully we will often see each other on the weekends."

Elizabeth hoped Morgan would be in some of her classes, too.

They had had a busy day shopping and had arrived back at the cottage. Everyone seemed to be tired.

Patricia thanked Mary for allowing Faith to spend the night, and Mary insisted she was grateful she was here and never minded watching over her.

"You have been so good helping me with Elizabeth all summer, and I could never pay you back for that," Mary said. "The girls always have fun, and we will get pizza for dinner."

Patrica agreed to pick her up around noon Sunday, hugged the girls and Mary, then left.

The weekend went by quickly. They all enjoyed being together, and the laughter from the girls gave Mary a peaceful feeling. She loved how Elizabeth and Faith got along so well, and because they had no other siblings, they loved being together.

Mary also got a little time to herself that she needed so much and was able to read for a few hours. She had not talked to Jimmy or spent any time with him.

Monday morning had arrived, and a new school year was here.

Elizabeth looked forward to meeting her new classmates and her 4th-grade year.

As they pulled up in the carpool line, Elizabeth reached over, kissed her mom, and said, "I love you, Mom."

Mary smiled and said, "I love you too, sweetheart. Have a great day at school, Elizabeth."

Mary stayed a minute or two and watched Elizabeth walk into the school. She heard a horn blow, and an impatient parent asked her to move out of the way. Mary quickly realized she was holding up the line and pulled away.

As she drove to work, Mary thought about how busy everyone was all the time and how so many memorable moments were missed because of it.

As Mary struggled to find a balance in her life, she realized, most importantly, that no matter what was happening around her, the Lord gives joy that no one can take away. "We must always keep our eyes on Him," she said out loud. Mary began to pray. *"Lord, thank you for the joy and peace you give me. Thank you for being my source of true peace, no matter what comes at me. Please bless Elizabeth and Faith today as they begin their new school year. Protect them, and may they enjoy their days with friends who love you. It feels hard at times, Lord, watching Elizabeth growing up in such an unbelievable world. My life also seems confusing to me now, but I know you know my comings and goings, my heart, and my future, and you will see me through whatever is before me. In Jesus' name, I pray, Amen."*

Mary quickly thinks of *Psalm 16:11*, *"You make known to me the path of life; you will fill me with joy in your presence, with eternal pleasures at my right hand."* This is the scripture I need to remember, Mary thought. This is so true. If we look to Jesus, He will lead us.

3

UNWELCOME SURPRISE

Mary had a busy day at the Inn. She had had back-to-back appointments all day and felt a little overwhelmed. Although feeling grateful that she had had a good day, she was pleased that the time had passed quickly.

Mary was excited about picking Elizabeth up from her first day of school. Elizabeth would skip after-school camp at Gymnastics, as the transition from summer to back to school would already be a long day for her daughter. Mary wanted to spend the rest of the day with her. Maybe we will go get some ice cream to celebrate, Mary thought.

Mary was eager to hear about her first day. Elizabeth always liked to tell her a story with a little drama in it, and Mary loved listening.

As Mary arrived at the school, she sat in the carpool line, waiting to reach the entrance where Elizabeth would be waiting. She thought of Elizabeth's first day of kindergarten and was reminded how the principal had persuaded her not to walk her in.

Mary felt happy but sad because she knew Elizabeth was growing up so quickly.

Mary had finally reached the entrance, and Elizabeth waved at her as she walked over to the car. She seemed very excited and was grinning. Mary had a feeling she'd had a great day.

Elizabeth excitedly said, "Mom, Morgan is in my class! We were so happy to see each other this morning. She is so nice, mom. I am so glad we are friends now!"

Elizabeth talked about her day and how much she thought she would like her teacher. She shared that her teacher wore small, thin, wire-frame glasses and reminded her of a librarian. She seemed very nice too. Elizabeth was also ecstatic that Faith had the same lunch schedule as her, so they could sit together to eat.

Mary was excited to hear the news and always loved Elizabeth's descriptive way of sharing.

"Well, Elizabeth, this makes Mom very happy. It sounds like you had an amazing day," Mary said.

"I did, Mom," Elizabeth told her. "But you'll never guess. I have homework already. I dread that part so much!"

Mary laughed out loud.

Elizabeth was surprised when Mary drove up to the ice cream shop. Giggling the only way Elizabeth knew how, she looked at Mary and said, "Wow, Mom, you're the best."

They walked into the ice cream shop to discover the line was very long.

"Everyone must have had the same idea," Mary said.

Elizabeth was looking around to see if she recognized anyone she knew. She didn't.

Finally, they had reached the counter and Mary and Elizabeth ordered their favorites on waffle cones.

They both said, "Yummy" at the same time. They were grateful for the treat. Mary thought they deserved it.

Mary looked at Elizabeth and said, "I am proud of you, Elizabeth."

Elizabeth, with a beaming smile, answered, "Thank you, Mom."

When they arrived home, they walked up the driveway to the cottage. It was then that they saw a package on the deck by the door.

"Hmm," Mary said. "I don't remember ordering anything. I wonder what that is?"

Elizabeth ran over to it and looked at the label. She looked up at Mary with a 'don't know what it is' look, shrugged her shoulders and darted into the cottage.

Mary picked up the package. Following her daughter into the kitchen, she sat it on the table and asked Elizabeth if she would take JJ for a walk. He was ready to go out. JJ was excited, running around the room while barking.

As Elizabeth and JJ walked out the door, Mary returned to the package and was shocked at what she saw. The return address label had Michael's name on it. What in the world is this, she thought. She did not want to risk Elizabeth returning and seeing her opening it, so she moved it into her bedroom and put it on a shelf in the closet.

Michael was Elizabeth's biological father. Mary unexpectedly met Michael on the beach years ago while walking. He had rented a beach house close to her to finish writing a book he was working on. Mary felt a connection to Michael. She guessed because he was also an author. They enjoyed their time together and spent a few evenings together preparing meals while enjoying sharing each other's stories. One evening after dinner, as Michael kissed her, Mary had allowed her emotions to get the best of her. This decision changed her life forever.

When Mary told Michael she was pregnant, Michael had no interest in having a baby and suggested an abortion or adoption. Mary, angry and heartbroken that Michael would even recommend this, and realizing he was not who she thought he was, asked him to leave. He never came back. Mary was left to bring up Elizabeth alone.

Mary never looked back and considered her choice as a blessing. After all Elizabeth had become her daughter and she could not have been happier about that.

After dinner, Elizabeth sat down to do her homework. Mary was surprised her daughter already had homework; she had to admit, she wasn't looking forward to doing that in the evenings. Homework was always a challenge, as it seemed to take hours to complete.

Mary often wondered why there was always so much to do after spending hours at school. "I'll never understand that," she thought to herself.

Finally, when it was completed, Mary asked if she could check through it. Mary was pleased as she had finished it all with very little help from her. Elizabeth was becoming much more independent now that she was getting older.

Elizabeth packed her books and notebooks into her backpack and hung it up on the hook by the door.

Elizabeth asked her mom if she could take JJ out for another walk.

Mary said, "Yes, but this time, please just take him around the yard."

"Ok, Mom, but I really wanted to take him to the beach."

Mary gave her a look that only Elizabeth understood.

When Elizabeth came back in, she called for Sunshine.

Sunshine became a part of Mary's life before Elizabeth was born. On a cold winter day during a snowstorm, Mary found her scratching on her door at the cottage. She brought her in, fed her, and rescued her from the winter weather. Sunshine was a gift from Jesus, and Mary loved her. She had brought a lot of joy into her home.

A few seconds later, Sunshine ran into the kitchen. Mary said, "She must have been sleeping. This is the first time I've seen her since getting home."

Elizabeth said, "Mom, she's always sleeping."

Sunshine was a great cat who always seemed to be content. As Mary reached down to pet her, she could hear her purring. "You are a happy Sunshine, aren't you, girl?" Mary said.

Mary called JJ over to feed him and checked the food in Sunshine's bowl. It was almost empty, so she refilled it.

It was getting late, and Mary knew Elizabeth was tired from school. She asked her to jump in the shower and put on her pajamas so they could relax for the rest of the evening.

"OK, Mom," Elizabeth agreed.

Mary entered her room while Elizabeth was in the shower and peeked at the box. She was amazed it was from Michael. She put it back on the shelf and closed her closet door.

Mary whispered a prayer, "Lord, help me, please! Give me peace and clarity in Your will for my life. This box has a purpose, Lord. I do not have any idea what it is. I can't bring myself to open it."

In just a few minutes, Elizabeth came out of her room. She was snuggly and looked relaxed. They decided to crawl into Mary's bed and watch a series they had begun to enjoy.

As the first episode finished, Elizabeth looked at Mary and asked if they could watch one more.

Mary smiled and said, "Just one more, young lady. I need to walk JJ, and you have school tomorrow."

They loved this program and could watch a few episodes a night but knew they needed to get some sleep.

Elizabeth loved snuggling up with Mary in her bed. She fell asleep just before the episode ended. Mary tucked her in tightly where she was and called JJ to go out.

When Mary and JJ returned, she entered her bedroom with JJ following her, crawled in next to Elizabeth, turned her lamp light off, whispered her prayers, and fell instantly asleep.

It was morning already, and when Elizabeth woke up, she was surprised she had slept in her mom's bed. Mary rolled over, looked at her with the sweetest smile, and said, "Good morning, princess."

Elizabeth giggled and said, "Why did I sleep here?"

While tickling Elizabeth's belly and giggling herself, Mary told her she had fallen asleep and looked like a little angel. She didn't want to move her. Elizabeth was happy. She loved sleeping next to her mom.

Thursday had come and the week felt long. She was tired and she was ready for a day to rest and write. Those days don't come often enough anymore, Mary thought.

As Mary was driving Elizabeth to school, she remembered telling her not to forget to get Morgan's phone number so she could call her parents. Mary also reminded her that Faith was spending the night, and Patricia would bring her over at six. They had planned to go to the pizza restaurant together.

The day was busy with meetings and clients. Mary had not thought about the box anymore until now. She needed clarification about what was in it and why Michael had sent it. This was troubling her.

She was still thinking about Jimmy and wondered what she would do. I know Jesus told me to love him, she thought to herself, but she had to understand what was being asked of her. She had to know this was God's will for their lives. This can't be it, she thought.

Mary's schedule was clear for the rest of the day, and she was excited about picking Elizabeth up. She left the Inn and drove to Gymnastics. While driving, she thought about Jimmy, the box in the closet from Michael, and felt confused. Mary had no idea what she was going to do.

When they arrived home, Elizabeth took JJ for a walk and returned to find Sunshine curled up asleep on Mary's bed.

Elizabeth was excited about Faith coming over and going out for pizza to celebrate the new school year.

The doorbell rang, and it was Patricia. As they walked in, Patricia hugged Mary. She looked at her strangely before saying, "Is there something wrong?"

Elizabeth heard Patricia and looked up at her mom.

Mary was surprised Patricia had picked up on her feelings.

Elizabeth asked Faith to come into her room. She wanted to show her a new toy she had gotten. This allowed Mary to show Patricia the package that had arrived.

Mary motioned for Patricia to follow her, and they entered the bedroom. As they walked in, Mary closed the door behind them. She walked into the closet and reached for the box.

Patricia was wondering what was going on.

As she got the box down, she looked at Patricia and said, "Look who this is from."

As Patricia looked down at the label, her mouth dropped open. "Are you serious, Mary? What? Why?"

There was a knock at the bedroom door. Mary said, "Just a minute, girls." She quickly put the box back on the shelf, and they left the room.

"Ok, girls," Mary said with a big smile. "It's time to go get some pizza."

Giggling, the two girls grabbed their things, and ran to the car.

Elizabeth had forgotten all about the package. After all, she had a friend with her and was happy to be going out.

Mary drove them to the restaurant, and Patricia sat in the front passenger seat. The drive was only a few minutes long, but they were all hungry when they got there.

On Thursday, the local pizza place was the place to be, as it was always packed. The restaurant had games for the kids to play while they waited for their food.

They sat down to order and decided on a large pepperoni pizza with extra cheese and salads. The salad was not the kids' favorite, but Patricia and Mary encouraged them to eat what they could, as it was healthy.

Elizabeth asked if they could play some games; Mary and Patricia happily agreed.

Mary said, "You two stay together and return in just a few minutes." They both ran off to play. Elizabeth was leading the way.

The second they were gone, Patricia looked at Mary and asked her what she thought was in the package.

"I have no idea what's in it," Mary said. "I haven't talked to Michael since before Elizabeth was born. What in the world could he be sending me now?"

Patricia knew Mary was troubled and attempted to comfort her.

The girls came back to the table laughing. They had a lot of fun together. Faith was bragging about beating Elizabeth in one of the games.

Elizabeth instantly spoke up, saying, "But you cheated."

Then they all began to laugh.

The food came to the table, and it all looked so yummy. Before eating, Mary thanked Jesus for their food.

As they sat eating, Mary received a text from Jimmy. She read it.

Hi, Mary. I just wanted to check on you. I have missed you this week and I hope you are having fun with your friend. Call me when you get the chance.

Mary was irritated with what she was feeling. She didn't like the neediness she felt was coming from Jimmy.

They all finished their meal and were excited about getting home for the evening. They had another day of school tomorrow to get ready for. Faith was spending the night, and Elizabeth was happy. Mary would take them both to school the next day.

As they returned to the cottage, Patricia hugged Faith goodbye and said, "You be good for Mary, baby, ok? I know you will."

Patricia hugged Mary and Elizabeth, then walked out the door.

Elizabeth and Faith ran to Elizabeth's bedroom to play.

JJ was standing at Mary's feet. She reached down to pick him up; she was so happy to see him. JJ always made her smile. He made the cottage a happy place. She put on his leash and took him out for a walk.

Mary loved the feel of Fall in the air, as Fall and Spring were her favorite seasons.

The summer had been scorching, and she felt more tourists were in the area this year than in the past. She was happy to finally get some cooler weather.

"Thanksgiving will be here before we know it," she said to JJ. She talked to him a lot. He always looked up at her, tilting his head as he listened. She then thought how nice it would be to take a week off during the holiday and spend time with Elizabeth. Mary's daddy and sisters had also considered coming, but their plans had changed. Mary was very disappointed as she missed her family so much. Then she thought, maybe Elizabeth, JJ, and I can take a road trip and surprise them this year. That would be so nice, she thought.

Mary and JJ walked back in. She could hear the kids laughing in Elizabeth's room. They were enjoying their time together.

She grabbed her laptop and decided to check her emails. "Oh, look at that," she said out loud. "An email from Michael!" Mary was happy Elizabeth didn't hear her. She read it with interest.

Hi Mary,

I'm sure I am the last person you want to hear from. Please hear me out. I have a lot of regrets that I wasn't there for you and the baby. I know this is hard for you to understand. I didn't tell you what was going on with me, and I made a mistake by not being honest with you. Mary, I had a bad divorce that I never could get over, and I didn't want to bring you and the baby through my emotional journey. I felt you deserved someone better, and I didn't feel as if I could provide you with what you deserved. I ran from you, scared of my past. I have finally understood my need to forgive and to be forgiven by the grace of God. My heart was broken in two, and I did not want to ever go through that again, so I guess, in a sense, I hid those feelings. When I understood Matthew 6:14-15, "For if you forgive other people when they sin against you, your heavenly Father will also forgive you. But if you do not forgive others their sins, your father will not forgive your sins," I realized the need for forgiveness of my own sins. I then knelt on my knees, cried, and asked God to forgive me. Peace has come into my heart now. I can forgive now. It was powerful, Mary! Jesus changed my life, Mary! I am finally feeling free!

I know it's too late, but I wanted to ask if we could talk on the phone sometime. I will try to understand if we can't. I hope you will message me back. I miss you and think of you and the baby all the time. I sent you both a gift. It should be there any day now. Maybe you have already received it. I wish I knew.

Love,

Michael

Mary slammed her computer shut and spoke out loud, "What? Another relationship stopped him from doing what he should have done! Seriously? And he is telling me this now!" She felt angry and hurt. Her heart was broken. She had done all this by herself for so long, and after eight years, he decided he could simply contact her like this and expect her to say, "Oh, ok. Welcome back!" NO! That is not going to happen!

Mary could feel her blood pressure rising. "Why was he doing this? Did he handle anything in his life correctly? I wish I had never met him!" Of course, then she remembered Elizabeth, and she found peace. I can't even imagine my life without Jesus or her, she thought. She then thanked Jesus for her life.

Raising Elizabeth alone had been hard, but no matter what, Jesus was with her, and He gave her the strength she needed to do what He had called her to do.

"Lord, now you are calling me to love Jimmy. How will I do that? I can't trust him to love and provide for us."

The Lord answered, "No, Mary, you can't. Not right now, anyway. But you can trust me."

Mary felt peace wash over her. She wanted so badly to have no fear and just walk in the path that He had called her to. She remembered the scripture in *John 4:18, "There is no fear in love. But perfect love drives out fear because fear has to do with punishment. The one who fears is not made perfect in love."* She began to pray, "Lord, please fill my heart with your perfect love; in Jesus' Name, I pray, Amen."

Mary entered Elizabeth's bedroom where the girls had turned on the TV. They were both falling asleep. "Girls, it's getting late, and you are very tired." Mary had them get up, brush their teeth, and put on their pajamas. As they crawled into bed, Mary tucked them in tightly, said a bedtime prayer, and wished them goodnight.

Mary took JJ out one last time for the night, walked into her bedroom to change her clothes, grabbed her laptop, and sat on her bed. She wrote for a while and began to get very sleepy. She closed her laptop, put it on the table beside her bed, cuddled with JJ, and drifted off to sleep.

Mary woke up at midnight to the sound of her phone ringing. Who was that calling in the middle of the night, she thought. Her heart started pounding as she reached over to pick up her phone to see who it was. Michael's name was on the caller I.D. Shocked, she sat the phone back down. Why would Michael be calling her now, she wondered. Her mind started spinning with thoughts she couldn't get out of her head. She had not talked to Michael since before she had Elizabeth, and there was no way she was letting him back into her life now.

Somehow, through all of that, Mary drifted back off to sleep. At 6 am, she woke up. As she looked over at the clock, she was reminded that it was a work and school day and about Michael's phone call at midnight. She was surprised she had slept once she remembered the phone call. Jesus must have filled me with His peace, she thought. She thought of *Philippians 4:7: "And the peace of God, which transcends all understanding, will guard your hearts and minds in Christ Jesus."*

As Mary got up and walked into the kitchen to switch on her coffeepot, she heard Sunshine running through the living room. She was the funniest and sweetest cat she had ever met. She still loved the idea of Sunshine being solid black, but the name Sunshine fit her so well.

JJ and the girls were still sleeping and had not gotten up yet. She walked into the room and gently woke them up as they needed to hurry and get ready for school.

Mary jumped in the shower, dressed, put on her makeup, and met the girls back in the kitchen. She made waffles, and they ate quickly. Then, she led them out the door.

The girls were enjoying their first week of another school year.

"Yay, today's Friday, girls," Mary said. She was excited!

Elizabeth and Faith were a lot more excited than even Mary was.

The day had been filled with many emotions. Elizabeth and Mary were both adjusting to another season - a season of joy, love, and some uncertainty. Both were continuing to learn to allow Jesus to lead as they trusted Him more fully.

Friday night had arrived, and Faith had begged Patricia if she could spend another night with Elizabeth. Of course, both Mary and Elizabeth were pleased. The girls enjoyed spending so much time together and they agreed it would be great.

Mary spent a quiet night writing while the girls played in Elizabeth's room. Bedtime had arrived, and neither of the girls wanted to go to sleep.

Mary told them they could lie in bed and watch a couple of episodes of their favorite show if they would like, and she would check on them before she turned in for the night. They changed into their pajamas, turned on the TV, and crawled into bed.

Saturday morning had come, and Mary was enjoying her morning having some much needed quiet time alone. Elizabeth and Faith would sleep in. After all, it was the weekend. Elizabeth loved Saturdays as she could stay in bed much longer. She was not much of a morning person, and it was hard for her during the weekdays when she had to get ready for school so early.

The coffee finished brewing, and Mary was happy. She needed her coffee every morning, especially with her favorite, Anderson's Pure Maple Syrup and creamer. As she poured her cup, she heard JJ walking into the kitchen. "Hey, buddy," she said. "I bet you are ready to go outside, right?"

The weather was beautiful, but a little overcast. Rain was expected, and she felt that it would be great as she could do some writing as the girls played. The temperatures were beginning to drop, and the leaves on the trees were changing color. "I love Fall," Mary whispered to herself. "My favorite time of the year."

When she was back inside, she fed JJ, checked Sunshine's food bowl, grabbed her bible and coffee, and sat down to read. She loved relaxing mornings when she didn't have to hurry out the door.

Mary felt sad because she had not spent enough time reading her bible and spending time with Jesus. She knew she needed Him in her life more than anything.

Her phone rang, and she got up to answer it. It was Jimmy. She picked up the phone and said, "Hi Jimmy, how are you?" He was happy she'd answered and asked if they could get together. Mary was reluctant because Elizabeth had company, but she told him he could come over after one o'clock.

Mary told Jimmy she would make dinner, but they had to make it early in the evening because she had to work, and Elizabeth had school the following day.

The morning was restful, and after Elizabeth and Faith woke up, Mary made waffles and warmed some of her favorite syrup to pour on top. They hung around in their pajamas for a while, and Mary talked to the girls about some of the concerns they had about their new school year. She spoke of a few of her favorite scriptures in the hope of comforting them, as she knew growing up and transitioning into another grade level of education would be a concern for them. As she read *Psalm 56:3-4, she said, "When I am afraid, I put my trust in you. In God, whose word I praise – In God, I trust and am not scared. What can mere mortals do to me?"*

The girls opened up to some of their concerns as they discussed each individually. Mary then realized she needed to remember this Psalm as much as anyone.

It was time for showers as Patricia would be there soon to pick Faith up, and Jimmy would be over not long after that. I need to decide what we will have for dinner, Mary thought.

The doorbell rang, and it was Patricia. As always, Faith was happy to see her mom.

Before Patricia left, Mary told her that Jimmy was coming over. She looked at Mary with concern, but Mary reassured her that everything would be okay. As Patricia and Faith left, Mary and Elizabeth sat on the couch next to each other and talked about Jimmy coming over. Elizabeth was excited to see him as she enjoyed his company.

The doorbell rang. It was Jimmy. He was tall and handsome. He had a beautiful smile, and Mary wanted so much to believe that he was a Godly man. She could see the changes in his character but knew of his past, and even after saying, yes, she was terrified of marrying him. She knew what God had asked of her and was still fighting to submit to His will. She was constantly reminded of her need to trust Jesus completely.

Elizabeth ran to the door as he walked in. He had a gift for her: a plush toy of a red dog. He hugged Elizabeth, and as he moved the toy around and brought it to her cheek, making funny sounds, she giggled a lot, and it made Mary smile.

Mary smiled at Jimmy and said hello. She felt happy that he was there. She also liked how Jimmy interacted with Elizabeth and how he would even allow her to play 'salon' with him. She would put bows in his hair, and they always showed Mary the new style as they all laughed hysterically. He loved making Elizabeth laugh, and regardless of what bows or their color, he always enjoyed the game. He knew this made her happy, and because she was pleased, he was too.

The afternoon was peaceful, Mary realizing that Elizabeth enjoyed having Jimmy in their home. Mary loved Jimmy. She didn't have a choice. God poured His love into her heart to love Him, and she knew she couldn't run from it any longer. He reassured her from His word in *Ecclesiastes 3:11, "He has made everything beautiful in its time. He has also set eternity in the human heart, yet no one can fathom what God has done from beginning to end."*

After a delicious dinner, Mary and Elizabeth said goodnight to Jimmy, and he walked out the door.

As Mary watched him drive away in the old truck the Mercy Center had given him, she realized that God was rebuilding his life, and she had to be a part of it.

4

GOD MAKES EVERYTHING BEAUTIFUL

The day was turning into night, and Mary felt happy. She was getting into more of a routine since summer was over and school had begun. She enjoyed structure and never enjoyed life when things felt unbalanced.

Jimmy had spent a lot of time with her and Elizabeth. Although she was still deciding whether to marry him, she knew God would give her the answer.

Jimmy had not spent time with his parents in over two years, which saddened Mary. She could not imagine thinking she'd not spent time with her own mom before she passed.

Mary was sure that because of the distance and subsequent long drive between her dad and sisters, she had not spent enough time with them. It was different for Jimmy and his family, however. Life's choices had taken him away from them.

Jimmy's birthday was approaching, and Mary wanted to surprise him. She picked up the phone to call Ann, their pastor's wife, to discuss the party, and they decided to have it at their house. Surprising him would be nice, Mary thought.

Ann and Mary decided on the few people they would invite, and Mary suddenly thought about asking his mom and dad over for the big party. She thought about how nice it would be to meet them, and she was sure they would be very proud of him and how well he was doing.

Ann and Pastor Butch were excited about the party. Jimmy didn't have much, so she was sure he would enjoy whatever presents he was given. He had no idea about the party. This would be a great surprise, she thought.

Mary only had a week to prepare, so she had little time. She suspected his parents needed lots of notice to make the long-distance trip, but she hoped they'd try. She was also unsure about their feelings about seeing Jimmy after all they had gone through together.

Jimmy's parents had long enabled him but later realized that was not the answer, so they had to distance themselves from him.

Mary decided to write to them and mail it priority mail so they would receive it quickly. She began to write:

Hi, this is Mary. I know we haven't met yet, but I am dating Jimmy, and we are having a surprise birthday party for him next Friday night. We will be having dinner and I'm planning on having just a few guests over. The party will be at our Pastor and his wife's home, Butch and Ann's. Jimmy has told me a lot about you, and I'm praying that you can come and surprise him. He would love it. I also realize there has been some tension between you because of his past mistakes, but I know God makes everything beautiful, and He is also making Jimmy's life beautiful. You will be very proud of him. I pray to meet you soon!

Mary

Mary was anxious to hear back from them and prayed they would be able to come to surprise Jimmy on his birthday.

Elizabeth had been in her room playing when she came out and saw tears in Mary's eyes. She walked up to her, hugged her, and said, "Mom, what's wrong?"

Mary said, "Elizabeth, I have been talking to Mrs. Ann about having a surprise birthday party for Jimmy. He doesn't have much, and I was thinking about how much it would mean to him."

Elizabeth smiled at her mom and said, "That sounds like a lot of fun, and yes, he would enjoy that. But, Mom, why are you crying?"

"Elizabeth, I know this is hard for you to understand, but you will one day. I will talk to you more about this later. I do have one question for you, however. Do you like Jimmy?"

Elizabeth answered with a determined yes!

Mary was slightly surprised but happy to hear how she felt about him.

Mary was exhausted, and it was time for Elizabeth to get ready for bed. A new work week was beginning in the morning, and they were prepared.

As Mary crawled into bed, she thought of Jimmy joining them for Thanksgiving at her family's. But the thought passed as she picked up her laptop to write.

Mary was close to finishing her second book and wanted to have it released around the holidays, but she felt she had missed her deadline. She opened her laptop, clicked on the manuscript's icon, and began writing.

"Wow!" She was delighted two hours later. "This one is almost finished."

She closed the page, placed her laptop on the table next to her bed, and began praying. *"Lord, I am feeling a little overwhelmed. I have so many things going on simultaneously, and I need clarity on everything. Please, Lord, give me confirmation that I need to move forward with my relationship with Jimmy. I know you know my heart, and I'm afraid. I do not want to make a mistake, and I need you now more than ever."* As she stopped praying, she immediately thought of *1 Peter 5:7, "Cast all your anxiety on Him because He cares for you.*"

Mary felt peace after sharing her concerns with Jesus. Soon, she fell asleep. Then, before she knew it, her alarm went off, and a new day had arrived.

Mary thought of taking the day off. She knew she could get caught up on her writing and possibly finish her manuscript by having a day at home. She reached for her phone and looked at her schedule for the day. It was clear, so she texted Mr. Henry to let him know she would not be in.

Mary was surprised when he responded almost instantly. "Mary, that's a great idea. Enjoy your day off, and while it's slow this week, maybe take off Tuesday as well. I realize you are going through a lot right now, and I completely understand. I will take care of whatever you need here. Don't worry, Mary, we'll cope."

Mary took a deep breath and felt so relieved. "A day off is exactly what I need," she exclaimed.

Mary walked into Elizabeth's room to wake her, but she was already up and getting dressed. "Good morning, my sweet girl," Mary said.

Elizabeth looked at her with sleepy eyes and said, "Good morning, Mom."

Mary went back into her bedroom to get dressed. She looked over at her laptop, thought about her writing, and prayed she could finish her manuscript. She got dressed and met Elizabeth back in the kitchen. Elizabeth had already taken JJ out and fed both him and Sunshine. Mary was blessed that Elizabeth was such a smart girl and had become very responsible in her chores.

Before walking out the door, Mary read her bible to Elizabeth and prayed with her. Elizabeth loved it when they read together and was beginning to understand how important it was to put God first in her life. Mary often shared with her the scripture that she had wished she had known at a young age, *Proverbs 4:23, "Above all else, guard your heart, for everything you do flows from it."* Mary wanted more than anything to be a great mom for Elizabeth but knew that no matter how hard she tried, she would not be perfect.

While driving Elizabeth to school, Mary thought about the box on the shelf in the closet. I may open it today, Mary thought. She had not received another email or call from Michael and wondered how he was doing.

Mary felt life had become very complicated. What happened to the balance that I had in my life? Nothing seems to make sense anymore.

When Mary arrived home, she opened her email and saw one from Jimmy's parents. They had got the letter, and were writing back to tell her that they could not make Jimmy's birthday party. Mary was disappointed but understood.

Mary closed her email and poured herself a cup of coffee. She sat on the couch while looking out the window at the ocean and thought about the box that Michael had sent. "Should I open it?" Mary said out loud. Before she realized it, she was walking toward the closet. As she reached up at the box, her heart began pounding. "Oh, Lord, help me!" She pulled the box down and just sat and looked at it for a few seconds. "I must know what is inside." As she tore it open, she saw there was a letter on top. Two boxes were inside wrapped in white paper with a blue bow. She picked up the letter, and read it:

Mary and Elizabeth,

I know this box will come as a surprise to you. I hope you are not angry with me. Please tell me you are not. I have thought of you so much, Mary, since I last saw you. I don't even really know what to say here except that I am so sorry that I wasn't there for you and Elizabeth. I thought I was making the right decision for you and should have been honest with you, but as I mentioned in my email, I knew the struggle in my life when you told me you were pregnant. That's why my reaction was as it was, and I did not want to drag you through any of it. Honestly, I didn't even know I would live through it to even be at this point in my life, but God helped me see the truth about my life through His Mercy, and now, here I am. What do I say? I don't know the answers, but I have prayed about it a lot. Anyway, I can't change the past, but I wanted you to have something from me, and I pray you can somehow forgive me for not being there for you both and not being honest with you.

Love,

Michael

As Mary sat holding the letter in her hand, she noticed a tear drop from her cheek onto the paper. She began to cry, and having no idea what any of this was about, she began opening the package with her name on it.

There was an envelope taped onto another wrapped box. She began opening it, and what was inside made her gasp. It was a check addressed to her in the amount of fifty-two thousand dollars. She began to tremble but somehow managed to hold it in her hand as she read what was written on a sticky note attached to the check:

Mary, this money is to pay child support for every month that I was not there for you. I realize money cannot undo the heartaches and the pain that I put you through, but as Elizabeth's biological dad, I am responsible for providing, and I pray that, in some way, this will make it up to you. I will be sending you a check in the amount of six hundred dollars every month from here on out. I respect your wishes if you never want me in your or Elizabeth's life, but I must do this.

Love,

Michael

Mary was totally shocked and had no idea how she would handle any of this.

As she began opening the other gift, she realized it must be a photo of some kind. She tore the paper off, and yes, it was a photo. The photo was of her and Michael on the beach when they first met and exchanged books. Every memory she had of Michael began coming back to her. The laughs they had together. Remembering Michael preparing her a meal in her kitchen at the cottage, everything just kept rolling over and over in her mind. She couldn't stop crying and knew at that moment that this would change her life forever.

As she sat there sobbing, she heard JJ walking into the room. He jumped up and sat beside her. She cuddled with him and said, "Thank you, JJ!" She knew he understood she needed a hug, and Jesus brought him to her just in time.

Mary shifted her focus and began opening the package for Elizabeth. She didn't know if Elizabeth would ever know what was in the package, but she knew that, above all else, she needed to protect her. She just wasn't sure how.

As she tore the paper from the box and opened it, she felt a warm feeling in her heart. It was a beautiful picture of Jesus with a lamb and scripture written from *Psalm 23*.

The Lord is my shepherd, I lack nothing. He makes me lie down in green pastures; he leads me beside quiet waters; he refreshes my soul. He guides me along the right paths for his name's sake. Even though I walk through the darkest valley, I will fear no evil, for your rod and your staff they comfort me. You prepare a table before me in the presence of my enemies. You anoint my head with oil, my cup overflows. Surely goodness and love will follow me all the days of my life, and I will dwell in the house of the Lord forever.

Mary read the scripture and then found a note inside that read:

Elizabeth, I don't know if you will ever receive this gift from me or even know who I am, but I wanted you to have this. As soon as I saw it, I thought of you. I have failed you as your earthly shepherd by not being there for you, but I am sure, knowing your mom, that she has explained to you that Jesus will always be your father, and I want you to know that, too. Be good to your mom, and always stay close to Jesus. I haven't always done that, and I have had to pay the price, as my choices have taken you and your mom away from me. I pray you can forgive me!

Michael

Mary felt Michael's heartfelt message but couldn't forget the lapse of time and the pain she had experienced from his betrayal in her and Elizabeth's lives. She had no idea how she would handle anything now that had come from him after all these years.

Mary put everything back in the box, including the check, and returned it to the shelf in her closet. She bowed her head and began to pray. *"Lord, please help me to do your will here. I can't do this by myself."*

Mary walked over to the kitchen, poured herself another cup of coffee, and then wandered out onto the deck. She decided to sit a while and look out over the ocean. She was still overwhelmed by Michael's package and didn't want to think about it - not now, anyway.

The phone rang, and it was Karen. Mary excitedly answered the call. She didn't get to talk to her friends as often as she wanted, and they barely got together anymore.

"Karen!" Mary said. "It is so good to hear from you."

Karen began telling Mary how much she had missed their friends' time together and wanted to see if they could get together soon for a girls' lunch out.

Mary totally agreed and realized more than anything how much she needed it. She remembered all that she had going on with Jimmy's birthday party and Thanksgiving coming up. Mary told Karen that they should have a Friendsgiving dinner at her cottage soon. "My weekends are full," she added, "so it would need to be a weeknight, if that's okay."

Karen agreed it would and suggested the following Tuesday night may work. She said she would send out a group text to check to see if everybody was available.

"Victoria is in Charlotte, so she would have to spend a night here, but she is welcome to stay with Elizabeth and me if she wants to. It is so good to hear your voice, Karen," Mary said.

"You too, Mary," Karen answered. They both said goodbye.

Victoria was a great friend to Karen. She was a beautiful girl with thin, long blonde hair and bangs. Victoria had a lot of adversity in her life growing up, and after beginning to follow Jesus, she strived to be a better person every day. She had a good sense of humor, which kept the girls laughing when she was around.

Victoria and her husband, John, lived in Charleston when Mary first met them, but later had to move to Charlotte because of John's new job. The job provided the family with more financial stability, and although they both wanted to stay in Charleston, moving was the best way to protect their future.

Mary and all the girls were very sad to see them move but knew that with Charlotte only being three and a half hours away, they could still see each other from time to time.

Not too long after they hung up, she received the group text from Karen. They had all agreed on the following Tuesday night at Mary's cottage. Patricia would bring Faith, and she and Elizabeth could play together while the girls all hung out and caught up.

Victoria had plans to leave Charlotte around noon and spend the night with Karen. The girls missed each other but were grateful that even with the changes in their lives, they always managed to figure out a way to stay close. They were all blessed to have each other and knew that their friendships were a gift from God.

Mary spent the rest of the day writing. If all went well, she was sure she could finish her manuscript the next day. She had gained so much experience writing her first book that she felt the editing would be much easier this time.

The time to pick Elizabeth up from school had arrived. Mary had already told her daughter that she could skip gymnastics camp since Mary would not be working and that she would pick her up from school.

As she arrived at the carpool line, Elizabeth was standing and waiting. Morgan was standing with her. Mary could see that they were talking about something important and wondered if everything was okay. Elizabeth walked toward the car, waving goodbye to Morgan as she went.

When Elizabeth got inside the car, Mary could tell something was troubling her. "Hi, Elizabeth," Mary said. "Did you have a good day at school?"

Elizabeth said she did but was concerned about Morgan. Morgan was going to Gymnastics without Elizabeth, and she shared with Mary about a girl there who had been bullying her. Elizabeth had known about it but not in very much detail.

"Mom, why are kids so mean?" Elizabeth said.

Morgan was having a hard enough time adjusting to the move, and she didn't need anything else to deal with. Mary then asked Elizabeth if Morgan had shared this with her mom.

Elizabeth didn't think she had.

Mary began explaining that bullying was wrong and that, in most cases, the reason someone bullies another is that they are very unhappy themselves and may even be jealous of the one they are bullying. "This must stop, Elizabeth! I will call her mom and talk to her about it. I will keep this private for now."

Elizabeth agreed and, with a concerned look, said, "Thank you, Mom!"

They had arrived home, and Elizabeth was happy to see JJ. Sunshine ran to the door to greet her as well. She loved them both and was very happy that God had given them to her. They were a part of the family.

Elizabeth ran JJ outside, came back in, sat at the kitchen table, and began doing her homework. She was happy that she didn't have too much to do, which seemed very unusual.

Mary had opened her laptop to check her emails, and she couldn't believe the number of readers asking when her next book would be out. This pleased Mary, and she was very excited that her manuscript was almost complete.

She opened her manuscript and began writing. She felt like she could fit in an hour of work before bedtime and needed to take advantage of the time she had.

The evening would be quiet as they had no plans, and Mary was happy about that. The rest of the week would be very busy, with the Friendsgiving celebration and Jimmy's surprise birthday party on Friday night. She knew they would enjoy their week but wished she could take the rest of the week off work.

5

GRACE

It was Tuesday morning, and Mary was sitting in her favorite chair by the window. She was happy to have another day off and had talked to Mr. Henry about taking the rest of the week off too. They agreed that she would work only on Thursday as she had an important meeting with a client that needed her attention for an upcoming Christmas party. The number in attendance would be close to five hundred. She was excited about the planning and knew this was one she needed to handle herself.

Mary stared out over the ocean as she thought about the final paragraph in her book. She was very excited to be finishing it and hoped that she would still have time to release it by the Christmas holidays.

As she looked back down at her laptop, she began to write the last paragraph.

Finally, she typed 'The End'. She had finished her manuscript!

Mary re-read the last paragraph and was pleased with the ending. However, she knew this was only the second book of three; she knew she had another one to write if she wanted to finish the story. There may be more, she thought.

The readers loved her books, and she loved writing them. She did wish she had more time to write, but life was busy for them, and her writing time had become very limited.

Mary saved her manuscript and then began drafting a letter to her publisher

Hello Jonathon,

I pray this email finds you well. I want to begin by saying thank you for your service and hard work with my books. With the busyness of life now, I didn't think I would get this one completed, but yay! Attached is my final manuscript for my new book. I know it's asking a lot but is it possible to have my book released before Christmas? It may need editing. However, I worked hard to get it as perfect as possible. I know you will take care of it. I am also excited to see the cover artwork for approval. Give me an update as soon as possible. Thank you!

Always Believe,

Mary

Mary was so happy that her manuscript had now been sent to the publisher. She was also happy that she had a few hours left before having to pick Elizabeth up from Gymnastics. She had not had time to talk to Morgan's mom, Pamela, and thought this was the perfect time to make the call.

She went to her purse to find the note the number was written on, and while looking for it, she remembered the cake that needed to be ordered for Jimmy's party. She found that phone number too but decided she would call Pamela first. The phone rang four times without an answer. Mary left a message for Pamela to call her back. She thought if she called back early enough today, maybe they could meet and have coffee this afternoon to talk in person.

Mary called the bakery to order Jimmy's cake. She decided on a chocolate cake with white icing and the words 'Happy Birthday, Jimmy' written on top in black lettering. She was excited about the party because she knew Jimmy needed to know he was loved and to have people around who cared about him.

Mary decided that since the party was on Friday, she had better go out and find him a gift. She thought of many things that he could use, but only one that she knew he would find invaluable. She grabbed her purse and keys and went out the door.

When she turned into the parking lot of the Christian bookstore, Mary felt happy. She felt peace in knowing the gift she wanted to buy Jimmy would be perfect. As she walked in, a lovely lady greeted her at the door. Mary told her she was looking for a leather-bound bible and asked if they did engraving.

The sales lady answered, "Yes, we can engrave it on site for you. Follow me, and I will show you a few you might be interested in."

They walked towards the back of the store, to where there was a shelf full of different bibles. Mary pulled out the biggest, opened it, and announced, "This is the one."

They took it back to the engraving area and had Jimmy's name engraved in gold letters. Mary was pleased. She knew exactly what she would write in it for him.

As she was paying for the bible, Mary's phone rang. It was Pamela. She still had a little over an hour before she had to pick Elizabeth up at gymnastics camp. As she answered the phone, she introduced herself to Pamela as Elizabeth's mom.

Pamela knew exactly who Elizabeth was and said, "Hi, Mary! Morgan has talked a lot about Elizabeth. I am so happy they met."

Mary proceeded to ask if she had time to grab coffee together at the local coffee shop. Pamela agreed they would meet there in fifteen minutes.

When Mary drove up to park her car at the coffee shop, she saw a beautiful blond lady standing by her car. That must be Pamela, she thought. She turned off the engine and locked her doors. She started walking over to the lady, and when she reached her, she asked her if she was Pamela.

The lady answered, "Yes, are you Mary? It's so nice to finally meet you."

Mary and Pamela walked inside together, ordered drinks, and sat down at a table in the back. Mary looked at Pamela and began telling her that she didn't want to interfere, but her heart was sad, and she wanted to discuss it with her. Mary had a heart for helping young girls in any way she could because of her life experiences. She also knew that kids could be so mean. Instead of beating around the bush, Mary just asked her if Morgan had told her that she was being bullied at school.

Looking very concerned, she answered that she hadn't

Mary proceeded to tell her that she would not have known had she not picked Elizabeth up from school yesterday and her daughter had told her Morgan was not going to Gymnastics. "Morgan and she were talking when I picked her up at the carpool line, and I guess Morgan must have been afraid to go to Gymnastics without Elizabeth. In the car on the way home, Elizabeth shared it with me, and my heart was broken. Pamela, we must stop this. These kids can't get away with it."

Pamela agreed and they decided to go together to speak to management when they picked the girls up.

Mary and Pamela sat for a while longer finishing their coffee together. They talked about the move and how difficult it was for the entire family. "My husband's work insisted we moved here, so we had to."

Mary talked about being an author and the enjoyment but the demands that went along with it. Mary then asked Pamela if she did any work other than in the home.

Pamela said, "Yes, I worked for years in the sales department at a major hotel chain until we moved. I really miss it, Mary."

Intrigued, Mary said, "Wow, I am the sales and marketing director at the Inn in town. Are you familiar with it?"

Pamela had heard about the Inn but had not yet been there.

Mary told her they should go there for lunch sometime. As she sat there, she thought to herself about how wonderful it would be to have another assistant to help her at the Inn and wondered if Pamela would be interested.

Before she knew it, she asked, "Pamela, would you like to meet Mr. Henry regarding working at the Inn?"

Pamela became very excited and said, "Mary, are you joking? I'd love to."

Mary wasn't joking! She had worked so hard for so long, and with her book selling so well, she felt like she could start working a little less and focus on her writing more. A little more time off would be good for me, she thought.

They arranged a time the next day to meet at the office. Mary realized she may have jumped the gun as she hadn't even spoken to Mr. Henry about any of this.

As she looked down at the time on her phone, she saw it was getting late. Their time together had been very pleasant, but they both needed to get going so they could pick Elizabeth and Morgan up at Gymnastics.

Mary and Pamela got up from the table, hugged each other, and said goodbye. "I'll see you in a bit at Gymnastics, and I will see you tomorrow, Mary, at the Inn. Two o'clock, right?"

Mary agreed that the time was good.

Mary and Pamela arrived at the gymnastics camp close to the same time. As they walked in, they could see Elizabeth and Morgan standing together with another young girl they didn't recognize. As they walked up, Elizabeth hugged her mom and introduced her and Pamela to their new friend, Alisa.

The introduction felt a little awkward. However, Mary and Pamela both smiled sincere smiles and told Alisa it was very nice to meet her.

Alisa looked a little shy but spoke up and said, "It's nice to meet you, too."

Mary asked Elizabeth if she had her things and said, "It's time for us to get going."

Elizabeth hugged her friends and said goodbye, and Mary told Pamela she was looking forward to also meeting her tomorrow at the Inn.

The drive to the cottage was very interesting as Elizabeth told Mary the story of forgiveness.

"Mom, you will not believe this! Alisa is the girl who was bullying Morgan! I was standing there when she came up to Morgan. As soon as we got to Gymnastics, Alisa started saying hurtful things to Morgan. Morgan looked at Alisa and said, "Alisa, I am not sure why you are saying such hurtful things to me, and I am not going to allow it. I don't know you, and you don't know me, but I would like to get to know you. Why can't we be friends?" Alisa seemed a little shocked, and as we looked up at her face, we saw a tear drop from her eye, Mom. It was beautiful. In no time, Alisa asked Morgan if she would forgive her for being so mean and asked if they could start over. Morgan agreed to forgive her and showed her God's grace. It was a beautiful blessing to witness it in real time. Jesus was there, Mom! Jesus worked it all out for us, and we didn't have to be mean back to Alisa. You had already told me that she may be hurting, so I talked to Morgan about that before the bell rang for class this morning. Morgan heard me and showed her grace! We are all friends now! Mom, I whispered a prayer to Jesus and thanked Him for giving Morgan words to say and the heart to love others even when we didn't want to."

Mary, with a tear falling from her eye, looked over at Elizabeth and said, "I am so proud of you girls."

Mary immediately thought of *Exodus 14:14, "The Lord will fight for you; you need only to be still."*

Elizabeth looked over at her mom and said, "Mom, I remember you telling me before how God spoke to you once and said, "It's not what comes at you, but what comes out of you that shows who you are in Christ." Today was a great lesson in that, wasn't it?"

With a heart filled with love, Mary looked over at Elizabeth and said, "That's exactly right! Jesus showed His love through you both today, Elizabeth. Mom couldn't be prouder of you. This is a lesson for all of us, isn't it?"

The evening was peaceful, and the lesson of the love of Jesus ran through Mary's mind all night. She was grateful for the lessons God had given her and more grateful for those lessons being instilled in her daughter's heart.

The alarm on Mary's clock rang, and she looked over to see the time; it was 5:30 a.m. As she reached over to turn the clock off, her thoughts immediately turned to Pamela's meeting at 2 p.m. She had not even talked to Mr. Henry and needed to do that as soon as she arrived at the Inn. She wasn't sure what his schedule was, so she reached for her phone and texted him, requesting a meeting with him.

When she jumped out of the shower, she quickly looked at her phone and saw Mr. Henry had texted that a meeting at 9 am would work perfectly. Mary was nervous as she knew this meeting was going to surprise him but also free up a lot of time for her if it went well.

Elizabeth was already up and dressed. When Mary walked into the kitchen to grab a cup of coffee, she saw the peace on Elizabeth's face. Mary hugged her and said, "Good morning, my little angel."

Elizabeth returned her greeting and smiled. Mary was still in awe at how she felt and realized how much this moment had impacted

Elizabeth.

After taking her daughter to school and arriving at the Inn, she drove slowly up the long drive, taking in the beauty of the colors the season had created. The leaves on the trees had not fallen and were bright orange and gold. It was spectacular! She loved driving up to the Inn, as it always gave her a sense of peace. In every season, she was reminded of God's glory on earth. She was also reminded that in every season of life, the lessons that God gave us were always a blessing, no matter what they seem to be at the time.

While sitting at her desk, she was thinking about her meeting with Mr. Henry. It was already 8:30 am, and she was getting a little nervous about sharing her thoughts about hiring someone to assist her. Pamela had the experience, and she felt great about having her work at the Inn. She also knew nothing was a coincidence, and the bullying from Alisa led her to Pamela, and she was confident everything was turning out this way for the glory of God.

Before going into Mr. Henry's office, she grabbed a cup of coffee. It was warm and tasty and would help to keep her spirits up if the meeting didn't go well.

The Inn's upscale restaurant took great pride in the service and the selection of foods, etc., it prepared for its guests. After all, they were not only guests; many had stayed so often that they had become almost family. Mr. Henry was a big part of why they came back as well. He loved serving the guests, and his smile was one that no one could ever forget.

As she walked into Mr. Henry's office, he looked concerned. Mary had not told him why she needed to meet with him, and she realized he must have thought the worse, and that she was coming to him with a big problem. "Mr. Henry, everything is okay," she assured him

Looking relieved, he motioned for Mary to sit down. After a little small talk, Mary thanked Mr. Henry for always being such a great friend and boss to her. She wanted him to know that, most importantly, Mary knew how difficult her life would have been without his friendship and understanding.

Mary told him that she had met a new friend who had moved here with her family as her husband had to take another job. Pamela was the assistant to the director of marketing at a large resort in the west. She went on to say that she had scheduled a meeting at 2 p.m. today to discuss Pamela possibly coming to work with Mary.

Mr. Henry instantly said, "Are you serious, Mary? I had thought of running an ad about this same position, and I was going to talk to you about it today."

Mary couldn't believe what she was hearing. She felt such relief, and most importantly, she knew that God was working everything out just the way He wanted it to be.

Mary said, "Well, then, Mr. Henry, I guess we are on the same page as usual, aren't we?"

Mr. Henry agreed and seemed very excited about meeting Pamela.

When Mary got back to her desk, she saw she had missed a call from Jimmy. He had left a message, so Mary picked up her phone to listen to it. Jimmy had asked if they could see each other during the week one night if she had a date open. Mary remembered her Friendsgiving dinner with the girls on Tuesday night, and she still had a lot to finish for his surprise party on Friday.

Mary picked up the phone to call Jimmy back. When he answered, he sounded a little down. She knew his life wasn't as hectic as hers, but he was busy assisting Ms. Lizzy with her new home, and he enjoyed the idea of helping someone so much. He had also been cutting down trees, helping to clear her land so they could plant a garden.

This was a new beginning for Jimmy, and she wanted to be a part of it when time allowed.

Jimmy was happy to hear from Mary and told her he missed her.

Mary told him she missed him too and reminded him of their date on Friday night.

Jimmy was excited. Mary smiled to herself; was he in for a shock!?

Mary told him she had a surprise for him, but he would have to hold on until Friday to find out what it was. He laughed and told her he would be thinking about her until then. She told him she needed to go as she had a lot of work to do. Jimmy understood and wished her a wonderful rest of the day.

2 p.m. came quickly, as the days went by so fast. As she looked up at her office door, Pamela was walking in. She was a beautiful woman. She had long, straight blond hair cut in layers angled toward her face. Pamela was almost 5' 8" and slim. She had a peace about her that drew Mary to her, and although they didn't know each other well, Mary was very excited about getting to know her better.

Mary got up from her chair and greeted her at the door. Pamela looked confident but maybe a little nervous too. She really wanted the job as she missed her time at work since moving to the town.

As they walked toward Mr. Henry's office, Pamela was mesmerized by the Inn and all its charm. She felt happy with the possible chance to be a part of it and prayed that God would allow it if it was His will.

When they arrived at Mr. Henry's office, they could see he was working on something that seemed important. However, when he saw them, he waved them in. He stood up from his desk to greet them and asked them to sit down.

Mr. Henry and Mary had talked about giving her a tour of the Inn, but first they wanted to spend time interviewing her for the job.

As always, Mr. Henry was dressed in an expensive suit and wore a smile that brightened the room. You could feel peace in his office. This feeling put Pamela at ease, helping her to relax.

The conversation went well, and everyone agreed that Pamela was a great fit for the Inn.

Mary would work full-time while she trained Pamela for a few weeks, and then she would transition over to part-time. Mary was excited and looking forward to spending more time writing. Also, Elizabeth wouldn't need to go to afterschool camp if she didn't want to.

Mary loved it that now Elizabeth would have a choice because of the change in her work schedule. Mary thanked God for the opportunity to spend more time with Elizabeth.

6

FRIENDSGIVING CELEBRATION

Mary and Elizabeth had arrived home after what felt like a very long morning, and they were happy to be there. JJ and Sunshine were also delighted they were home. Mary had picked Elizabeth up early from school because they had friends coming for a Friendsgiving dinner. Everyone was excited as they did not seem to have a lot of time to spend together. Things had changed for everyone, and life just kept trundling along. Unfortunately, this left them little time to share in person. Mary loved her friends and missed them greatly. Faith was also coming with Patricia. This made Elizabeth very happy as well.

Patricia's personality was unique to most. She had a Southern accent that everyone enjoyed. Whenever she walked into a room, everyone noticed her. Her presence felt like the love of Jesus, and people wanted to be around her.

Patricia and Paul had one child, Faith. Faith was a smart girl and independent as she had spent most of her time with Patricia at home. Faith was an only child, like Elizabeth, and they had become best friends.

Patricia married her high school sweetheart, Paul. Later in their marriage, he became a youth leader in their church and always strived to love Patricia as Jesus does. They had a happy, thriving marriage, and everyone who knew them knew that. Patricia was blessed to have Paul as her husband. He adored her, and his actions always conveyed that.

While Mary began preparing the dressing and cutting up the vegetables that she had planned to roast in the oven, Elizabeth took JJ for a walk and played with him for a while. JJ was lonesome during the day, but he was getting much older now and seemed to enjoy resting more.

Patricia had roasted chicken breasts to bring and baked homemade rolls.

Victoria had arrived in town, and she and Karen were preparing a fresh cranberry salad with lots of fruit and a green bean casserole.

Mary was also preparing corn pudding and mashed potatoes. The corn pudding was Elizabeth's favorite. Mary had already baked her favorite cheesecake for dessert. She couldn't wait until everyone was there.

Elizabeth was sitting on the couch watching TV, and Mary was finishing up her homemade lemonade and sweet tea when the doorbell rang. It was Karen and Victoria. They both looked so pretty. You could see the joy in them as they hugged everybody.

There was something about Karen that was different, though. Mary couldn't decide what it was.

Elizabeth said, "Hi." She took the food from them and placed it on the counter.

Seconds later, Patricia and Faith were there. As the doorbell rang, Elizabeth ran to the door. As polite as Elizabeth could be, in her excitement at seeing Faith, she only managed to share a quick "Hi" to Patricia, before she and Faith ran off to her bedroom.

The food smelled wonderful, and although they were all getting hungry, Mary poured each of them a glass of sweet tea and asked if they wanted to walk out on the deck to catch up for a while. They all happily agreed.

As soon as they had all sat down at the table on the deck, Mary felt Karen wanted to say something. "Karen, I know you all too well, and you look like you need to share something with us. Go ahead, girl. We're all ears!" Mary said with a warm smile.

It only took her three seconds of looking away and back at her friends to say what she wanted to say. "Girls, I'm pregnant!"

Everyone screamed in excitement.

"Karen, oh my goodness! I am so happy for you!"

Mary got up, ran to her friend, and hugged her with a hug that felt much like genuine love.

Mary could not be happier for her friend.

Patricia got up from her chair and ran over to Karen, giving her a big hug too. As she did, she realized a tear had fallen from her cheek.

Karen felt the joy and love from her friends, which she needed at that moment.

God had created a special bond between all of them.

They all began asking all the right questions and, in their excitement, they wanted the answers right now.

Karen began sharing with them that she was already three months pregnant, and she didn't want to tell anyone until at least close to the end of her first trimester. She told them about all her doctor's appointments and was so pleased that everything was going so well.

Karen could feel the energy of joy and excitement all around them. She had wanted to be pregnant for so long, and her time had finally come.

As a tear fell from Mary's eye, she thanked Jesus for her friends; the news of Karen's pregnancy could not have made any of them any happier.

This is going to be a great day, Mary thought.

Victoria spoke up to say, "Well, my news couldn't come at a better time! I am so excited to tell you that John has taken a new position in

Charleston. Girls, we are moving back home."

Everyone stood up from the table, ran, and hugged Victoria. They were all very excited about Victoria moving back home, as they had missed her so much. Although Victoria had visited as often as she could, she knew that they would see more of each other if she didn't live so far away.

The news of Victoria moving back home brought lots of joy to each of her friends.

Mary remembered the feeling of sadness when Victoria told her they were moving.

Mary asked the girls if they were ready to eat and said, "All of this excitement is telling me we need to celebrate with a great meal."

They all agreed and walked back inside.

Mary called Elizabeth and Faith into the kitchen and told everyone she would like to pray over their meal. Elizabeth and Faith had been giggling in Elizabeth's room, and the peace of hearing the girls laughing while sharing stories also filled the cottage with great joy.

Elizabeth, in her sassy way, said, "Yay, it's time to eat!" Faith followed behind her.

 Mary began to pray.

"Father, we come to you today and thank you for the great news about Karen becoming pregnant. Lord, we pray that you protect her and the baby, and as she and John prepare to be parents, we pray that you give them joy that's unspeakable. Carry them, Lord, in your presence, nurture them, and protect them. Father, thank you for the news of Victoria and John moving back to Charleston. We have missed them both so much, and we are grateful. Father, I thank you for my friends. You have blessed me beyond measure. Thank you for this food, and as we prepare to break bread together, we ask that you use this food to nourish our bodies and bring us closer to you. In Jesus' name, we pray. Amen."

The food had already been placed on the bar for everyone to enjoy. As the girls all lined up to get their food, Mary spoke up to say that she felt Karen should go first and then Victoria, as their news certainly put them at the front of the line. Mary wanted to honor her friends. She immediately thought of *Romans 12:10, "Be devoted to one another in love. Honor one another above yourselves."*

The stories that were told around the table during their meal brought many different emotions. They laughed and occasionally cried. They all knew that God had given them each other to go through life with, and they could not have been more thankful.

The news of Karen being pregnant and Victoria moving back home was a blessing, and the timing could not have been more perfect.

Mary thought of the sadness that she knew Karen had felt many times at not becoming pregnant sooner, but she now realized the timing could not have been more perfect. It had taken Karen a long time to get used to not working, as her job had truly become her identity, and she needed this time to grow within herself and with Jesus. The life she had now was wonderful, and her time at home was comfortable for her.

The food was delicious, and everyone couldn't believe that they had eaten almost everything.

The cheesecake was perfect. The conversation was needed, and the Friendsgiving celebration was another memory for each of them that would be cherished forever.

Sadly, it was a school night, and all too soon it was time for everyone to leave.

Mary had hoped that they could have done this dinner over the weekend, but with Jimmy's party on Friday night, her weekend was too busy.

As they all began packing everything, Mary hugged her friends and told them how much she had missed them and loved them.

As Mary and Elizabeth stood on the deck and watched everybody leave, a special feeling came over both of them. They looked at each other and with a look of gratitude, said, "This was a wonderful night."

It was time for Elizabeth to get ready for bed. She went into her room to take a shower while Mary ran JJ outside.

When Elizabeth came into the living room, Mary had opened her laptop, and there was an email from the publisher. She was excited to read it but decided she would wait. She didn't want to be up all night thinking about her book, as she needed to rest for work the next day. She closed her laptop and went into Elizabeth's room, where she was waiting in bed for her mom to pray and tuck her in tight.

Elizabeth always cherished her mom's goodnight prayers and hugs.

The sound of the alarm rang, and Mary jumped. She had been dreaming. As she reached over to turn it off, she felt something in her heart that she wasn't familiar with. She then realized that she had been dreaming about Michael, and it wasn't a dream that she ever wanted to remember.

As she got up to wake Elizabeth. Mary had decided she never wanted to see Michael again, but in this dream, he had shown up at her office. This frightened Mary! She wished this dream never happened.

After Mary finished a cup of coffee and read her bible and devotion, she went into her room to shower. Elizabeth was already dressed and ran JJ out to potty. When Mary entered the kitchen, Elizabeth had already fed JJ and Sunshine. Mary was so pleased with the responsibility that Elizabeth had taken on her own, and she told her so.

Mary felt that Elizabeth must have felt the responsibility to help her as it had only been the two of them in the cottage for so many years.

Elizabeth smiled at her mom and said, "Mom, I enjoy helping you when I can."

Mary was right. She hugged her and said, "Thank you, Elizabeth. How did you sleep?"

Elizabeth proceeded to tell her that she woke up a couple of times thinking about Alisa and how well everything went with Morgan showing her God's grace the other day. She was very excited to see God work through Morgan and how it changed everything.

Elizabeth, like Mary, always enjoyed seeing God working and longed for those moments.

Mary thought of Michael and immediately felt convinced that no matter what Michael had done to her, she needed to show him God's grace as well. She just wasn't sure how she could. She also hoped that he would never show up at her office, like in her dream, because she knew that wouldn't go over very well.

God was working in Mary's heart.

Mary had forgotten all the pain she had felt from him walking away, and she loved her life now just exactly as it was. Of course, now she was dating Jimmy and still very puzzled about that as well.

The one thing Mary did know was that God was with her, that He would lead her, and that He would not leave her or forsake her.

Mary prepared some oatmeal with granola for Elizabeth. They sat down together and ate while talking about how good God was in every situation they faced. Mary prayed that they would both be protected throughout the day and that God's peace and protection would be with them.

It was very close to time to leave, and Mary realized rain was in the forecast, so she asked Elizabeth to grab her rain jacket. "We better get going now," she said. They both petted JJ. Sunshine couldn't be found, so they shouted goodbye to her too.

During their drive to drop Elizabeth off at school, they talked about the dinner the night before and how well it had gone. Mary realized how much she missed her friends and how much she desperately needed them. They talked about trying to get together for dinner a couple of times a month. Of course, Elizabeth loved that because she had a friend come too, and she loved having Faith over.

As they were pulling into the carpool line, Elizabeth saw Morgan and Alisa standing outside together. Elizabeth hugged her mom and ran to catch up with them. Mary waved to each of them as she drove away.

During her drive to the Inn, Mary recalled her dream about Michael and prayed that God would give her peace.

Her thoughts changed to Jimmy's birthday party on Friday night, and she realized she only had two days left until the big event. She was excited about the party and knew that Jimmy would be surprised. So far, no one had slipped up and told him about it. They had plans to go to dinner, but Mary was going to say that she needed to stop by and pick something up at Ann's before they went to the restaurant. She wasn't sure how he would react when he walked in to see everyone there, but she couldn't wait to see his expression.

Mary had reached the drive up to the Inn, and she was trying to change her focus on her workday. As she drove up the long drive, she was mesmerized by all the colors once again. She never got tired of the beauty God had created. It was always so beautifully landscaped and gave the most peaceful feeling. God's glory shined through on each side of the driveway. It was always refreshing for Mary.

Mary had reached the front entrance and parked her car. She pulled the visor down to check her makeup. As she wiped the smudge of mascara away from her eyes, she wondered why she had tears in them. She was struggling today and knew she needed to get herself together quickly.

Mary grabbed her purse, locked her car, and walked into the Inn. She had a 10 a.m. appointment to get ready for and had a couple of questions for Mr. Henry before the meeting.

Mr. Henry was standing in the lobby as Mary walked toward her office with the biggest smile she had ever seen from him. "Well, good morning, Mr. Henry. You look very happy today," Mary said with a tone of gratitude. She needed to see his smile, as it always brightened her day.

Mr. Henry told her why he was feeling so happy. He had had another check-up for his previous cancer, and there was no sign of it returning.

Mary hugged him and said, "I just knew the Lord was going to take care of you, Mr. Henry! Now, I have a question for you; suppose I had taken your job here at the Inn? What would you be doing now?"

Mr. Henry looked at Mary with the sweetest look and said, "Well, I'm not sure, but the Lord took care of that too, didn't He, Mary?"

Mary returned the smile and agreed. She was so happy that Mr. Henry was following Jesus now. She could feel His presence in him, and she was so grateful. They discussed her 10 am meeting, and her questions were answered. They also discussed the day that Pamela would start working, and they agreed on the following Monday.

Mr. Henry expressed his appreciation for Pamela and felt that her previous experience would make her a valuable asset to the Inn.

Pamela taking the position would also free up a lot of time for Mary to write. Mary was excited about that. She felt like she had been on an emotional rollercoaster for so long and was looking forward to having better balance in her life.

Mary opened her laptop and began checking her emails. She had totally forgotten the message she had seen from the publisher the night before. She felt her heart skip a beat as she opened it.

Mary, I am excited to announce that the editing of your book has been completed; you did a great job with your manuscript. Congratulations! I must say that I love the cover illustration, which reminded me of your first book, When Jesus Calls. You have an amazing graphic designer, Mary.

If we can get the signed approval form back before the end of the week, we can schedule print, and we should have it published before Christmas.

Your second book is better than the first, and that is a big compliment because your first one was amazing! Keep writing, Mary. Your readers love you and your books. The world needs more writings like yours.

I look forward to hearing from you,

Jonathon

Mary was overly excited about the email and the possibility of her book being published before Christmas. She wanted to click on the link for the book cover, but she knew she had already had enough distractions for the day and needed to focus on her upcoming meeting. She closed her laptop in hopes of seeing it when she got home and settled in for the night.

As soon as she closed her laptop, her cell phone rang. Jimmy was calling. She didn't want to but ignored the call so she could get some work done. She texted him quickly to say that she would call him a little later. He responded with the words, "Hurry, I miss you." Mary put her phone down and attempted to focus on her meeting.

It was 10 a.m. and the time came very quickly as her morning seemed to be full of distractions.

Just as she was finished with all the details of her meeting, her client walked in. Mary enjoyed working with this company. They had their Christmas party there every year. Mary enjoyed watching the company grow each year, and this year is going to be the largest party in number by far. The guest number in attendance would be over five hundred.

They discussed the details of changes from previous years and added additional items to the menu. Italian was always the favorite entrée, and the Inn always prepared the most authentic Italian food in the city. They were well known for this, and because of it, the restaurant was always fully booked up every weekend.

After all the details were completed, her client told Mary that he wanted to talk to her about something a little more personal.

Mary looked up with a look of concern when he proceeded to tell her that he had read her book, "When Jesus Calls", and that he loved it!

He said, "Mary, I am one of those, like so many, that never really felt worthy of God's love, and I wanted to tell you in person that while reading your book and the scriptures you shared, it really touched my heart. I have given my life to Jesus, Mary, and I have you to thank for that!"

Before Mary knew it, a tear fell down her cheek. She knew that this was the very reason she wrote her book, and that was where her heart was, so she told him, "Seeing people come to know Jesus in a more personal way has blessed me more than anyone could ever imagine. Thank you for sharing your heart with me; I am so happy for you."

With a humble smile on his face, he got up to go. Mary hugged him. They discussed another meeting time to finalize everything they had discussed, then he left.

Mary was overwhelmed! She was so happy that her book, "When Jesus Calls," was touching hearts and thanked God for allowing her to be, in some small way, a conduit in helping others.

Mary never wanted to receive any glory for the writings that she knew God had given her, but He always seemed to continue to make her shine in His grace and love. Mary was never one to be a person wanting any kind of attention; however, she had accepted the fact that her writings were a gift from the Lord, and she didn't want to be too proud not to enjoy what He had given her to share with others.

7

A SPECIAL BIRTHDAY PARTY

Friday had finally arrived, and the anticipation of Jimmy's birthday party gave Mary a feeling of gratitude. She couldn't help but feel joy for a life that had been changed. She was also excited that the gift she was giving him could be one that could also be read to change hearts, for God's Glory was very satisfying to her. She knew Jimmy needed so much more, but she had carefully written these words in his new bible: "So you always know what is first and most important in your life". She was excited to see his expression when he finally received it.

Mary had taken off early from work and had a few hours before having to pick Elizabeth up from school. She spent her afternoon preparing food for the party. Jimmy had talked about wanting a fried turkey for Thanksgiving, so Ann and Pastor Butch were deep-frying one for his party. She had a cake with white icing and black letters on it that read, "Happy Birthday, Jimmy".

Mary was sad that Jimmy's parents could not attend the party, but she knew she could take pictures to send to them. After all, there was not enough time for them to plan a long-distance trip like this, and she understood.

Mary had told Jimmy that she would pick him up at the Mercy Center at 5 p.m., and they would have dinner shortly after that. Elizabeth wanted to stay with Faith since there would be no children at the party for her to play with, and Mary agreed that it would be fine. Patricia would pick her up at the cottage around 4:30, and Mary would pick her up on her way home.

With all the busyness of getting everything together, the hours had flown by, and it was soon time to pick Elizabeth up. After walking JJ out, Mary left to drive to the school.

On her way there, Ann called and asked if she could pick up some ice cream and, of course, Mary said she would. She would pick it up when she picked up the cake.

Mary could feel her excitement escalating. She knew Jimmy would be so happy that others loved him enough to do something special for him like this.

When she arrived at the school, she saw Elizabeth standing with Morgan and Alisa. Elizabeth instantly saw her mom, waved goodbye to the two girls, and ran over to the car.

Elizabeth was excited about spending time with Faith and was even happier that she had no homework for the weekend. She loved the weekends because she could sleep in a bit and not have to go to school. She loved school, but like most kids, a break from it was also fantastic. Their two-week Thanksgiving break had begun, so not only did she have the weekend, but she also had two weeks with her mom, which made her super happy.

Mary was delighted to see Elizabeth. She began asking her about her day at school.

Elizabeth told her she had had a wonderful day, as for most of it, she'd played, and hardly had to do any work at all. She laughed and said, "I wish every school day could be like today."

Mary laughed with her and told her she understood.

Mary and Elizabeth ran by the grocery store to pick up Jimmy's cake and ice cream. Mary was reminded that JJ and Sunshine also needed more snacks, as they would be out of them before the first of the week. As they walked into the store, Mary looked over at the register and spotted her friend, Tiffany. Mary waved to her, hoping her line would open when they checked out.

Mary had met Tiffany a while back in the same line at the grocery store. Mary recognized that Tiffany was feeling a bit down and left her card with her so she would have her number. To encourage her, she told Tiffany that she wanted to be her friend if she ever needed anything. Tiffany later called, and Mary met her for lunch. It turned out that she did need a friend, and Mary was able to give her some wisdom that helped her in a decision she was about to make about having sex with her boyfriend. Their friendship had become one of God, and it saved Tiffany from making a bad choice that would change her life forever.

They grabbed what they needed and began walking back to the front of the store. Tiffany asked them to come to her checkout line, so they were happy. Tiffany smiled at Mary and said, "I have some great news for you!"

Mary smiled back. "I'm all ears."

Tiffany excitedly began to tell her that she had met a lovely guy and had been dating him for a few months.

She looked down at Elizabeth and said, "Elizabeth, always listen to your mom. She has much wisdom, and she has saved me from much pain." She went on to tell Mary about her new boyfriend and how everything they had talked about at lunch that day was not a problem for them at all. "As a matter of fact, Mary, just after we had lunch, my dad took me on a daddy-daughter date and gave me a promise ring. God protected my heart, Mary! Thank you again for taking the time to help me."

Tiffany walked around the register and hugged Mary. Elizabeth looked up at her with a beautiful smile, and Tiffany bent down and hugged her as well. A feeling of love surrounded them, and they knew that the love was a gift from Jesus.

Jimmy's cake was beautiful. Mary carefully picked it up and handed Elizabeth the bag of snacks for JJ and Sunshine. Then they left the store.

It was getting close to 4 p.m., and they needed to get home. Patricia would be at the cottage at 4:30 p.m. to pick up Elizabeth, and Mary needed to pick Jimmy up shortly after for the party.

When they arrived home, Mary set the cake down on the kitchen counter, and Elizabeth ran to her room to grab a couple of things she wanted to take to Faith's. As soon as she set the cake down, the phone rang. Patricia was on her way and wanted to ask if she needed her to bring anything. Mary, with excitement, stopped to think for a second then said, "Thank you, Patricia, but I think we have everything."

Patricia told Mary they would be there in about five minutes, and they hung up.

Mary quickly grabbed Jimmy's birthday present and set it by his cake.

The doorbell rang, and it was Patricia and Faith. Of course, Elizabeth and Faith began to giggle as they were excited about spending a few hours together. After all, it was Friday night, and their two-week Thanksgiving break had started, so they were both happy.

Patricia walked over to the kitchen to see Jimmy's cake and told Mary how much she liked it. Mary agreed that the bakery had done a great job decorating it. She hoped that Jimmy would like it, too.

Elizabeth hugged her mom and told her she would see her soon. Mary reassured her she would pick her up after the party on her way home. They all said goodbye and walked out the door.

Standing alone in her kitchen, Mary stopped, took a deep breath, and thanked Jesus for her friend, Patricia. She prayed that Jimmy would enjoy his birthday party and that it would be a great memory.

Before leaving to pick up Jimmy, she ran JJ outside, put his and Sunshine's food down for dinner, looked around the cottage, and thanked Jesus again for their peaceful home.

Mary picked up Jimmy's gift and took it to the car, placing it in the back seat. Then, she went back inside to get his cake and ice cream. The drive there wasn't long, so she felt the ice cream would be OK.

When she reached the Mercy Center to pick up Jimmy, he was happy to see Mary. He was wearing jeans and a cream-colored dress shirt. He seemed excited to go to dinner with Mary alone.

During their drive there, she mentioned she had to run by Ann and Pastor Butch's house to pick up something. She asked if he would come in with her when they pulled into the driveway. He agreed.

As soon as they walked inside, everyone shouted, "SURPRISE!" Jimmy stood there in awe with no words. He was surprised without a doubt and seemed overwhelmed. The love in the room was beautiful, and Mary couldn't have been happier. Everyone greeted Mary and hugged her and Jimmy, saying, "Happy Birthday!"

Ann said, "Well, alrighty then, let's get this party started."

Their friends Bob and Karen from the Mercy Center were there with big smiles. Bob worked at the Mercy Center and had significantly influenced Jimmy's life. Karen, Bob's wife, had been a big part of Jimmy's life as well. They had often invited him to their home for dinner and fellowship. They cared for him deeply. His friends Joey and Karen, also from the Mercy Center, were there. Mary was pleased they could all attend. She had hoped to have his parents there, but it wasn't God's will at the time. After all, His timing is perfect, and this wasn't His time. She felt reconciliation would come.

Mary helped Ann set the table while Jimmy talked with everyone. Everything looked beautiful. Jimmy's cake sat on a buffet table by the wall with dessert plates stacked up next to it. His gifts were there too.

Jimmy may not have felt worthy of a party so lovely, but Mary was reminded of God's word regarding the prodigal son in *Luke 15:32, "But we had to celebrate and be glad because this brother of yours was dead and is alive again; he was lost and is found."* Mary thought this was something to celebrate for sure.

God was making all things new in Jimmy's life.

The laughter and smiles in the room were delightful. Everyone was happy, especially Jimmy. Ann had him sit at the head of the table. After all, this was Jimmy's birthday, and everyone was celebrating it with him.

The conversation around the table was great. Everyone seemed joyful as Jimmy's birthday celebration was going very well. The fried turkey was also a surprise to Jimmy and was delicious. He was grateful!

When everyone had finished their meal, Mary and Ann stood up to clear away all the dishes.

Jimmy sat at the head of the table with a humble look of gratefulness. Mary put his cake on the table, added the candles, lit them, and they all began to sing Happy Birthday. He seemed to be glowing at that moment. Jesus was with him.

Jimmy had a great personality, and everyone who knew him enjoyed being around him. He stood up to blow out his candles, and Mary began slicing the cake while Ann grabbed the ice cream from the freezer. As everyone enjoyed the cake and ice cream, the conversation flowed.

The birthday party was indeed a joyful time.

The time had come for Jimmy to open his gifts. Everyone got up to pick up their gifts and put them before him. He looked excited to open them. One by one, he unwrapped each gift and read the cards aloud. Mary felt her eyes welling up. She could see what Jesus was doing in Jimmy's heart, which touched her greatly. Mary couldn't stand it any longer as he had not opened her gift yet.

Mary put his gift in front of Jimmy and, with a smile, said, "Open it."

Jimmy began unwrapping the gift and saw it was a bible. He then took it out of the box and read his name engraved in gold letters on the bottom right. He thumbed through it and said, "This looks like a preacher's bible!" Little did he know then that God was calling him to preach the gospel, but time would also reveal this. He was happy with everything that was given to him and thanked everyone.

The look on Jimmy's face was priceless, as she felt Jimmy had no idea that he would ever be worthy of preaching the Gospel. Still, God had already given Mary that vision, and she was reminded once again of *1 Corinthians 1:27*, "*But God chose the foolish things of the world to shame the wise, God chose the weak things of the world to shame the strong.*"

Mary also knew that with God, all things were possible, and just like *Acts 4:13 says*, "*When they saw the courage of Peter and John and realized that they were unschooled, ordinary men, they were astonished, and they took note that these men had been with Jesus.*"

Jesus had called Jimmy to share His goodness and preach the Gospel, and he knew it. Mary thought it was time for him to understand that now. She also realized that her timing was not God's timing, and He would finish what He started.

Would Jimmy follow the will of God in his life? Mary hoped so.

8

A QUIET DAY AT HOME

It was Saturday morning, and Mary awoke to the smell of coffee brewing in the kitchen. It took her a minute to realize it was Saturday, and she had no plans for the day. She was happy about that, as it seemed she had no time for herself lately. Mary loved writing but seemed to never have the time to do it. "Where does the time go?" she asked herself.

Mary sat up in bed, stretched, got up, and walked toward the kitchen. She saw Sunshine run across the living room to greet her. JJ was coming behind her, wagging his tail. Mary smiled as she loved her cottage and her life with Elizabeth, JJ, and Sunshine.

While pouring her coffee, she thought of Jimmy and his birthday party the night before. She felt it went well and was happy to have been able to do this for him. She then began thinking about her life and struggled to figure out how she would fit Jimmy into it. Although she was a single mom, Mary was content. She had found a balance that worked for everyone, and she had no desire to make a change.

Thanksgiving Day was the following Thursday, and she still hadn't decided if she would take Jimmy with her to visit her family or if they would even make the trip. Mary wanted to see her dad and sisters but knew how awkward it would be to bring Jimmy along with her.

Mary's daddy was looking forward to seeing her and Elizabeth, but she thought they were still struggling with the idea of her dating Jimmy, and she didn't want to deal with that during the visit.

Mary knew she would figure it out, so she changed her focus and sat down with her coffee to read her bible. More importantly, Mary had come to know that her time with God was crucial, and she wanted to spend time alone with Him every day. She had faith that God would lead her in the right direction; that was where she left it for now. Of course, she had to decide on her plans for Thanksgiving as she wanted to see her family and spend it with them.

Mary stared out of the window over the ocean and caught a glimpse of two seagulls flying by. As they landed together at the edge of the water in perfect uniform, she thought of the beauty and significance of God's creation. She was reminded of the scripture, *Matthew 6:25-34, "Therefore I tell you, do not worry about your life, what you will eat or drink; or about your body, what you will wear. Is life not more than food and the body more than clothes? Look at the birds of the air; they do not sow or reap or store away in barns, and yet your heavenly Father feeds them."* Are you not much more valuable than they? By worrying, can any one of you add a single hour to your life?" Mary tended to worry, and as God nudged her to trust Him, she found much peace.

Mary desired to become more like Mary in God's word, and she felt she was learning more and more every day to learn to trust Him and worry less. She was grateful!

While taking her last sip of coffee, she could hear footsteps coming into the room. As she looked over, she saw Elizabeth walking toward her with sleepy eyes. "Good morning, my sweet girl," Mary said.

"Good morning, Mom," Elizabeth answered. She sat down next to Mary, rested her head on her shoulder, and hugged her.

Mary was so grateful for the love and affection that Elizabeth always showed her.

Elizabeth was a beautiful child and had such a sincere heart. Mary knew she was a gift from God.

Being a single mom had been hard for her, but God always reassured her that all would be okay, giving Mary the strength to persevere.

Mary often wondered how Elizabeth felt, and once or twice attempted to talk to her about it, but she would not open up about her feelings. Elizabeth appeared happy with their life together and Mary didn't want to encourage negative emotions if none were there. After all, Elizabeth was a gift from God, and Mary couldn't doubt that. She did her best as she sought direction from the Lord.

Occasionally, however, Mary would try and jump ahead of the Lord without waiting for His answer and always had to pay for the consequences. Those times were never fun, but the lessons she learned from them were always very rewarding. Mary was continuing to learn to let Jesus lead.

Mary asked Elizabeth what she wanted for breakfast, and they began discussing their plans for the day. Elizabeth was happy that they would be home for the day and were going to enjoy some time together.

As Mary got up to prepare breakfast for Elizabeth and herself, the phone rang. As she reached into the refrigerator, she looked at the caller ID, and saw it was her sister, Beth. Mary excitedly answered the phone and felt sure she knew why she was calling. Mary thought it was time to decide about Thanksgiving; today must be that day.

Beth began asking her how they were doing and if they had plans to come for Thanksgiving.

With a smile of confirmation, Mary looked at Elizabeth and decided they were going home for Thanksgiving and would bring Jimmy.

Beth was excited, and although Mary was a little nervous about Jimmy coming, she knew she was wrong to judge and thought spending more time with him and her family would benefit everyone. Beth talked about their daddy and how well he was doing. They had all agreed that they would have dinner at her house because she had the space, and since their mom had passed away, it worked out better.

Mary began to tell Beth that they would leave early on Wednesday morning so they could get there to help Beth and Sarah with things that needed to be done. They had planned to stay until Saturday then leave that morning so they would have Sunday at home to prepare for the week ahead. They were all very excited about being together. Holidays were always special, and family time was a blessing that Mary had not enjoyed enough of with her busy schedule. But this is going to change, Mary thought.

The temperatures outside were getting much cooler. Mary missed the summer because she enjoyed so much more time with Elizabeth when school was out, but each season brought something new, and adjustments were always needed. She was pleased that they had a few days off for Thanksgiving.

As they sat down to eat their breakfast, Mary thought about the box from Michael. She wondered how she would tell Elizabeth or if she ever would. What will I do with the check that he sent, she thought. Should I cash it and pay it toward the cottage or put it in a trust fund for Elizabeth? She didn't even want it and knew she wouldn't be cashing it anytime soon.

A thought suddenly came to Mary's mind, and her heart began to race! Just the thought of telling Elizabeth about him was terrifying to Mary. How in the world will I do this, she thought. I can't! That's just how it is. Elizabeth doesn't deserve any of this. I don't think she even needs to know. Mary's mind began spinning, and she couldn't shake it.

Elizabeth could tell something was wrong and looked concerned. "Mom, are you okay?" Mary realized that her emotions were now affecting Elizabeth, and she hadn't even known.

Mary answered, "Mom's okay, baby."

After breakfast, Mary and Elizabeth went to their rooms to dress. As she opened the closet, her eyes fell on a box perched on the shelf. A surge of regret washed over her, transporting her back to the day Michael left her to face it all alone. A solitary tear escaped a poignant reminder of the pain she had buried. She yearned for the nightmare to end, for this was a chapter she had long avoided. "Not now, not ever," Mary said with a painful tone.

Mary closed the closet door and jumped into the shower. She began to pray for peace and the answers she needed when she suddenly felt this warm sensation. She felt the presence of God, and the fear she was facing abruptly left her. Mary loved how Jesus constantly reminded her that He was there with her, and she knew she needed that above all else.

What happened next surprised Mary. As she stood in the mirror looking at herself, she began to speak out loud. "How do I ever forgive him, Lord?" Mary realized she had spent years not dealing with the pain she had felt, and God was bringing it back to her. Mary was sure there was a purpose for it and hoped He would heal her broken heart. This is for me and Elizabeth, she thought.

The phone rang, startling Mary. As she reached for it, she saw it was Jimmy. This brought a smile to her face. She surprised herself. When she answered the call, she excitedly asked him if he would like to go with her and Elizabeth to visit her family for Thanksgiving on Wednesday.

Jimmy had hoped she would ask as he wanted to be a part of her family and instantly answered, "Yes!" They made plans for him to drive over early on Wednesday morning, and they would take Mary's car as his truck was old, and they couldn't trust it on a long-distance trip. They all seemed joyful about the plans, including Elizabeth, but especially Jimmy.

Elizabeth, who had finished getting dressed, came into Mary's bedroom carrying JJ. She had on a cute cotton dress and was barefoot. JJ was happy, too, as he loved the attention. Mary told Jimmy she needed to go for now and that they could talk later. She felt he wanted to come over for the afternoon, but Mary had already decided that today she was going to focus on only her daughter.

Jimmy will be fine, she thought.

Mary and Elizabeth were enjoying their day together. They took JJ for a long walk on the beach and found a couple of unique seashells to add to their collection. As they looked at each one they had collected, it seemed to bring them back to the moment and their exact emotions when they found it. They were all extraordinary. The beach, however, had a different meaning to Mary since meeting Michael there.

Mary was afraid that the memories of their meeting and the mystery of it all would never leave her. She often wondered why things had ended the way they did. Now she guessed she knew; but now she faced the challenge of telling Elizabeth. She wished she didn't have to.

It was lunchtime, and they were getting hungry. Mary thought a picnic on the deck would be nice. Elizabeth agreed, so Mary made sandwiches and put chips and fresh hummus dip that she had made on their plates, and they walked out on the deck. They each had a glass of water with a slice of lemon to drink, and after such a long walk on the beach, it was refreshing. As they sat at the table, Mary wondered if it was the right time to share with Elizabeth about Michael. Her heart began to race, and as she looked at Elizabeth, she just couldn't do it! Mary also realized she could never shield her daughter from the pain and confusion it would bring to Elizabeth's life, no matter when she told her. She decided it would not be now, however. She wanted to wait a while longer and let them both enjoy their Thanksgiving Holiday without all of that drama.

When they were almost done with their lunch, the phone rang. Mary answered to the sweetest voice on the other end. "Daddy, it's so good to hear from you!" He called to let Mary know how excited he was that she and Elizabeth would be home for Thanksgiving.

"Are you bringing Jimmy too, Mary?" her daddy asked.

Mary said, "Yes. Is it okay, daddy?"

"Of course," he said.

Mary's daddy was such a humble man and never said anything negative about anyone. What he said next comforted Mary.

"Mary, you are a very smart woman, and I know you will make the right decisions. I'm happy he is coming if you and Elizabeth want him to."

Mary was so happy to hear her daddy's support. He was always her biggest cheerleader, and although she knew this situation with her and Jimmy's past was concerning to him, he never once said anything that would discourage her either way. Mary needed that!

Monday had arrived, and Mary knew the next two days would be long and stressful.

Mary was sitting at her desk when Pamela walked in with a vision of confidence in her beautiful navy suit. Pamela was excited about her new job at the Inn and eager to get to know the staff better. Mary shared in her excitement, but sadness lingered beneath her smile. She had been fiercely protective of her job for many years, and now, with Pamela's new role, she was faced with the bittersweet reality of being able to focus more on her writing career.

Mary stood to greet her and asked if she wanted to get some coffee.

Pamela giggled as coffee was one of her favorites, too.

As they walked into the restaurant and found a table to sit down, Mr. Henry came in behind them. He welcomed Pamela to the Inn and shared how excited he was that she was joining the team.

Pamela smiled, agreed that she was just as excited, and thanked him for the opportunity. Mary asked Mr. Henry if he wanted to join them for coffee, and he agreed.

The laughter at the table filled Mary's heart, confirming that Pamela was a perfect fit for the job. She felt they all knew the bond would grow to be just as beautiful as the relationship she and Mr. Henry had.

They sat at the table, and the waiter brought each of them a cup of coffee and asked if they needed a breakfast menu. They all agreed that coffee would be all for now.

They began discussing their ideas for the day.

Mr. Henry asked Mary if she planned to go over the computer system and how they kept everything organized.

Mary laughed and said, "How do you know me so well, Mr. Henry?"

Mr. Henry said, "Well, Mary, you have no idea how much I will miss you being here every day. It has always felt as if we could read each other's minds."

Mary agreed.

Monday and Tuesday were filled with training, and Pamela did a great job adjusting to the system and the workflow that needed to be done. Mary introduced her to the staff, who seemed to enjoy meeting her. Mary felt confident that hiring Pamela was the right choice for the Inn and Mr. Henry. So far, everyone seemed to be satisfied.

Mary was feeling confident that they had made the right decision about Pamela and was happy that now she would have more time doing what she truly loved: being with Elizabeth and writing.

9

THANKSGIVING WITH FAMILY

Wednesday morning came quickly, and as the alarm on Mary's clock rang, it was time to get up and get ready. The car still had to be packed for the trip to visit her family for Thanksgiving. Mary had not slept well and felt it was because she was anxious about bringing Jimmy to spend a holiday with her family. She wanted them to like him so much and had so much confidence in God's vision of Jimmy. Mary wanted so badly to see nothing but good come out of their relationship.

Mary's faith was undeniable. She also felt the jolt in her heart when God called her to love Jimmy, and she didn't have a choice. She desired to follow Jesus above all else and knew that sometimes she would be called to do hard things. After all, faith is believing what you can't see, and Mary knew this too. She certainly couldn't predict the future but wished she could. Security was vital to Mary, and she knew this need-ed to be a definite priority for Elizabeth. Her home had always been warm and filled with love and peace. She never wanted this to change.

Jimmy would meet them at the cottage at 7:30 a.m., and time was passing quickly. Mary walked into Elizabeth's room to wake her and saw that she was already dressed. Mary smiled at her and gave her a warm hug. "Elizabeth, are you excited about our trip?" Mary asked. "Are you happy Jimmy is going with us?"

Elizabeth agreed she was excited and looked forward to Jimmy coming with them.

Mary wanted more than anything to do the right thing for Elizabeth and knew the Lord's calling to love Jimmy must be the right answer for them both. "How could I go wrong here?" God went on reminding Mary not to be afraid. Of course, she was scared and knew that in all of this, there must be a lot for everyone to learn.

The doorbell rang and, as Mary opened the door, she saw Jimmy standing there. He was about fifteen minutes late, but this was common for him. Somehow, he always seemed to have an excuse for not being on time. This troubled Mary, as being on time was a priority for her. She welcomed Jimmy inside, and Elizabeth ran out of her room to greet him. He smiled at Elizabeth and back at Mary with a look of joy. This made Mary happy, and she forgot all about him being late. However, they needed to get on the road. Mary's dad knew she was always on time, so she hoped to make up for the difference on the journey there. She didn't want anything going wrong on this trip and hoped everyone would enjoy their time together.

Mary went inside to get JJ, and they put the last bag in the car. Karen would stop by the cottage daily to clean Sunshine's litter box, feed her, and check the mailbox for her. Mary was so blessed to have friends who always made themselves available to help her whenever needed.

Everyone was in the car, and Mary decided to drive. JJ sat in the back seat with Elizabeth. Mary felt awkward because it had been years since she had taken anyone home for a holiday. This feeling will pass, Mary thought.

Mary dreaded the long drive, and the traffic was heavy, but she was still excited to see her family.

As Mary looked down at her gas level, she realized she needed to stop and get gas. She pulled off the interstate and into a truck stop to fill up. Jimmy got out to pump her gas, and Mary said, "How nice is this, Elizabeth? Mom doesn't have to pump the gas."

She looked back at Jimmy, who she saw was eating a honey bun. She thought that was strange and wondered why he was doing this. Is he trying to hide this from us, she thought. But why? When he got back in the car, not saying a word, Mary said, "Jimmy, how was that honey bun? You have icing on your face." She began to laugh.

Jimmy laughed too, but his face turned red with embarrassment.

Mary was perplexed. Why would he sneak a honey bun while pumping gas? That's deceitful, she thought.

The rest of the drive was easy, and the conversation was great. Elizabeth took a long nap with JJ, and the peace of Jesus filled the car.

Mary often felt like she was on a rollercoaster in her mind when she was with Jimmy. She didn't like this. She knew she didn't like the chaos in her heart either, but she knew those feelings were fear. She immediately thought of a bible scripture that she referred to often. *1 John 4:18, "There is no fear in love. But perfect love drives out fear because fear has to do with punishment. The one who fears is not made in perfect love."* She began to whisper a prayer. "Lord, please help me to remain in your perfect love!"

Finally, they arrived at her sister Beth's house. The energy in the room was electric. Beth was delighted to see Mary and Elizabeth. It had been too long.

With a smile, Mary looked at Jimmy and said, "Beth, say hi to Jimmy."

Beth smiled and said in a confident voice, "Hi, Jimmy. Welcome to our home."

Jimmy said hi to Beth. "Thank you for having me. This is a special time for me, and I am honored to be here."

Although it felt awkward, Mary looked happy; she prayed everything would go well.

It was early afternoon, and they had planned to prepare some dishes for their Thanksgiving meal to get ahead for tomorrow. Mary asked Jimmy if he would bring the cooler that held some of the items she had brought for a special dessert she had planned to prepare. This was one of her dad's favorites, and she wanted to surprise him.

Beth had already begun preparing some of the casseroles to be put in the oven. The kitchen smelled amazing, and Mary realized they had not eaten lunch. Elizabeth was happy to see her family, as she hadn't had the opportunity to spend much time with them.

Mary would soon be working only part-time and hoped to spend more time with her family. Of course, she was also looking forward to her writing, and her readers were waiting for the sequel to her already-published book.

Jimmy came in with the cooler and a bag of chips. Mary laughed and grabbed the chips from him. He looked at her, laughed, and said, "Oh, you're hungry too?"

Mary quickly replied, "Yeah, I am, and I didn't eat a honey bun like you did." They both laughed.

Beth realized they had not had lunch and went to the refrigerator to get the lunch meat, homemade bread, mayonnaise, mustard, and homemade pickles that she knew both Mary and Elizabeth loved.

Mary thanked Beth and called Elizabeth into the room. Before Mary realized it, a tear had fallen onto her cheek. She missed her family so much, and her love for them was indescribable. She hoped they knew how much!

The phone rang in the background as they sat down to eat a quick lunch. It was Sarah. Beth had her on the speaker phone so they could all hear the conversation. Beth was very excited that they had finally made it there and shared with them that she would be over in an hour or so.

Jimmy got up to hug Mary with what looked like a tear in his eye. He spoke softly to her and said, "Mary, thank you for bringing me."

Mary hugged him back and said, "Jimmy, of course." She felt the sincerity in his heart and thanked Jesus for His love, which allowed her to love Jimmy. Even when it didn't make sense, she also realized that without the love that Jesus gave us, none of us would be capable of loving anyone.

The doorbell rang, attracting everyone's attention. Beth walked over to answer the door, and Mary stood up in anticipation of seeing who was there. "Daddy," Mary said as she ran to him and hugged him. With tears welling up, she looked into his eyes and said, "Daddy, it is so good to see you!" Of course, her daddy cried too and smiled at Mary. She quickly realized that she had left Jimmy alone and motioned for him to come over to where they were. He began walking over, and Mary introduced him. Jimmy looked concerned and hoped her dad would approve of him. Understanding his background gave Jimmy a sense of insecurity, and he desperately needed the approval of Mary's family. Her daddy reached for his hand to shake his hand and, with a firm handshake, welcomed him.

As Jimmy shook his hand, he could feel a bit of tension and, under his breath, said, Lord, help me to be the man you desire me to be for Mary. Jimmy was still learning that he was worthy because of Jesus and that the feelings of fear and shame did not come from God.

After the introduction, a sense of peace settled in the room, but Mary's heart was still heavy. She understood her family's concern, but it was hard for them to comprehend what she believed God was doing. Despite this, she was determined to follow His will, trusting He would take care of all the details.

Mary's heart swelled with joy as they were busy with the preparations. The sight of Elizabeth in the kitchen, wearing an apron and working alongside the family, filled Mary with the happiness she had longed for.

They had planned to stop baking around 4 p.m. so they could start preparing dinner.

Jimmy and James, Beth's husband, were going to grill steaks, and they had planned to bake potatoes and roast vegetables. Mary had also already prepared her favorite strawberry cheesecake at the cottage, and it sat in the cooler, waiting to surprise everyone.

JJ also spent a lot of time in the kitchen. Occasionally, he would find a dropped morsel on the floor. Although he was under everyone's feet, he was also a part of the family, and everyone loved him. JJ also felt at home there and loved the attention he was getting.

Mary found herself praying silently. As she meditated on the gratefulness in her heart, she thought of *Romans 12:10, "Be devoted to one another in love. Honor one another above yourselves."* She could see what God was doing as she felt His presence in the home.

Finally, everything was prepared and was now sitting in the refrigerator. The Thanksgiving meal would be a heartwarming experience filled with the warmth of their togetherness, and everyone was eagerly looking forward to it.

The doorbell rang, and Sarah came through the door. Everyone stopped what they were doing to greet her. She looked happy and held a vegetable tray with her favorite homemade dip in her hand.

Mary walked over to hug her, and Elizabeth took the platter and dip from her to place on the bar. Elizabeth was always so attentive to the needs of others, and this pleased Mary.

Sarah got hugs from everyone, and once again, Mary realized that Jimmy had not met her. She called him over and introduced the two of them. This time, Jimmy felt more at peace. Sarah didn't show him any emotion of concern, which also pleased Mary. She was happy that all was going well and realized again how supportive her family was of her.

James called Jimmy over to the grill. He had a platter of already seasoned steaks for grilling. Jimmy loved to grill, and Mary was pleased that James had included him in this part of their evening.

Jimmy asked Mary's daddy if he would also like to join them outside, and he agreed.

The girls all hung out in the kitchen, catching up on what they'd all been up to. Mary sliced vegetables, Beth prepared the potatoes for the oven, and Sarah sat with Elizabeth; JJ sat at their feet. Beth had made two loaves of homemade sourdough bread and thought she would slice one for their evening meal.

The laughter was contagious in the room, and their time together was priceless. Mary couldn't imagine her life without her family, so she whispered a prayer to thank Him. The bible scripture in *Colossians 3:13* came to her mind. *"Bear with each other and forgive one another if any of you have a grievance against someone. Forgive as the Lord forgave you."* She remembered there were often times in life when people had to forgive each other and was so grateful that, most importantly, God had forgiven them. This time, a new test was in front of them. Jimmy also needed to be forgiven and loved, just as Christ had called Mary to do.

Sarah got up to set the table and saw Mary standing at the French door, peaking out at the BBQ grill. Sarah smiled, tapped Mary on the shoulder, and said, "How is it going out there?"

With a big smile, Mary answered, "It looks like it's going very well. Daddy is laughing at something Jimmy said, and I can only imagine what that was."

Sarah laughed and walked back over to the table to finish setting it.

Jimmy had a great personality. He was handsome and had so much to offer in life. Mary was often sad to hear some of the stories he had shared with her, such as how being caught up in peer pressure at a young age almost destroyed his life. He was grateful that God never left him and always knew that he had a special calling in his life. He had difficulty believing that he was worthy of any calling from God but was now beginning to accept it. Mary hoped so.

Just in time, the men with the steaks were coming in the door. Beth took the vegetables and potatoes out of the oven and placed them on the bar next to the platter of meat. Sarah had buttered the bread and added garlic for toasting. It was ready, too. Mary filled all the glasses with sweet tea and added lemon to the top of the glass.

Everything came together just as planned. It was time for dinner!

Before they began to eat, Beth asked Daddy if he would say the blessing.

He replied, "Of course!" He began to pray, *"Father, thank you for this time with my family and the joy and laughter in the room. Thank you also, Father, for allowing Jimmy to spend time with us. May we all show the love You freely give us and be a bright light in the world that desperately needs You. Because of You, we can do that, and because of Your love, hearts change. Thank you for this food and the hands that have prepared it. In Jesus' name, I pray, Amen."*

Jimmy thought of his family and how much he had missed them. It had been a couple of years since he had seen them. He hoped that one day, God would restore their relationship, and Mary could be a part of his family. He loved them so much; unfortunately, his choices had brought much division between them. He also believed that if he kept walking with Jesus, God would restore his life, and maybe they could be a family again. This hope for reconciliation and forgiveness was a powerful emotion filling the room, touching everyone's hearts.

After all, it was Thanksgiving, and they all had so much to be thankful for.

Everyone began filling their plates to sit at the table. Mary's daddy started the line. Beth had requested this, as her dad was so special to the girls. While everyone was enjoying their delicious dinner, compliments kept coming up about how good the steak was. James and Jimmy did a fantastic job grilling. All of the food was delicious.

Now, the time had come for dessert. As everyone began looking at Mary for the surprise, she got up from the table, walked over to the cooler, and had everyone close their eyes. She placed the large strawberry cheesecake in the center of the table and brought dessert plates for everyone. The strawberries were fresh and filled the top of the cake.

Beth spoke up and said, "Mary, okay, you have made us wait long enough."

Everyone began to laugh.

Mary told everyone to open their eyes, and the noise in the room was so rewarding. Mary was happy the cake made the long trip without damage and loved serving others. She began slicing the cake and gave each one a slice. Mary was delighted that everyone was pleased.

Elizabeth started giggling, and no one knew what she was giggling at, so Mary asked her. She began telling them that she was just happy and loved the look on her mom's face as everyone ate the cheesecake that she knew her mom had worked so hard on. Mary got up and hugged Elizabeth and said, "You are the sweetest girl on the planet, baby." Elizabeth was a sweet girl and always took notice of how hard her mom was always working.

After dinner, the men walked outside, and the girls got up to wash the dishes and clean the kitchen together. Beth commented that they needed to eat all the food they had prepared the next day because she couldn't find any more room in the refrigerator for anything else.

Mary spoke up and said, "Oh, Beth, don't worry. We will eat it."

Sarah started laughing, and Elizabeth did, too.

The kitchen was clean, and everyone was stuffed.

Jimmy asked if everyone wanted to sit by the fire pit for a while. Everyone grabbed a sweater and agreed that this would be great. They all walked outside to find the fire blazing.

James and Jimmy had made the fire. After a great meal and conversation with the family, Daddy sat down to rest.

Jimmy had already picked out three chairs for Mary, Elizabeth, and he to sit in. Before sitting down, Jimmy hugged Mary and thanked her for allowing him to be a part of such a beautiful family Thanksgiving.

One by one, stories were shared around the campfire,. There was laughter, tears of sadness, and tears of joy, and the love felt was beautiful.

This was a day to remember forever.

As the hours passed, it began to get late, and although each heart felt a sense of not wanting the day to end, Mary realized they must get some rest. The next day, there was much work to be done, and she knew they could pick up from where they left off.

As they all got up from their chairs to go back inside for bed, Daddy stood up to say a final word of the day: "Thank you for such a great meal and for all of you loving me the way you do. It was a fantastic day! One that I needed." Hugs were given, and everyone went inside.

It was six a.m., and Mary was one of the first up. She brewed the coffee, took JJ for a walk, and picked up her bible to read. She chose a window with a view of the pond, and as she reflected on the day before, she realized that she had a heart full of love.

While she was praying, she heard footsteps coming toward her. It was Jimmy. He sat down beside Mary and reached for her hand. As he held her hand, he looked peaceful.

Jimmy began to tell Mary that he was so grateful for the time spent with her family and how much he had needed it. "Mary," he said, "I haven't felt this close to anyone, nor felt so much love, in so long. I miss my family, Mary. I see Jesus here and pray I can spend many more holidays with your family."

Mary felt the sincerity in his words and was blessed that Jesus had given him a glimpse of His love through her family.

As Mary and Jimmy sat holding hands, everyone began coming into the kitchen. It was Thanksgiving Day, and they were excited to spend it together.

Beth put some fresh ground sausage in a pan and prepared French toast. Mary got up to help when Sarah came in to help as well. The girls worked well together.

Breakfast was delicious, and the kitchen was cleaned once more. It was time to begin baking the dishes for their Thanksgiving Day meal. They had planned to have a late lunch and an early dinner and were shooting for three p.m.

The parade sound was heard from the living room as James, Jimmy, and Daddy sat and talked. The sisters were in the kitchen talking as they went over the menu and told stories of growing up. The joy felt was beautiful, and the memories they shared were also heard by Daddy, who tuned in to hear as many of them as he could. Occasionally, he would chime in to comment on a story one was telling, and they could all feel their daddy's love in their hearts.

It was already another beautiful day.

As the timer on the double ovens went off and other casseroles were placed in the oven to bake, they were very close to completing their meal. It was time to prepare another couple of pies Beth knew were their favorites. Their mom had always made homemade chocolate pies, and Beth seemed to be the only one who knew exactly how to make them. As she began getting all the ingredients out to prepare it, Mary could feel the memories of her mom as they all sat together eating the traditional chocolate pie. It was wonderful to Mary how memories could bring her back to that moment. They all felt that way, and in some small way, Beth's chocolate pie always seemed to be a favorite part of their meal on Thanksgiving Day.

The island was filled with the colors of great casseroles and desserts.

The turkey was sliced and served on a platter Mary's mom gave her. Rolls came out of the oven, and the table was set with Beth's finest china. She enjoyed serving as much as Mary, and they always prepared the most amazing meals together. Sarah was also very good at baking, but with her career, she didn't have as much time.

Mary asked Daddy if he would call everyone into the kitchen and if he would bless the meal. As he got up to get everyone's attention, he felt something in his heart that he knew he needed to share with everyone.

The family and Jimmy stood in the kitchen when Daddy began to speak. "I want to thank all of you for being here. Mary, you, and Elizabeth had a long drive. I realize things are so different now that your mom has left us, and she loved the Thanksgiving holiday so much. She loved her family, and I know all of you miss her as much as I do." There wasn't a dry eye in the room except for Jimmy. He had a sweet look of love on his face, and Mary realized how much he must have missed his family.

Their daddy began to say the blessing as they all held hands to form a complete circle around the room. *"Father, thank you for my family. Thank you for our time together and the love we all feel in this room. You have blessed each one of us beyond measure. Thank you for this food and for the hands of my sweet daughters who have prepared it. In Jesus' name, I pray, Amen."*

The laughter in the room was contagious as they all sat and enjoyed their meal. The words "yum", "oh my goodness", and "wow" were heard throughout the room. As always, the food was delicious, and everyone was stuffed, although everybody left a little room for the pies!

Like most, the day flew by, but everyone, including Jimmy, would remember it forever.

Saturday had arrived, and the time to drive back home had come. Mary felt sad as she longed to be with her family. As she and Elizabeth hugged everyone goodbye, tears began to flow. She knew this would be difficult for her and Elizabeth, but she knew she had to get back home as she was training Pamela on Monday. Mary was looking forward to her new journey as a part-time employee and focusing more on her writing. She felt more trips to see her family would be a part of that journey.

10

A REUNION WITH JIMMY'S FAMILY

After weeks of training Pamela at the Inn, Mary's new journey of part-time employment had come. It was a sad time for everyone, and Mr. Henry had planned a luncheon for the staff. Although Mary would still be there, it would not be the same.

Mary, however, was very excited about spending more time at home with Elizabeth and writing a lot more. Her published book had been read by many, and with the busyness of her life the last several months, she had not even been able to stay in touch with her readers. This troubled Mary. Her writing career meant a lot to her, and she began feeling like she had failed everyone. It's time to change that, Mary thought to herself.

Sitting at her desk, Mary stared out of her office window into the garden, to the bench she used to spend a lot of time sitting on during her lunch breaks. She remembered when it was just her and living in the apartment alone. She thought about when Karen took her to meet JJ and how he came home with her. The memory of her applying for the loan for her new cottage made her smile as she remembered being so overjoyed at her new home that she still loved so much. She thought of the sweet moments when Elizabeth was born and how frightened she was to bring her home all by herself. She thought of Sunshine and how Jesus brought her to their front door on a cold winter day. The thought of ever leaving the cottage was one she hoped would never become a reality as the memories there were all so precious to her, and she couldn't imagine ever living anywhere else.

The phone rang, startling Mary. As she almost jumped out of her chair, she looked at her phone and saw that Jimmy was calling.

As she shifted her focus, she answered the call. Jimmy sounded sad. Mary asked him what was up. He told her how much he had missed his family and children and thought he was ready to revisit them. Mary shared with him that she felt he needed to call them. He agreed that he would. However, what he said next was hard for Mary to hear.

"Mary, I would like for you to go with me. Would you?"

Mary took a deep breath and said she would have to consider it. Jimmy hoped that she would go as he knew he needed the support.

Mary didn't say anything but didn't know how she could be without Elizabeth for four days. They had not been apart for more than a night. Jimmy thanked Mary for listening and she told him she would call him soon.

As Mary put down the phone, Mr. Henry walked into her office and saw the sadness on her face. "Mary, are you okay?" he asked.

Mary responded, "Yes, I'm okay, Mr. Henry, but you know how much I will miss you, don't you? We have been doing this together for so long, and even though I know I will still be here part-time, it will not be the same."

Mr. Henry walked toward her, and as she stood up from her chair, he motioned for her to come to him. He hugged Mary, and tears began to flow from her eyes. She had no idea how hard this would be, but she discovered it wouldn't be as easy as she had hoped.

Pulling away, she thanked him for always being there for her and believing in her. While looking up, she saw a tear in Mr. Henry's eyes and realized that this wasn't easy for him either.

Mr. Henry was the best boss Mary had ever had, and she couldn't be more thankful that she would still spend some time with him.

"Well, I didn't expect all this," Mr. Henry said with a chuckle. "I came in to tell you that your luncheon was prepared, and everyone was waiting for you."

She began to laugh, too, and together they walked out of her office to enjoy a great lunch and time with her friends.

The restaurant was full of everyone Mary loved. The smell of the food was incredible. Looking around the room, she could see and feel everyone's emotions. The tables were beautifully decorated, and Mary could only feel the love that everyone had for her. She thought of the bible scripture in *1 John 4:12, "No one has ever seen God; but if we love one another, God lives in us, and his love is made complete in us."* She knew at that moment that God had brought all of them together and that they could all love each other in the love that He had given them. Mary realized that it started with Mr. Henry as the leader of the Inn. He had developed an incredible staff, and everyone there knew it.

The celebration was over, and it was time for Mary to leave to pick up Elizabeth from Gymnastics. As she began to walk out the door, everyone started to give her hugs. She was happy again and knew that her season was changing, and she had to embrace this change.

Pamela walked her to the car to say goodbye and thanked her for believing in her for the sales position at the Inn. Mary thanked her for taking it and said, "God knew this would happen long before we did."

Pamela smiled.

Soon Pamela would be alone for the first time, as Mary planned to take a vacation and write while enjoying the cool days in the forecast. They hugged goodbye, then Pamela stood and watched as Mary drove away.

While driving to Gymnastics, Mary thought about her call with

Jimmy. "How could I leave Elizabeth for that many days? Should I go or not?" She needed to support Jimmy but had no idea what to expect. She wanted to be there for him, and she had the time off to do it, but she wanted to spend it writing and not traveling. "Oh, my! Why isn't anything easy?" Mary asked herself.

Mary arrived at Gymnastics, and Elizabeth was outside waiting for her. She gave her usual wave and began walking to the car. As Elizabeth entered, she told Mary hi and asked how her day was. Mary, of course, told her all about the luncheon Mr. Henry had set up. Elizabeth was happy for her. Mary thanked her and gave her a warm smile.

After arriving at the cottage, Mary began preparing dinner while Elizabeth did her homework. She thought about talking to Patricia about the trip to see Jimmy's parents and possibly taking care of Elizabeth while she was gone, but the thought quickly left her. She could feel her heart racing at the thought of leaving Elizabeth for almost a week. "This may be something I need to do," she thought. She began to whisper a prayer. "Father, please lead me to where you want me to go. Help me follow your will for my life."

Mary and Elizabeth sat down to eat dinner out on the deck. The cool breeze was refreshing, and they could hear the waves crashing onto the shore. Elizabeth loved their cottage as much as Mary did. It was home and the only home that Elizabeth had ever known.

After dinner, Elizabeth decided to take a shower and put on her pajamas while Mary cleaned the kitchen. Mary couldn't quit thinking about Jimmy and how sad he sounded on the phone. She knew she had to be there for him, so she picked up the phone and called Patricia.

It only took Mary a second to begin explaining to Patricia what was going on and asking what she thought. Patricia understood the sadness Jimmy must have felt and Mary's feelings about it.

"Of course, I will take care of Elizabeth, Mary! It would be my honor, and yes, I think you should go." Mary could not believe what she was hearing and had hoped she would tell her not to go. After all, she would need to leave in only a few days. Mary agreed to talk to Elizabeth before bed and told her she would let her know. She thanked Patricia, and they hung up the call.

When Elizabeth came out of the bathroom and into the living room, Mary was sitting on the couch with JJ. Mary asked Elizabeth if she could talk to her about something, and Elizabeth sat beside her and smiled.

Elizabeth had no idea what her mom was about to say but she could see the concerned look on her face. Mary began to tell Elizabeth a little about Jimmy's life and shared with her that it had been two years since Jimmy had seen his parents. Elizabeth looked sad. She couldn't imagine not seeing her mom, but she did know what it felt like not having a dad in her life. She listened intently, and as soon as Mary told her that Jimmy wanted her to go with him to see his parents for the first time in two years, Elizabeth said, "Mom, you need to go!"

Mary couldn't believe what she was hearing from her and felt a little strange. She told her that she had already talked to Patricia, and she had offered to take care of her and JJ if she decided to go. Elizabeth loved the idea of being able to spend the night with Faith for that long and encouraged her mom to go. Mary hugged Elizabeth and said, "Thank you, baby! I love you so much!"

Elizabeth didn't have school on Friday or Monday as they were out for teacher workdays until Tuesday. Mary guessed she would leave on Monday and come back on Thursday. She wasn't sure of all the details, so she picked up the phone to call Jimmy. He answered on the second ring and seemed excited that she had called. Mary proceeded to tell him that she had been praying and that she had talked to Patricia and Elizabeth. She told him she would go but would only stay three nights. Mary knew she was using her vacation time to take the trip and wanted to finish writing before returning to work. Although part-time, she still had to work, and the change would also require an adjustment.

Jimmy seemed so happy and agreed to talk to his parents and look up flights. "At such short notice, I'm not sure what the cost will be, but let's look." Jimmy thanked Mary and said they would confirm the plans the next day.

Elizabeth was in her room watching a series that she loved. Mary crawled into bed and snuggled with her. Her love for Elizabeth was strong, and she was grateful to God for her daughter. She wanted to be the best mom in the world and feared failing her and God.

It was time for bed, and Mary gave Elizabeth a big hug, prayed with her, and tucked her in tight. Elizabeth looked happy, which always made Mary happy, too. They said goodnight, and Mary went into her room.

As soon as she walked into her bedroom, the phone rang. It was Jimmy. He had found a couple of Monday flights and talked to his parents, who had agreed to pay for them.

"Mary, can we talk about the times so my mom and dad can book the flights? I am so excited to see my family again. Thank you, Mary!"

Mary picked up the phone to call Patricia to ask if Monday through Thursday was okay with her. As they talked, Patricia could tell Mary was feeling a little uneasy.

"Mary, of course, Monday through Thursday is fine, but are you okay?" Patricia asked.

"Yes, but I'm a little nervous about this," Mary said. "I feel God telling me to go, Patricia, but I'm unsure I want to. It's a lot to deal with."

Patricia agreed it was a lot, but felt Mary would be blessed because of her obedience. Her words comforted Mary, and she was beginning to get excited about the trip.

As soon as she hung up the phone with Patricia, she texted Jimmy to say all was good and that she would take the trip with him. Jimmy was very excited, but she could also sense a little anxiety from him. After all, this was a reunion he knew would not be easy for anyone. Mary encouraged Jimmy by telling him that God was restoring his family, and it would be wonderful. Jimmy loved how Mary encouraged him, and her faith was indescribable. He had never felt what he was feeling before.

This was all new to him. Jimmy soon hung up the phone excitedly so he could call his parents back to tell them the good news.

Mary was very excited about meeting them and his children. James was only 6, and Maddie was 11. I believe, Mary thought, this was going to be a trip to remember.

Before she knew it, it was morning. The sun shone through the window, and she could hear Sunshine running across the floor, chasing her toy. JJ was still snuggling next to her in bed. She sat up, stretched, and put her feet into her slippers. She entered the kitchen to turn on her coffee pot and open the blinds. As she looked out at the ocean, she thanked God for their cottage and even thanked Him for the new season that she was in. She still wasn't sure what He was doing but knew it was His will, and she needed to walk in it.

Monday morning came quickly, and Jimmy was scheduled to meet her at her house at 9:15. Their flights were scheduled for 12:15, but she still had to get Elizabeth to Patricia's and pack some last-minute items she didn't want to forget. She could tell Elizabeth was happy about spending time with Faith, and she was glad for Jimmy that he would revisit his family and children.

The doorbell rang as Mary was finishing washing the last of the breakfast dishes. It was Jimmy. Elizabeth ran to the door to let him in, and he was excited to see her. Mary smiled and said, "Hi, Jimmy." He could see their luggage was already in the kitchen by the door and asked if he could take it out for them. Mary thanked him.

The drive to Patricia's went without incident. Mary had a tough time leaving Elizabeth for so long and she hoped her daughter would cope okay.

Faith ran out the door to the car to greet Elizabeth as they arrived at Patricia's. Mary smiled and said, "Those girls are too much!" Mary gave Patricia a copy of the flight schedule and important documents, such as Elizabeth's insurance card, in case they were needed.

Patricia smiled at Mary and said, "You are the most organized person I know, Mary, but everything will be okay."

Mary smiled and nodded. Then, after hugging Elizabeth extra tightly, she and Jimmy walked out the door.

Before they knew it, they had arrived at the airport. It was a direct flight, so she had hoped it wouldn't be too bad. Mary loved to fly but was unhappy that Elizabeth was not with her. But she suspected her daughter was coping a lot better than she was.

As they boarded the plane and the captain informed them to fasten seat belts, she knew it was too late to back out. She began to pray. *"Lord, please protect Elizabeth while I am away from her. Protect Jimmy and me, and please make this a beautiful reunion for him and his family. In Jesus' name, I pray, Amen."*

She could tell that Jimmy was excited but nervous. His family loved him so much, and sadly, it had come to this, with the pain and hurt of his choices. Mary hoped that his future would be different, as she knew this was what God had shown her anyway. She wanted so badly for Jimmy to turn his life around. He had so much to offer, and the testimony that God had given him to share and be there to help guide others was incredible.

The flight seemed quick and comfortable. They arrived at the airport, and after they exited the plane, they began walking to the escalator to go to baggage claim, where they would meet Jimmy's dad. As they stepped onto the escalator, Mary saw someone standing at the bottom, looking up at them. As they got closer, she looked up at Jimmy, who had tears in his eyes, and trying to understand it all, she saw the man again. With tears flowing down his face, she immediately realized it was Jimmy's dad. Chills ran through Mary's body as she could see what was happening and began to pray. "Lord, you are showing me the prodigal son right before my eyes. Jimmy is coming back home, and his dad is so happy!"

As they reached the end of the escalator, Jimmy's dad grabbed him, and with tears flowing, they hugged, not saying a word. Mary could see God restore two broken hearts, and the love she saw was indescribable.

She knew now why she had taken this trip and would not have changed the blessing God had shown her for anything. Mary saw the power of God at that moment as she had never seen it before.

Mary enjoyed his dad's company and couldn't believe how much Jimmy favored him. Their personalities were similar, and Mary loved their conversations. She was looking forward to getting to know Jimmy's family better.

Jimmy was so happy to see his dad, and because everyone was hungry, they stopped at a BBQ restaurant to have lunch. Jimmy's son, James, was in kindergarten, and Jimmy was picking him up at school. He was expecting him and knew he was nervous about it. It had also been a very long time since they had been together.

The BBQ was yummy, and everyone was full. The day had been tiring as they had all gotten up very early. Mary texted Patricia to let her know they had made their trip safely and shared a bit about how Jimmy's dad had been waiting for him at the end of the escalator and how she could see God's word right before her. "Patricia, God showed me the prodigal Son coming home!" It was incredible!

Patricia shared with Mary how well Elizabeth and JJ were doing and that she had been by the cottage to check on Sunshine. Everything was going well. Mary was overjoyed to hear the great news, and the trip was more than she expected.

They had arrived at the school to see James, and while Jimmy was looking for him, he could see him coming around the corner. Jimmy ran to him, picked him up, and hugged him tightly. James smiled at his dad, and you could see the love between them. You could also see pain. The time apart had been very painful for everyone. As Jimmy introduced James to Mary, she smiled at him, picked him up, and, while giggling, twirled him around and around. He liked Mary, and Mary already loved him.

Mary could see Jesus' reconciliation in Jimmy's family at that moment. She could feel the fear leave and the love of Jesus return.

Jimmy's mom was not there to meet them at the airport as she was working. Mary wondered if fear had kept her from coming to the reunion as she chose not to be there. Mary had hoped she would see her but knew she would in the evening. She was also happy to have the opportunity to spend time with her.

The day had been filled with God's goodness. As they drove away from the school with Jimmy's dad and son, Mary could see Jesus picking up the pieces of a broken life and putting them back together again. Mary thought of *Hebrews 12:14, "Make every effort to live in peace with everyone and to be holy; without holiness, no one will see the Lord."*

Mary sat listening to the conversation and thought of the pain that Jimmy's parents must have felt being away from him for so long. She believed the fear they must have felt for him would be challenging for everyone. Mary thought of the goodness of the Lord and how she felt He would use their life story for good, bringing Mary peace. She thought of *Genesis 50:20, "You intended to harm me, but God intended it for good to accomplish what is now being done, the saving of many lives."* Mary knew then that what she witnessed was from God and would be used for His glory!

The memories of this time will be cherished in Mary's heart forever. Jimmy was finally at home again.

11

SURPRISE VISIT FROM MICHAEL

The trip to see Jimmy's parents and children was a memory that both Jimmy and Mary knew would never be forgotten. The love and forgiveness felt through God's love were profound. Mary knew that only Jesus could bring this kind of unity, and she was grateful she was given the blessing of witnessing it first-hand.

The next few days at home would be quiet days of writing. Mary had a book to write, and she had to get caught up on emails from her readers that she had not purposefully ignored. Her readers were very special; she never wanted to take them for granted.

The morning seemed to go by too fast. After taking Elizabeth to school and catching up on chores, Mary finally sat in her favorite chair by the window overlooking the ocean. As she sat down with her warm glass of ginger tea, she felt a sense of relief and began thanking the Lord for the time she had to write. Her life had become exceptionally busy, and while still trying to find a balance, she felt that with her beginning to work part-time, those days were coming.

Mary opened her laptop, looked out at the ocean, and thought about Michael. She had not heard from him again since the last email, and the package had arrived. She remembered their time on the beach when they met and how exchanging books was a beautiful time for her back then. Although she felt in her heart that God had sent him to her, after all the years that had passed, she was still questioning how things went so wrong and so fast.

At that moment, the phone rang, and when she looked down at her phone to see who was calling, it was Michael. "No Way," Mary said. "Oh, God, help me, please!" She ignored the call, laid it back down, and began to look over the last chapter she had written. It had been a while since she had had the opportunity.

The phone beeped, indicating she had a voicemail, and the distraction got the best of her. Mary picked up her phone to hear what he had to say, and after listening, she dropped it. "This can't be, Lord!" Michael was back at the beach in the same rented house he had been in when they met. His voicemail sounded cheerful, and he asked if he could see her somehow.

Mary's heart began to race out of her chest. "There is no way! I will never see him, and how in the world am I going to avoid him? He is practically next door!"

Mary's heart was troubled. She began thinking about Elizabeth. How will I ever tell her? She began to pray. *"Father, please help me! I do not know what to do here, and I do not want to see Michael again."* She was immediately reminded of Colossians 3:13. *"Bear with each other and forgive one another if any of you has a grievance against someone. Forgive as the Lord forgave you."* This is so hard, Lord!

Mary did not return Michael's call and began to write. Two hours had passed, and she was well into another chapter of her book when the doorbell rang. As she stood up to stretch, she wondered who it could be. Is it Michael, she thought. Her heart began to race, but as she peeped out onto the deck at the front door, she saw Jimmy standing there with a single rose in his hand. She began to feel more relaxed and realized she had a smile on her face.

Mary knew in her heart that God had called her to love Jimmy, and He had put that love in her heart for him, but she was still fighting within herself to get too close to him. She still had a fear of his past life and didn't want to be a part of any of that either.

Mary walked to the door. When she opened it, Jimmy handed her the red rose. She smiled and thanked him. While looking away from him, she immediately thought of when Michael would visit, and how, each time, he would hand her a single rose as he walked in. The memories of Michael were still everywhere, and Mary didn't like it.

Jimmy began to speak. "Mary, I hope I'm not interrupting your writing. But I wanted to stop by to thank you for visiting my family and children with me. I can't tell you how happy it has made me, and the unity and love I now feel between them has been so refreshing. I never want to be apart from them, and I can't imagine doing that alone. You are a very special person, Mary, and I just wanted you to know that."

Mary was touched by his words and thanked God for allowing her to witness such a reunion.

She invited him in and shared that she had just gotten up to take a break from her writing when the doorbell rang.

"Great timing, Jimmy. Let's sit on the deck for a few minutes," Mary said.

Mary went into the kitchen to find a vase for her rose. They then walked out onto the deck. It was a beautiful afternoon, and although the temperatures were cool, the sun was shining brightly, and it felt great to be outside.

Jimmy moved two chairs closer to the deck rail, away from the table, so that they could look out over the ocean. The sound of the waves crashing into the shore was so relaxing.

As she looked at Jimmy with a smile, Mary began to talk about their trip to see his family and how much she enjoyed meeting everyone. She spoke about his mom, how beautiful she was, and how her job kept her busy. Although she didn't get to meet her at the same time she met his dad at the airport, she was blessed to spend much time with her in their home.   Mary realized that God's plan had worked out perfectly.

Jimmy began telling Mary how his dad had retired years ago and how well he handled things at home while his mom continued to work. She loved her career and wanted to work as long as she could.

Jimmy stood up from his chair. Mary looked at him and said, "Where are you going?

Jimmy replied, "Mary, let's go walk on the beach. Do you have time?" She immediately thought about Michael being practically next door, and her heart began to race again. She had not told Jimmy about Michael at any length, and she didn't even know he was in town until a few hours ago. Jimmy looked a little perplexed and asked Mary if she was okay

Mary quickly answered, "Yes, I'm OK. But I don't have very long, Jimmy. I only have a few hours before picking Elizabeth up from school, and I wanted to write this afternoon."

Jimmy reached for her hand. She grabbed her keys from inside the cottage, locked the door, and they both began walking hand in hand down the walkway to the ocean. When they reached the shore, Mary turned to the right. She was trying to avoid Michael at all costs. Jimmy, nudging her, said, "Let's go this way. It looks like there are a lot of seashells on this side for some reason."

Reluctantly, Mary agreed.

As they laughed together, Mary's heart was torn. She could only pray that Michael would be nowhere around. She began to whisper a quick prayer. "Lord, please protect me. Please don't let Michael be anywhere close!"

Jimmy let go of Mary's hand as he saw something along the shore's edge. As he ran toward it, Mary followed behind him. It was a beautiful conk shell. It was perfect. Jimmy put it up to his ear to see if he could hear the ocean and then, with a child-like giggle, placed it on Mary's ear so she could hear it, too.

The laughter and fun they were having took her mind off Michael for a few minutes, but as soon as the joyful thoughts left, they returned.

Walking further down the beach, Mary suddenly realized they were directly in front of the house Michael rented. Looking up, she could see Michael standing on the deck, looking down at them. As their eyes made contact, Mary felt a shiver run down her spine. Turning away, she looked out at the ocean and began sobbing.

Confused, Jimmy walked over to Mary, put his arms around her, and said, "Mary, are you all right?"

Mary didn't answer. "We need to get back to the cottage, Jimmy."

They began walking back up the beach; this time, Mary walked ahead of him. Jimmy was so confused. He had no idea what had just happened,

As they reached the cottage, Mary turned to Jimmy and thanked him for coming by and for the rose. She also told him that what just happened wasn't about him. "Jimmy, please don't think it is. It is something that I must work through myself."

Jimmy thanked her for seeing him and for their stroll on the beach.

Mary walked inside, closed the door, locked it, and went to her bedroom.

After crying for what felt like an hour, her eyes were red and swollen. Mary knew she had to pull herself together before it was time to pick up Elizabeth.

The day that she had dreaded for eight years had come, and she wasn't ready for it.

Mary picked up the phone and called Karen. The phone rang several times before she finally answered. "Karen, I need to see my friends! Is there a time we can all get together?"

Karen knew instantly something was wrong; not only did she miss

Mary, but she was also concerned about her too. Karen answered, "Hi Mary! I was thinking about you and Elizabeth just today and how much I have missed you. I will send a group text now. Let's make it soon!"

Mary agreed that the time between meeting with her friends had stretched on for too long and meeting up needed to be a priority. Mary talked about beginning to work only part-time and how she hoped this would allow her to spend more time with the people she loved.

Karen talked about her pregnancy and how she was seven months now. She had been doing very well. Everything had gone as planned so far. Sam was enjoying Karen being at home, and Karen had adapted very well after leaving her career. Life was different for her now, but she knew that with the baby coming soon, it would be so rewarding. The thoughts of her having to go back to work were frightening to her, and she was very happy that Sam had suggested she leave to get adjusted, as her job had become her identity, and they both knew it. The months of being at home had helped her find her identity in Jesus as well as herself. She loved who she had become.

They talked about Victoria and John and how nice it was that they had moved back home, but they had hoped they would have had more time together. Mary said, "We must change that. I have missed all of you so much! We need each other, Karen. I need you all very much."

Mary looked down at her phone, and saw Karen had already sent the group message. They had all responded that the following Saturday would be a great time to meet at their favorite Italian restaurant. This time, Faith and Elizabeth would be there, but Mary knew they would enjoy each other, and it would be great to include them as well.

Karen was also very excited. They had not been together often, and with her being seven months pregnant, a lot had changed.

In the busyness of all their lives, they had not even thought about a baby shower for Karen, and Mary felt terrible. She realized this was something she needed to begin planning right away.

How could I forget my dear friend's baby shower, Mary thought. "Okay, we need to make our time together a priority from here on out. Life can sure keep us busy, can't it?" They agreed that this would be one of the topics of conversation when they got together on the following Saturday. They agreed to meet at 11 a.m., and they were all excited about spending a little time together.

When they hung up the call, Mary realized it was soon time to pick Elizabeth up from school, and she was exhausted. She felt as if two days had run into one and, what with the call from Michael, Jimmy coming over to surprise her as well as seeing Michael, her day had not gone as planned. Mary began to pray for peace, as she needed it badly. Her day started with plans to write, and she was grateful for the writing time that she had had, but, wow, it had been a confusing time.

Taking a deep breath, she walked out onto the deck and looked out into the ocean as far as her eyes could take her. A smile began to form as she saw three dolphins in the distance. As they went under and came back up to the surface of the water, she had another thought that didn't surprise her, really. She began to pray.

"Lord, watching those dolphins go under and come back to the surface reminds me a little of how I feel right now. So many times, I feel as if I am drowning in fear and as I begin to sink, you continue to carry me and bring me back to the truth in the fact that you already know the plans you have for me. You tell me not to fear, and I trust you, Lord. Please give me peace that only you can give, as I know you are with me. In Jesus' name, I pray, Amen."

Walking back into the cottage, Mary realized the peace that she was now feeling, and the confidence of knowing that Jesus was with her through so much uncertainty in her life gave her courage. She knew that she could never do it without Him.

She was happy to be leaving to pick up Elizabeth from school as she enjoyed being with her so much. When she arrived, she sat in the carpool line until she got to the entrance. As she got closer, she could see

Elizabeth waiting for her. Elizabeth had a compassionate heart. Mary often knew how difficult it was for her, in a sense, not having a dad at home, but it was all Elizabeth had ever known, and she seemed to be very happy regardless. After all, Mary had made her a priority and was very careful to ensure Elizabeth had the security and structure she needed as a child. She seemed confident and knew how much Mary loved her.

Mary worked hard to be everything she could be for Elizabeth. She also knew she was a blessing from the Lord, and she never wanted to let Him down even though being a single mom was often a struggle. She had learned that, although she wanted to be the perfect mom, she couldn't be. This realization was difficult for Mary.

12

FRIENDS, FORGIVENESS, AND CLOSURE

Mary spent the remainder of the week at home doing what she loved. Writing. She was looking forward to meeting her friends for lunch on Saturday, as she felt she needed to see them. So much had happened since they were last together, and she felt it would take hours to get caught up on all of the changes in everyone's lives.

Mary stood up to stretch. Then, with Tiffany on her mind, she went to prepare lunch. She hadn't talked to her in a while and remembered the last conversation they had about her new boyfriend and keeping herself pure before marriage. She thought about the wisdom she had given to Tiffany and how it had kept her from going down the wrong path of having sex with her last boyfriend. Her thoughts turned to prayer as she thanked the Lord for using her life story and the pain that she had endured to help others.

As Mary opened the refrigerator to pour herself a glass of fresh lemonade, she reached for the phone. She found Tiffany's contact number and called it. Tiffany picked up the phone on the third ring.

"Mary, it is so good to hear from you! I was just thinking about you.

I have great news."

"That's wonderful, Tiffany. How are you?"

Tiffany began to share the news of her engagement. Mary was so excited for her and so happy that Tiffany had met such a nice young man who respected her and her wish to keep herself pure until she was married. Mary knew that God would bless their marriage and couldn't stop thinking about the example that Tiffany would be setting for so many. God was using her, and this made them both happy.

Tiffany's conversation was enjoyable and lifted Mary's spirits. You could hear the joy and excitement in her voice. They were planning a summer wedding, and Tiffany asked Mary for her address so they could send her an invitation. Mary was delighted! Before hanging up the call, Mary prayed with her. Tiffany loved Mary and was grateful for their friendship. Mary was grateful as well and thanked God for bringing Tiffany into her life.

After the call, Mary thought about Michael. She was curious to know his thoughts about seeing her with Jimmy and why he was even there to start with. As soon as the thought came to her, the phone rang. It was Michael. Mary felt her heart skip a beat when, before she even realized it, she answered the call. It was early afternoon, and she had hoped he was going to tell her that he was leaving forever and would never return.

The voice on the other end sounded different. "Mary, hi, it's Michael."

Mary couldn't speak. She never dreamed she would ever hear from him and felt as if she was going to be sick.

"Mary, are you there?"

She wanted to hang up but finally spoke. "Yes, I'm here."

Michael began the conversation with small talk, and Mary was very uncomfortable. She never wanted to live through this day, and she began to whisper a prayer, "Lord, help me!"

Mary hadn't spoken another word until Michael asked if he could see her. She asked why he needed to see her, and he told her he had something that he needed to share with her. Mary reluctantly agreed to walk down to the ocean to meet him. She still had not had lunch, but grabbed her lemonade and keys, locked the door behind her and began walking down the dock to the ocean. As she got closer to the water, she could see Michael looking up at her. Her heart felt as if it was going to explode out of her chest. She was getting closer and closer, and the closer she got, the faster her heart was beating. She realized how much hurt and anger she still had towards him and knew this was not good for her. After all, she knew the scriptures. She knew she had to forgive him. She knew she needed closure to a part of her life that had given her the most beautiful gift in the world, Elizabeth.

Mary finally reached Michael, and as she stood there looking into his eyes, she couldn't speak. A tear fell from her eye when he reached for her hand. Mary stepped back; but he seemed to understand her feelings of anger that she still had toward him. Michael was sure the package that he sent her would explain and bring the reconciliation that he desperately needed and wanted. He was wrong! The box only brought more pain, confusion, and sadness. Mary had thought so many times how the years that had passed could have been avoided if he had been strong enough and had less pride so that he could have shared with her his concerns. They could have talked through it, she thought. But no, that wasn't the plan, as they could both see, and the feelings of bitterness needed to end and end now. Maybe today is the day, Mary thought.

He looked toward the water and began to speak. Mary, standing behind him, could hear his words.

"Mary, I already know how wrong I was. I already know that I probably lost the best gift I could have ever received from you and Elizabeth. I have struggled deeply with that, and I need you to forgive me." He turned toward her. "Mary, will you please forgive me? I realize coming back here was a shock to you and I am sorry. I feel like we both need to get through this part of our life so we can both move forward. Mary, I can't change what has already happened. I have prayed for forgiveness, and I know the Lord has forgiven me. Mary, please forgive me too."

Mary began to cry. She wanted to forgive him. She wanted to move on from all the questions she'd had for so long. She really wanted to forget their relationship had ever happened. She couldn't. She had to, and she knew the only way she could. She thought of all the wrong she had done against God and how many times he had forgiven her. She thought of all that He had done for her even though she didn't deserve it. She thought about her beautiful daughter, Elizabeth, and the gift she was to her, and she began to feel peace coming over her like she had never felt before. She looked into Michael's eyes and said, "Michael, I forgive you." She knew that holding on to all the bitterness that she had built up inside of her would never be anything good, and she had to let it go.

Michael gazed into Mary's eyes, his heart brimming with gratitude. "Mary, thank you! Thank you for forgiving me. I saw you with someone on the beach the other day, and you looked happy. When we made eye contact, I saw you look away and I could feel your hurt from here. Mary, I can't keep you from falling in love with another man, and I would never try because there is no one that I know on this earth that deserves to be happy and in love more than you. Because of you, I'm changed, Mary. You showed me Jesus when we were together through your honesty and love, and my relationship with Him is stronger than it has ever been. I am grateful!" His words were filled with sincerity, and Mary could feel the depth of his transformation.

Mary listened to his heart intently and thought about Elizabeth. "I can't tell Elizabeth about you right now, Michael. I can't allow you to see her. I have never even told her about you. She will never understand any of this, and it will tear her world apart."

Michael understood, and although disappointed, he knew he could not push the issue. She told him that she would pray about how to handle this and let him know. The most important thing she wanted to do was protect Elizabeth, and if she never knew Michael, then she would always have a Father in Heaven who would never let her down. Mary's resolve to protect Elizabeth was unyielding, and it was clear that she would do whatever it took to ensure her daughter's happiness and well-being.

Michael began to speak when he noticed tears flowing from Mary's eyes, and what he said next shook her to the core. "Mary, I have met someone, and we are getting married in a few months. This was one of the reasons I wanted to come here as well. I needed to let go of you and feel some closure as well as hear you tell me you forgive me. She will never be you, Mary, but she loves me and needs me. She has two children who need a father, and I feel that I am the one God has sent to be that for them."

Mary, in anger, exclaimed, "REALLY MICHAEL! Okay, you are very strange. I raised Elizabeth for 8 years by myself and never heard from you until one day I received a package in the mail filled with gifts and a check that you thought was going to fix everything. Well, it didn't! Oh, and speaking of the check, I haven't cashed it, but I think I will now. I will put it in an account for Elizabeth. I guess that's the least you could do! Now you come here, and you seem so sympathetic in asking for forgiveness when the real reason you are here is so you could leave a ton of guilt so you can get married and raise someone else's kids."

Mary's emotions shifted again as she remembered what Jesus said to her once, "Mary, it's not what comes at you, but what comes out of you that shows who you are in me." She looked into Michael's eyes and, with a sincere heart, said, "Michael, I told you I have forgiven you, and I have. Elizabeth and I have a great life, and God is a very forgiving God. You told me that He has forgiven you. Go and get married, raise those girls by teaching them to lean on and trust Jesus. Love your new wife as Christ loves, respect her, do not be harsh with her, and make a beautiful life with her if this is how you feel led. I'm happy for you.

"God has a beautiful life planned for me, and He will get me through all of this. God has a beautiful life planned for Elizabeth, too. She has never known you, and she never will."

Mary turned and began walking back toward her cottage and thanked Jesus that that part of her life was over. She didn't have any more questions because she knew, most importantly, that God had protected her above all else and that His plan, regardless of what it was, was the right one for her and Elizabeth. Mary was strong. She had to be. But, most importantly, she was strong in Jesus and He was there with her, and He would lead her through this part of her life. She was confident in that.

Mary had arrived back at the cottage, and JJ met her at the door. She had a couple of hours before having to pick Elizabeth up at school. She looked over at her favorite writing chair and, while staring at her laptop, took a deep breath. She was instantly reminded of God's word in *Ephesians 5:25-27* "*Husbands love your wives, just as Christ loved the church and gave himself up for her to make her holy, cleansing her by the washing with water through the word, and to present her to himself as a radiant church, without stain or wrinkle or any other blemish, but holy and blameless.*"

Mary realized that she had given Michael the word of God, and God's peace came over her! She had said what she needed to say, and she had forgiven Michael. She had prayed God would help her, and He did. She couldn't ask for anything more, but she was exhausted. She thought of taking a nap and began walking to her bedroom, with JJ following her. She laid down on the bed, snuggled under her favorite blanket with JJ curled up next to her. She set the timer on her phone for an hour, sat it on her bedside table, and thanked God for loving her and Elizabeth. Her last thought before falling asleep was a prayer, "*Lord, I pray someone loves me one day, just like your word says. Is Jimmy the one that you have called to do that, Lord?*"

The alarm went off, and as Mary was fumbling for her phone, she realized her nap had gone way too quickly. She wished she could stay there until morning. She sat up, stretched, and walked to the kitchen. Sunshine ran out from under the bed toward her and she brushed her face against Mary's feet. Mary reached down to pet her and thought about the peace that she had in her heart. JJ came into the kitchen, too, and Mary spoke to them both. "You two are very special to me, do you know that?" Mary, with a sigh and a deep breath, thought, I am so happy that part of my life is over, and although I don't know how I will ever tell Elizabeth, I don't have to tell her now. In time, she thought.

13

BACK TOGETHER AGAIN

It was Saturday morning, and Mary and Elizabeth were excited to meet their friends for lunch at Eleven, their favorite Italian Restaurant. They were happy not to rush to get out the door for school or work. However, Mary's time off was soon coming to an end. She had decided the two days that she would work at the Inn would be Wednesday and Thursday. These were the busiest days as they were preparing for weekend functions that were always important. Christmas would be there before they knew it, and neither of them was looking forward to the cold weather ahead.

Mary was standing in the kitchen at the coffeepot when Elizabeth walked in. "Well, hello beautiful, you're up early for a Saturday morning," Mary said.

"Hi, mom. I couldn't sleep," said Elizabeth. "I'm so excited about our luncheon today and spending time with Faith."

Mary smiled at her and said, "Come here and give Mom a hug." Elizabeth walked over, and Mary gave her the tightest hug ever. She asked, "Do you know how much I love you, sweetheart?"

Elizabeth giggled, giving her a loving hug back and answered, "Mom, I love you, too!"

As Mary gathered all the ingredients for homemade pancakes, Elizabeth sat on the floor, playing with JJ. Sunshine was playing with a ball, and as it rolled across the floor while jingling, she would chase it. Elizabeth laughed out loud while watching her play.

Mary loved the peace that surrounded her cottage. She prayed that it would never change.

The oil in the cast iron skillet was getting hot enough to put in the pancake mix Mary had prepared from scratch, and as she dropped it on the skillet, the sizzling sound made her tummy growl. They were both hungry. She pulled out the plates for herself and Elizabeth, the butter, and their favorite, Anderson's Pure Maple Syrup. Mary loved that brand of syrup as she felt supporting a family-run business was important, and after almost 100 years of proven quality, she knew she was providing Elizabeth with the best. This was very important to Mary as a mom.

Breakfast was ready. Mary called Elizabeth to the table.

While skipping across the floor with a big smile on her face, Elizabeth was rubbing her tummy as if to say, yummy. She told Mary how great the pancakes smelled, and she was sure they would be perfect. As they tucked in, they sat and talked about their day and the excitement they had about getting together with their friends and getting caught up on life's changes. Mary couldn't wait to see Karen as she knew she looked a lot different as now she was seven months pregnant.

Elizabeth, in a grown-up conversation, said, "Mom, I'm so happy for Karen!" She has waited a long time to have a baby, and I pray that everything goes just perfectly for her. She is going to be a great mom, just like you."

Mary didn't feel like a great mom because some of her choices left a lot of uncertainty in Elizabeth's heart, but she was doing the best that she could to compensate for her daughter not having a dad in her life. She wanted more than anything in her life to be a great mom for Elizabeth. She prayed that God would lead her and immediately thought of *Psalm 31:3, "Since you are my rock and my fortress, for the sake of your name, lead and guide me."* Mary was continuing to learn to lean on Jesus for her strength as she knew that without Him, she would fail.

Breakfast was delicious, and while Mary cleaned the kitchen, Elizabeth went to her room to shower and get ready for the day. Before getting in, she looked through her closet and decided on her white-washed jeans with a sweater that Faith had given her. She loved Faith and wanted her to know how much she loved the gift that she had given her.

Mary began walking into her bedroom to shower when she thought about the box from Michael. It had been a while since she had opened it. She closed her bedroom door, locked it, and opened her closet. Her heart felt peaceful this time. She realized seeing Michael was the closure that she had needed. Although it did not change the fact that Mary had hoped her life would be different, she understood more now and how to be okay with it. After all, she had done this by herself for so many years, and she was sure no matter what she had dreamed about, changing it would never work anyway. "It's time to move on," Mary said.

Opening the box felt different this time. She already knew what was inside and remembered the panicked feeling she had had when she opened it the first time. As she opened it and reached inside, she felt she needed to at least save the picture of her and Michael. One day, I will show this to Elizabeth, she thought. The check he had sent was still sitting on the top. She reached for it and felt as if this would be a way to add to Elizabeth's savings anyway. "Elizabeth deserves at least that from him," she said out loud. She peaked at the picture once more, turned it over quickly, then closed the box. It went back on the shelf with the gifts inside, but the check for Elizabeth was still in her hand. She thought she would cash it and deposit it into her savings account the following day.

Mary was running out of time, and she still needed to get dressed. She had not even had a shower yet. She jumped in, pulling her hair back so it wouldn't get wet. After a few seconds, she heard knocking on her bedroom door and Elizabeth calling for her. Mary had forgotten to unlock it. Getting out of the shower, she wrapped a towel around herself, calling to her daughter that she'd be right out.

Elizabeth was happy to hear Mary's voice and called back, "Okay, Mom."

Mary never wanted to have secrets from Elizabeth but felt as if she now had one for sure. This made Mary feel uncomfortable, but she knew this would be too much for her to process and wanted to protect her.

Mary had pulled out of her closet her dark blue jeans and a linen top with pastel colors in a flower pattern. She dressed before opening the door.   As she walked to the door to open it, she saw Elizabeth still standing there. She had a look of confusion on her face. Mary saw it and said, "Hey girl. Mom was just looking at a box that needed to be put away."

Elizabeth, still confused, said, " Okay, Mom."

"Well, you look adorable, Elizabeth," Mary said.

"You do too, mom," Elizabeth answered.

You could feel the awkwardness in the room, but Mary knew it would soon be over. It was! JJ was standing at Elizabeth's feet. Elizabeth reached down to pick him up and put him on Mary's bed. She also laid down on the bed and started to chat away to her Mom. Mary loved her so much, and she knew there was nothing she would not do for Elizabeth. Sadly, she thought, this time, I have no control. Mary recalled *Matthew 11: 28-30, "Come to me all you who are weary and burdened, and I will give you rest. Take my yoke upon you and learn from me, for I am gentle and humble in heart, and you will find rest for your souls. For my yoke is easy, and my burden is light."*

Mary stopped, looked at Elizabeth and JJ, and thanked God for her baby girl, her adorable pets, and her life. She knew that no matter what she had to go through, God was with her, and He was her best friend.

Finally, she was ready to go. It was 10:30 a.m., and they needed to meet their friends at the Italian Restaurant soon. Elizabeth looked over at her mom and said, "Mom, you look happy. I am excited, are you?"

Mary began to giggle, hugged Elizabeth, and said, "Let's get JJ outside before we leave. I'm excited, girl. This will be a fun day."

They both decided to walk JJ together. Mary never wanted to be away from Elizabeth, although she had to be at times. Elizabeth was growing up, and she knew their time together would be more limited as she got older. Mary wasn't looking forward to that day.

Mary was looking forward to seeing her friends. It had been way too long!

As they arrived at the restaurant, she saw Karen getting out of the car. She looked so beautiful. There was a glow about her that Mary had never seen before. She also looked very pregnant, and Mary couldn't believe it had been so long since they had been together.

She parked her car and as Elizabeth got out, they also saw Patricia and Faith pulling in. Elizabeth was smiling from ear to ear. Mary walked over to Karen, gave her a huge hug, and as she looked into her eyes, she could feel joy. Mary was so happy for Karen.

Patricia and Faith also walked over to the car where Mary, Elizabeth, and Karen were standing. The love that was felt in that parking lot was so noticeable to everyone. They were all happy to be together!

As they all began walking into the restaurant, they saw Victoria coming in behind them. They had not seen her in the parking lot. She also looked happy to be there. The hugs that were given at that moment by friends were only a beautiful gift from God. They all knew it, too!

The hostess motioned for them to follow her, and before they knew it, they were sitting in a private room in the back. They must have remembered them as if they had spent way too much time there the last time, they were together having lunch. They remembered how rude they had been by holding up the tables from other customers and felt this was what they were trying to prevent. "We probably owe them an apology, as our time together goes so quickly," Mary said.

All the girls were happy as now they didn't have to be in any hurry and wished they had asked for a private room when making the reservations. "Anyway, they have it worked out for us now," Mary said with a giggle.

Victoria, like all of the girls, needed this time together as much as any of them.

The waitress came into the room, said hello, and handed each of them a menu. Elizabeth and Faith sat at the end of the table together. As they all looked over the menus and talked about what they would have, they decided on two appetizers that they could share. They each ordered a glass of water with Lemon. The waitress left the table to go turn in the order of appetizers and to bring the water they had ordered. The conversations around the table were joyful.

The waitress returned to the table with the appetizers and water, and they each placed their orders. Everyone was having a great time, and the appetizers were just as they had remembered them. Mary looked over at Elizabeth and before she had realized it, she had reached for one. Mary quickly reminded her that they needed to pray and thank Jesus for their food.

With an apologetic look, she whispered, "Mom, I'm sorry." Mary smiled back at her and said, "It's okay, baby; mom understands. I am hungry, too!" Mary began to pray, *"Lord, thank you for the food that you have provided us. Thank you for our friendship and the time that we have together. You have blessed each one of us so much, and the stories of your love and grace in our lives have been so refreshing. Use this food to nourish our bodies and fill our hearts with your peace, Lord. In Jesus' name, we pray, Amen."*

Elizabeth waited for the others this time, as she was reminded of how impatient she had been. Mary noticed and reassured Elizabeth that it was okay.

Mary looked over at Karen and felt something was wrong. She asked if she was okay. She had her hand over her forehead, looking down.

Karen became the focus of the room, which made her uncomfortable, but she quickly said, "I just had a sharp pain in my belly!"

Mary got up to walk over to where she was sitting and put her hand on her shoulder. "Karen are you okay," Mary said with a gentle tone.

Karen looked up at her and said, "I think so, Mary." The pain quickly left, but Karen was feeling a little frightened. Mary felt it! She reassured Mary that she was okay, and she went back to her chair.

The mood in the private room they were seated in changed a little as everyone there loved Karen and wanted to be sure she continued to do well with her pregnancy.

The waitress came to the table with another server, bringing the entrée they had each ordered. The smell in the room was fabulous: the aroma of fresh garlic, oregano, rich tomatoes, and freshly baked bread filled the room.

Mary caught a glimpse of Patrica looking over at Karen as she was also worried about her friend. She and Mary had both had great pregnancies, and they all wanted everything to continue to go well for Karen too.

Karen, who didn't seem to be eating her lunch, suddenly grabbed her belly again and stood up. They all immediately stood up and walked over to her.

Karen began to laugh. "I'm okay, I promise, girls! He or she just kicked so hard that it startled me."

They all remembered those times, too, and felt relieved that she was okay.

Mary walked with her around the room for a minute, hoping that the baby would settle down a bit.

Patricia, with a giggle, said, "Oh, well, we know who else loves Italian food!"

The girls were all so grateful that Karen was okay.

The mood in the room changed again to lots of laughter and a few tears as they shared stories of their lives while trying to catch up on their time apart. Elizabeth and Faith were seated at the end of the table, and while occasionally joining in the conversation, they were more interested in each other and sharing their own stories.

Everyone had finished their meal when the waiter came back into the room with a dessert tray. The sounds of, "Oh, that looks so good, Yummy, chocolate, and I'm not going to do it." These were the words of everyone. They all refused dessert except Mary. Mary decided on the chocolate mousse brownie.

As everyone began to laugh, Mary said, "I am not going to share it, either!" Everyone laughed hysterically. Chocolate was one of Mary's favorites, and they all knew it. While they all sat there wondering if she would refuse the temptation of dessert, they were certain she would not. They were right!

Mary remembered the chocolate cupcake with the sparkler on it that Mr. Henry had given her for the loan approval on her cottage, and the sweet memory filled her heart with so much love. Mary had been so blessed with so many amazing people God had put in her life.

When the chocolate brownie arrived at the table, everyone was admiring it.

Mary asked the waitress for extra spoons and said, "We can each have a bite."

The laughter in the room was contagious, and it was just like Mary to share her dessert.

Their time together was meaningful, and no one was ready to leave, but they had to. Another private party was coming in within an hour, and the restaurant had to clean up the room and prepare it for them. After all, they had been there over two hours, and they sure didn't want to be rude again.

Before leaving, they had planned to meet the following week at Mary's cottage to discuss the final planning for Karen's baby shower. Mary felt terrible that they had not already had her shower, as Karen had been so attentive to hers for Elizabeth. Mary felt she had let her friend down, and she apologized to Karen.

Karen said, "Mary, you are an amazing friend. Don't be so hard on yourself. We have plenty of time."

As they were walking to the car, Mary saw Karen stop and grab her stomach. She and Elizabeth ran over to her, and she seemed to be in a lot of pain.

"Karen, I'm calling Sam!" Mary said with a voice of concern.

Patricia and Victoria saw what was going on and ran over to Karen as well.

Mary had Karen sit down in her car, and she picked up her phone to call Sam.

The phone rang twice when Sam answered. "Mary, is everything okay?"

Mary, in a panicked voice, asked if he could call her doctor and meet them at the restaurant.

"Of course, I'm on the way," Sam said.

It felt as if it had been thirty minutes before Sam arrived, but it had only been a few minutes. He hurried to his wife's side, and when he arrived, Karen began to cry. Sam put his arms around Karen and reassured her everything would be okay. Although trying to be strong for Karen, his heart was beating out of his chest. They had waited so long for a baby and were both scared of what could happen. Karen still had almost two more months left of her pregnancy, and they both knew this could be serious.

Sam told them he'd called Karen's doctor on the way there, and the doctor had told him to bring his wife in right away. Sam and Karen both promised to call the girls as soon as they knew what was happening.

Then, filled with concern, everyone drove away.

While driving, Mary began to pray and thought of the scripture, *Philippians 4:6-7, "Do not be anxious about anything, but in every situation, by prayer and petition, with thanksgiving, present your request to God. And the peace of God, which transcends all understanding, will guard your hearts and your minds in Christ Jesus."*

Once again, the Lord gave Mary peace, and she shared the scripture with Elizabeth, who also seemed very concerned for Karen.

Mary and Elizabeth had arrived home, and they were happy to be there. JJ met them at the door, and while Elizabeth grabbed his leash to take him for a walk, the phone rang. Sam had called just to let Mary know that they had arrived at the doctor's office, and he was doing a few tests. He would give her an update as soon as he could.

Mary tried to remain calm and continued to pray for her friend. She picked up her phone to text Patricia and Victoria to give them the update when she saw they had already texted. They were anxious as well, so Mary gave them the news and shared with them the scripture that the Lord had given her. Mary wanted to stay positive and reassured them all would be okay.

Thirty minutes had passed and there was still no update from Sam. Mary could feel herself getting more anxious and had to work hard to stay calm.

She walked out on the deck and looked out over the ocean. There were very few places that she'd rather be when she was concerned than here. The ocean gave her such peace. As she stood there, she saw a dolphin swimming and another one behind it. She thought of God's creatures and how precious each one was. She loved it when she could see them playing together.

The phone started ringing, and Mary quickly grabbed it. It was Sam.

Sam sounded relieved but still somewhat shaken up. He began to explain that Karen would need to be on bed rest for a few days.

"Everything is good; the baby is fine, and she is okay, but she started with some premature labor pains, so the doctor wants her off of her feet and resting for a week or so."

Mary, with concern, immediately agreed to help in any way she could. She could hear Sam beginning to cry. "Mary, the baby's going to be okay!"

Mary could feel herself choking up, too, and said, "Yes, the baby is going to be okay, Sam! God has you three, and we just have to help Karen slow down a bit. We will come over and keep her company each day. I will talk to the girls and see if they can also help."

Sam thanked Mary and hung up the call.

Mary called the girls on a group call to give them the update. They were very relieved to hear from Mary. As they chatted, they worked out how best to plan their days so they could also sit with Karen. Everyone was concerned about Karen, and Mary asked them to pray for her.

Karen and the baby were going to be okay; Mary just knew it!

14

CHRISTMAS DECORATING

The weekend was going by too quickly, and Mary wanted to do some Christmas decorating. She usually had the cottage decorated by now but this year she had not had the time. Elizabeth was excited, as she always looked forward to helping her mom decorate the tree. And Mary enjoyed sharing her memory of collecting the ornaments with her daughter.

It was 8 am on Sunday, and Mary woke up to the sound of rain on her window. As she slipped her feet into her slippers, she walked over to the window. The mornings were getting very chilly. As she opened the blind to look out, she could see the cloud cover and had not even realized the rain was in the forecast. This will be a great day to stay in our pajamas and decorate, she thought. She knew Elizabeth was looking forward to spending the day with her mom.

She walked into the kitchen and turned on her coffee. She then grabbed her jacket and called JJ to go out. She heard him jump off the bed. He hated going out in the rain, but he had to. Mary put on his cute little rain jacket to protect him from getting wet. JJ didn't like it very much, but Mary did.

When they came back inside the cottage, the coffee was ready. Mary loved the smell of freshly brewed coffee and knew its warmth would warm her up a bit.

After putting JJ's food down and checking Sunshine's bowl, Mary heard a bell jingling across the floor. Sunshine was carrying her toy mouse in her mouth. She loved her toys, and the sound of her bell jingling was always so cute. Mary loved her pets; they were a part of the family, and they brought so much joy to the cottage. They were a blessing to her and Elizabeth, and the cottage would not be the same without them.

She sat down on the couch in the living room and was just pulling out her bible to read when she heard footsteps coming into the room. Elizabeth sat down next to Mary and JJ jumped up too. As they all sat together, Mary picked her bible up and began to read aloud the story in *Luke 15* about the parable of the lost son. As she read each verse, she thought about her trip to see Jimmy's parents and how God showed her this in real life. The memory of his dad standing at the bottom of the escalator would be one she would remember forever.

After she read the scriptures, she began talking to Elizabeth about Jimmy. She hadn't said too much about his life before now, but she wanted her to understand and know how much God loved him.

"Elizabeth, Jimmy made some poor choices. We all have. Sadly, so many feel unworthy of God's love. The pain they have is real, and they have buried it so deep in their hearts that they run from it. Sometimes, they run to things that they feel will ease the pain, but it doesn't. It may seem like it for a few minutes, but it's a fantasy and the pain never goes away. It is only an escape from reality, so the cycle continues.

"Jesus is the only way to truly be fulfilled in this world. We all forget that at times! Elizabeth, remember the trip Jimmy and I took to see his mom and dad and children? God showed me this very scripture we just read right before my eyes. Remember I told you that he had not seen his parents in over two years?" Mary proceeded to tell the story, and Elizabeth listened intently.

Her daughter understood some of what she was hearing, and as soon as Mary had finished talking, her mom could see in her face that Elizabeth had something to say. "Mom, can we invite Jimmy to our house today to help us decorate the tree?"

Mary shrugged her shoulders, looked at Elizabeth with a look of gratitude and said, "I love you so much Elizabeth! Do you know that?"

With a child-like giggle, Elizabeth said, "Well, mom, can we?"

Mary agreed that she would call and invite him over a little later.

Mary got up from the couch and went into the kitchen to pour herself another cup of coffee.

Elizabeth came running in behind her and said, "Can we make French toast?"

Her mom, of course, agreed, and while pouring out the ingredients to make them, she thought about Jimmy. She thought about her book that was very close to being published as Jonathon said it should be available before Christmas. She thought about Karen and the baby and how she would find the time to spend with her and help her. She knew she had to. Karen had been there for her so much!

As her mind began to spin, she turned her focus toward Jesus and whispered a prayer. *"Lord, please help me!"* He will help me through this season, Mary thought.

Elizabeth was sitting on the couch with JJ when Mary called her into the kitchen for breakfast. The French toast smelled so good, and as she walked in, Elizabeth could see the butter still melting on top.

Elizabeth was excited and said, "Mom, you're the best! This French toast smells so yummy!"

While eating their breakfast, they talked about their day. Mary thought she would have Jimmy come over after lunch. This would give them time to relax a bit and get out all the Christmas decorations from the attic storage.

Mary was also excited about Jimmy coming over, and she knew he would enjoy their time together.

The phone rang, and Mary got up from the table to answer it. It was Jimmy! Elizabeth could see the joy on Mary's face as she looked at the caller ID. Elizabeth was excited and hoped that Jimmy would be able to come over to help decorate the cottage for Christmas.

When she answered the phone, Jimmy sounded a little down. Mary asked him what he had been doing.

Jimmy said, "Not much, just thinking about you and Elizabeth."

Mary asked if he had plans for the day and asked him if he'd like to come over to help with some Christmas decorating.

Jimmy's voice perked up as he had hoped that they could spend some time together. "Of course," he answered. "What time?"

Mary told him that one o'clock would be good if that was okay with him. He agreed and asked if there was anything he could bring. Mary couldn't think of anything but told him that she had some beef filets in the freezer and asked if he minded grilling in the rain.

Jimmy laughed and said, "No, as long as you have an umbrella."

Mary said that was not a problem and that she had a few and giggled. Jimmy's tone completely changed from the beginning of the call, as he seemed very happy to be coming over.

When they hung up, Elizabeth ran to her room to get into the shower, and she and Mary laughed as they realized their pajama day was not going to happen.

Mary finished cleaning the kitchen from breakfast and went into her room to shower.

When Mary came out of her bedroom, she was wearing a red sweater and jeans. Elizabeth was sitting in the living room and, as she walked in, they both started laughing hysterically. They'd had the same idea of wearing red to get in the Christmas mood and were both dressed in the same colors.

"Great minds think alike," Mary said.

Mary thought of going into the attic to get everything down, and Elizabeth agreed to help her. They loved going to the Christmas tree farm and cutting down fresh trees, but Mary was allergic to them, so she bought a beautiful artificial tree a couple of years ago that she loved.

After walking into the attic, Mary looked to the left and was pleased. She saw the stacked red and green totes and remembered how well she organized everything before putting it up last year and knew it would make decorating much simpler. Mary moved each one closer to the steps so it would be easier to bring them down. Elizabeth would stay up in the attic so she could hand her the ones that she could carry. One by one, the totes were brought downstairs, the last item being the tree. It was stored in a large red canvas bag and Mary saved it for last as she knew this one would be difficult to bring down. She remembered having to have some help to get it up the steps the year before.

Mary had a thought that she loved and told Elizabeth. "Hey, Jimmy's coming over. He can help me get the Christmas tree down."

Elizabeth smiled back. "Good plan, Mom."

Before taking everything out of the boxes, Mary wanted to spend some time reading her bible and praying with Elizabeth. She asked her to come and sit by her as she reached for the book.

Elizabeth looked forward to this time with her mom, so she happily walked over and sat on the couch beside her. JJ was sleeping on the floor by Mary's feet. Mary said a silent prayer asking the Lord to show her what scripture to read, and she found the one that gave her peace. *Proverbs 19:21, "Many are the plans in a person's heart, but it is the Lord's purpose that prevails."* Mary read the scripture aloud to Elizabeth and began talking about her life. "Elizabeth, Mom had no idea that our life would be like this! I always thought I would be married and have a beautiful family. The ones you read about in the storybooks; you know? You and I both know that is not how it has turned out for me, and I am okay with that. God gave me you, and I am so grateful to God for you." She realized a tear had fallen onto her cheek, and she looked into Elizabeth's eyes and said, "I'm so sorry that you don't have a dad right now. I know it's hard on you at times to see other children with dads. Our family is different, isn't it?"

Elizabeth spoke back with the sweetest look on her face and said, "Mom, my father is in heaven. He is always with me."

This made Mary smile because she knew that what Elizabeth was saying was the truth. Mary hugged Elizabeth and said, "One thing I have learned in my life for sure is that we can't always plan the life we would have, but thank God we know Jesus, and no matter what, He is with us, always!"

In all of Mary's planning and dreams of a perfect life, she realized that it wasn't possible, and without expectations, she would never be disappointed. She had many expectations in her life and had been disappointed many times. We have to focus on our life one day at a time as Jesus asks us too and walk in His will not our own. I have failed at this at times for sure. Mary wanted Elizabeth to think this way, so she didn't have the expectations of her life that she had had. "God has a plan for all our lives, and I think when we begin to understand that it makes it much easier. After all, He says in *Romans 8:28, And we know that in all things God works for the good of those who love him, who have been called according to his purpose.*" "We will make mistakes in our life, but God turns the bad into good, Elizabeth, if we have the desire to walk with Him. If we choose to walk away from Him, there are always consequences, too," Mary said. "All we can do is our very best and leave the rest up to Him."

Mary looked at Elizabeth and, with tears flowing from her eyes, said, "Elizabeth, do you know you are the greatest gift from the Lord that I could ask for other than knowing that He is my Savior and understanding how much He loves both of us."

Elizabeth hugged her mom, and the presence of Jesus filled the room.

JJ had gotten up and walked toward the door, so Elizabeth asked if she could take him for a walk. Mary agreed but reminded her to stay close to the cottage.

Mary reached for her laptop to check her emails. She had an email from Jonathon at the publishing company. Attached was the final cover and interior of the book for her to approve before being published. The email read: *Mary, your book is complete and ready for publication. Could you please review and sign the approval letter? Next week, I will send it to the printer. Mary, this one will be a bestseller. You are an amazing Author. I enjoy working with you and look forward to many more books from you.*

Jonathon

Mary was happy that her book was ready. She thought she would review it after Jimmy left so she could get back to Jonathon.

Mary and Elizabeth were sitting on the floor with open totes surrounding them. While Mary looked through some of the décor that would be hung and placed around the room, Elizabeth was pulling out the ornaments for the tree. The memories that filled the containers brought lots of emotions back to each of them.

As Mary and Elizabeth shared their feelings about items, the room was filled with their love for each other. Their bond was indescribable, and Mary knew nothing could separate the bond God had given them as mother and daughter.

The doorbell rang, startling Mary and Elizabeth. JJ, sleeping next to them on the floor, they all quickly got up to see who was there. It was Jimmy. He had a small box in his hand that was wrapped in beautiful Christmas paper. When Mary opened the door and asked him to come in, he handed her the box. Elizabeth ran to him and hugged him with a warm, friendly smile on her face. Jimmy looked happy. Mary motioned for him to come in and said, "If you can get around all the mess that we have made."

Jimmy smiled and said, "This looks like a decorating party, and you both started without me."

Mary quickly responded with, "Oh, no, we saved the best for you. We wanted to ask if you could get the tree out of the attic for us."

Jimmy agreed he would, so Mary showed him where it was and described the bag it was in. He climbed the steps, and as hard as Mary felt it would be to get it down, Jimmy made it look so easy.

Mary was so grateful for his help.

Mary asked Jimmy if he wanted something to drink and remembered she or Elizabeth had not even had lunch. They decided on snacks and lemonade, so Mary went into the kitchen to prepare a plate of snacks for them all. Dinner would not be too long, so this would hold them over until then. "This is perfect," said Elizabeth and Jimmy at the same time. They all laughed.

Jimmy had already taken the tree parts out of the bag and begun putting them together. Mary walked over to him to help. Elizabeth stood there and watched. She was eager to see it together and the lights shining brightly.

Jimmy placed the top segment on the tree. Mary thought about the years that it had just been she and Elizabeth and how nice it was to have Jimmy over.

Mary had longed for a Godly man in her life and a great father for Elizabeth. She had prayed for that for years.

Mary asked Jimmy if he would marinate the steaks for dinner while she and Elizabeth added the ornaments to the tree. He agreed, as he loved feeling like a part of their lives and wanted to do what he could to help.

Mary walked him into the kitchen and pulled out the beef filets. She asked how he wanted to marinate them and what ingredients he needed. She showed him where everything was and said, "Ok, you're on your own now." He looked peaceful, and Mary was happy.

When Mary walked back into the living room, Elizabeth had already begun putting the ornaments on the tree. Her favorites were all in one place, and she enjoyed examining them as, one by one, she added them to the tree.

Jimmy entered the living room after marinating the steaks. He just stood at the door watching Mary and Elizabeth and thanking Jesus for his time with them; he began to pray a silent prayer. *"Father, thank you for this time here with Mary and Elizabeth. Thank you for another chance to be your example in the lives of two people that I know are missing a man, a leader under your direction, in their lives. You have blessed me beyond measure, and I am grateful."* He thought of the scripture in *Daniel 9:9*, *"The Lord our God is merciful and forgiving, even though we have rebelled against him."*

Jimmy was thankful for his time at the cottage with Mary and Elizabeth and was so happy to spend this special time with them. They were happy he was there, too.

Mary saw Jimmy standing by the door and, with a warm smile, invited him to come and help put the ornaments on the tree.

Jimmy walked over to the table where Mary had placed the box that he had brought her and picked it up. He then handed it to Mary. "Open it, Mary."

Mary looked at him and said, "Now?"

"Now is as good of a time as any," he answered, smiling back at her. Elizabeth, who was watching, walked over to them.

Mary opened the box, and what she discovered inside surprised her. It was a glass Christmas ornament in the shape of a heart with the picture imprinted on it that they had taken when they first met. Mary, with a tear in her eye, hugged Jimmy and said, "Thank you! This is very special, Jimmy." Elizabeth peaked at the ornament, and as she looked up at both Mary and Jimmy, she had a look of approval on her face.

Jimmy was sincere about his love for Mary and Elizabeth, and Mary knew she was still showing signs of reservation. She knew she had to, and she still wasn't sure how to let go of the fear that she had. She was trying, and God was helping her as He continued to encourage her to keep walking in His will with the words in *Proverbs 3: 5-6, "Trust in the Lord with all your heart and lean not on your own understanding; in all your ways submit to Him, and he will make your paths straight."*

Mary was still learning to submit to God's will, and she wanted to!

The tree was beautifully decorated, and the white lights glimmered throughout the cottage. One thing was different this year, though. A new ornament placed on the tree had changed the lives of five people, and Mary knew God was the reason for it all.

The cottage was beautiful, and finally, everyone was in the Christmas spirit. "Now we can start buying gifts to put under the tree," Mary said with a happy tone. She then thought about her family and wanted to see each of them so badly that she prayed that God would bring them together for the holidays.

The rain had stopped, and Jimmy was grateful. Although he would grill steaks in the rain, he was certainly happy he didn't have to.

Mary went into the kitchen to get the steaks out of the refrigerator that Jimmy had marinated. "Um, these look really good!" Mary said. Jimmy loved the affirmation that Mary always gave him. She thought about baked potatoes and asparagus. She had bought some organic vegetables the day before and couldn't decide which ones she had a taste for, so she asked Jimmy which he preferred. "Asparagus it is, then." Mary said with a flirtatious look.

Mary began washing the potatoes and turned on the oven to roast them when Jimmy asked if she wanted him to light the grill. They were all hungry and decided an early dinner would be good because they had only had a few snacks for lunch. Mary also knew that she had to go over the book that Jonathon had sent her and needed to make it an early night as Elizabeth also had school the next day.

Jimmy walked out onto the deck to light the grill, and as soon as he walked out, he saw five dolphins swimming by. He ran inside and called

Mary and Elizabeth to see them, too, and they all stood there watching them together.

Jimmy loved the ocean as much as Mary did.

Mary returned inside to get everything ready and thought about the bread she had just made the day before. The steaks were ready to go on the grill, and the potatoes and vegetables were ready to be roasted in the oven.

Elizabeth loved helping her mom in the kitchen. Mary knew that one day, she would need to prepare her own meals, and she wanted her to be ready for that day, so she allowed her to help her anytime she wanted to.

Her daughter set the table for three, and as she looked at the third plate sitting on the table, she looked up at Jimmy and smiled. She loved having him there with them.

Jimmy was coming in with the steaks from the grill, and Mary had already put the potatoes and vegetables on the table. The bread was in the oven toasting, and Elizabeth had already taken her seat.

"It smells good in here!" Jimmy said. Mary agreed with him, and while pouring water into the glasses, he placed the steaks on the table. It was time for dinner, and they were all ready for it.

Mary pulled the bread out of the toaster oven, buttered it, and as she was slicing it, she could hear Jimmy and Elizabeth talking at the table.

Jimmy was asking her about her time at school and how her friends were doing.

Elizabeth shared with him that they were all doing well and told him about her and Faith's time together with the girls on Saturday. She also explained about Karen and what happened at the restaurant.

Jimmy, with a concerned look, asked Mary if Karen was okay.

Mary brought the bread to the table and sat down. She began to share that Karen would be okay but that she and her friends were going to need to help her as she was on bed rest for a few weeks.

Mary asked Jimmy if he would say the blessing for their food, and he agreed. He began to pray: *"Father, thank you for this food and for allowing the rain to stop so I didn't have to cook the steaks in the rain. Thank you for my time here with Mary and Elizabeth and for bringing them into my life. Thank you for this food. In Jesus' name, I pray, Amen."*

Mary and Elizabeth both said Amen at the same time, and they began making their plates.

Mary proceeded to talk about Karen and how concerned she was for her. Sam had planned to take a few days off with his wife as he wanted to be close to her, but he knew he would not be able to take two months off even if that was what was required for her to keep her and the baby safe. Mary didn't know what to expect exactly, but she knew that no matter what, she would be there for her friend.

Jimmy began talking about their time with his family and how he had wished Elizabeth could have come. "My mom and dad love you, Mary," he said. "Mom said she first thought you must have been unstable because our story made no sense, but now she knows you're not."

Mary agreed none of it made sense, and she could certainly feel the uncertainty about it all. She looked over at Jimmy and said, "But I know God makes everything beautiful."

Jimmy, with a look of gratefulness, said, "Thank you, Mary!"

Mary, Elizabeth, and Jimmy had a great day. The cottage was finally decorated for Christmas, and Mary was confident that God was making all things beautiful!

15

CHANGING HEARTS

Mary had already taken Elizabeth to school, had two great cups of coffee, and was excited about spending a couple of hours with Karen. Sam was taking time off work for a couple of weeks but needed to run some errands in the afternoon.

Mary had plans to be there at her house around 12:30 for a couple of hours, but prior to arriving at her house, she wanted to catch up on her emails from her readers. The words they were saying about her book, *When Jesus Calls*, and the excitement they had about her new book being published encouraged Mary. She needed her readers and saw a glimpse of God's love in each one of them. Her story wasn't easy to write at times as the painful memories in her life came flooding back, but she knew God was using her story to encourage others, and that's exactly where her heart was. The reviews they were leaving about changes that God had made in their hearts were worth it all. She loved her readers and, as God had connected them to her, she never wanted to let them down. She was also continuously reminded of the forgiveness, love, and grace of Jesus, and this kept her going. God had been so good to Mary, and in all her struggles, He never let her down. After all, He was her Savior, and she knew it. He was also her best friend.

Mary sat in her favorite writing chair next to the window, opened her laptop, and began reading her emails. The ministry that God had created through her writing was so important to Mary. As she answered them, she prayed for each one.

One of her emails grabbed Mary's heart in a powerful way:

Mary, the words on the pages brought me into a place that I never knew I would be in. Since I was a little girl, I had always known that Jesus died on the cross for my sins, but I had no idea until recently how much He loved me. I never felt worthy of His love as I have chosen so many bad paths in my life. Reading your book brought me to my knees. I could see how you continued to receive the grace and love of Jesus and how you didn't allow the enemy to defeat you. Yes, you had times that you did, but you got right back up, repented, and fell right back into Jesus' arms. Mary, I fell into Jesus' arms after I read your book, When Jesus Calls. I have felt the presence of God like I never have before, and He has also become my best friend! Thank you for sharing your life, your struggles with the world, and the redemptive power of Jesus Christ! Keep writing, Mary!

God Bless You!

Sabrina

Mary began to cry. She never dreamed that God could use her life in any way and felt so comforted, realizing that if He could use her, He could use anyone. She immediately thought of the scripture in *Matthew 19:26: Jesus looked at them and said, "With man, this is impossible, but with God, all things are possible."*

Mary knew God was doing it all.

Mary closed her laptop and thought about Jimmy. She had gotten a phone call from him yesterday but had not returned it, so she picked up the phone to call him.

Jimmy answered the call on the 2nd ring. He sounded happy to hear from her.

Jimmy began telling her about a phone call he had had the day before. Pastor Butch had called to share with him that God had woken him up at 3 am to write their wedding vows.

Mary couldn't speak at first and then spoke with a very firm voice, "He did what?"

She could feel God tugging on her heart about what He had shown her when they first met, and she knew she loved Jimmy in a way that only God could love, but she was still very undecided about marrying anyone. Mary was happy with her life just like it was, and she didn't want to change it.

As the conversation continued, Jimmy said, "Well, Mary, you told me yes months ago; what are we waiting for?"

Struggling to know what to say, she finally said, "Jimmy, I don't know exactly what the Lord is doing here, and until I do, I can't marry you. I'm sorry."

Mary could tell her words hurt Jimmy, but she thought he should certainly understand her feelings.

Mary had already turned Jimmy down three times and she didn't care if he ever asked her again. She wanted to follow God's will for her life more than anything, but how could this be His will, she thought? She was still scared, and as her faith continued to waiver, she felt the conviction of the Lord heavy in her heart.

It was eleven a.m., and Mary needed to grab a quick lunch and get ready to visit Karen. She had only an hour before she told Sam she would be there, and she always tried to keep her commitments. He and Karen were counting on her.

While Mary was finishing up her lunch, she thought about her call with Jimmy again. She began to pray, *"Father, why would Pastor Butch write our wedding vows in the middle of the night? Is this your will for my life? What about Elizabeth? Will Jimmy be a great dad to her? What if he's not? Lord, Please show me something more. In Jesus' name I pray, Amen."* Mary had so many questions, but what she realized she had mostly was doubt. She had trusted God so often in her life, but this time it was different. This time, it didn't just involve her life; Elizabeth would have a big adjustment, too. As her mind began to spin, she was reminded once more of the words God had given her so many times in *Matthew 8:26,* "He replied, *"You of little faith, why are you so afraid? Then he got up and rebuked the winds and the waves, and it was completely calm."*

Mary knew she couldn't do alone what God was asking her to do; and without His continuous encouragement, she would never be able to overcome the waves of doubt that she was feeling. He will be with me, she thought. Mary kept reminding herself that God would never fail her.

Mary then thought about the concerns she had had when they met, that they were not equally yoked, but she knew now they were. God is doing something here in my heart, too; I need to pay close attention, Mary thought. After all, it's not about me; it's about Jesus. He desires that we completely trust him and walk in His will for our lives. "This can be very hard to do at times," Mary spoke out loud.

The drive to Karen's was quiet, other than the questions about Jimmy that kept swirling around in her head. God's conviction to follow Him was strong, and she knew that eventually she would have to commit. But how will I do this, she thought?

Realizing she had pulled into the driveway at Karen's, she had to quickly get her focus back to what she needed to do next. She needed to encourage her friend and be there for her just like Karen had always been there for her.

As she parked the car, she pulled her mirror down and looked at herself. She had mascara under her eyes, so she began wiping them when she saw Sam come out of the door. Mary got out of the car and greeted him.

Sam, with a smile, told Mary, "Thank you for coming to sit with

Karen." He proceeded to tell her that she was not handling bed rest very well, and he thought she seemed to be a little down. "Maybe you can cheer her up, Mary!"

Mary walked into the house and down the hall to where Karen was lying in her bed. She had water and a book on the night table, as well as a few crackers that sat on a small plate. As Mary walked in, she saw a smile on Karen's face.

Karen was bored and having to stay in bed was very difficult for her.

Karen sat up to give her a hug and thanked her for coming. "You have brightened my day, Mary," Karen told her.

Mary gave her a gentle hug and a warm smile. There was a small chair by the bed facing Karen, and Mary sat down. She looked closer at the book on the table and realized it was her book. Mary said, "I see my book on the table, Karen. I thought you had already read it."

Karen replied, "Are you kidding me, Mary? Of course I had already read it, but I go back and read a few of the chapters again and again as they speak to my heart and encourage me so much."

Mary had often thought that in some way, *WHEN JESUS CALLS* with all the scripture references in it, was like a devotional. In fact, she often thought of writing a devotional for it.

"I think you just reminded me of how great it would be to have a small book handy to reference some of the ways God encourages all of us."

Karen was excited about the thoughts of her writing a devotional as she loved Mary's book so much.

Mary was happy to see a smile from Karen after the conversation she had had with Sam. She began asking Karen how she was doing and if she could get her anything.

Karen was just happy that her friend was there and having girl time and conversations she could relate to. It was just what she needed.

Karen was doing very well physically but was having a very hard time just lying in bed and resting. This was the doctor's order, and she knew she had no choice. She was getting excited about her next doctor's appointment as she would find out if she could get up and be a little more active. Her appointment was the next day at 9 a.m., and she was getting very anxious about it. Sam was, too!

Mary shared with Karen the phone call she had with Jimmy that morning. Karen was surprised but was starting to enjoy seeing her and Jimmy's relationship growing. This surprised Mary, coming from Karen, as she had always been the one who had such a guard up about it all.

Karen shared how she had been praying for an answer and felt God was doing something special between them, especially in Jimmy's life. "I can see the peace that he has."

Mary nodded. "I can see he's changing, but this could take a long time."

Karen agreed and said, "I know Mary, but remember a grown tree wasn't grown in a day, and *John 12:24* tells us, "*Very truly I tell you, unless a kernel of wheat falls to the ground and dies, it remains only a single seed. But if it dies, it produces many seeds.*" Mary, trust Jesus! He knows how long it will take for all of us to finally get it, and He will walk with us, continue to teach us, and change us along the way."

Karen then said to Mary, "Do you also remember in *Matthew 17:20, He replied, "Because you have so little faith. Truly, I tell you, if you have faith as small as a mustard seed, you can say to this mountain, 'Move from here to there,' and it will move. Nothing will be impossible for you.*"

Karen got up, sat on the bed beside her, looked into her eyes, and said, "Thank you for being such a great friend. My life would be so much harder without you in it, and I am so grateful to God for you!" She hugged her gently, and they both had tears in their eyes.

Karen asked Mary if she wanted a cup of coffee, and Mary said she'd love to.

Mary knew where she kept her coffee. She walked into the kitchen to brew each of them a cup. Mary needed this time with her friend too.

While she was waiting for the coffee to brew, she could see a few dishes in the sink that Sam had left, so she washed them, dried them, and put them away.

Mary reached into the cabinet and picked out two cups, one of them being the cup she had bought Karen for her birthday the year before. It looked a little worn, and she was happy that she had been using it. She poured the two cups then, careful not to spill any, she went back into Karen's bedroom.

Karen was waiting patiently for her to return.

Mary sat while they sipped their coffee together and talked.

Karen shared how strong the baby seemed to be with the kicks that she was feeling and how excited they both were to have the nursery finished before she had to be put on bed rest. Occasionally, she would cheat and go into the nursery when Sam wasn't looking. He caught her there one time, and they sat quietly together while thinking about how their lives were going to change. They were both sure it would be a welcome change.

When Sam walked in, he could hear Mary and Karen laughing in the bedroom.

Sam smiled and said, "Well, how can she make you laugh, Karen? I haven't been able to."

Karen replied, "Well, you know how it is, don't you?"

Sam walked over to her, kissed her on the cheek, and said, "I love you, Karen."

Karen was blessed to have Sam as her husband, and Mary was grateful.

Mary hoped that if Jimmy was the one God was really calling to be her husband, she would be just as blessed.

Mary glanced at the clock on the wall, and realized she needed to get going. It would soon be time to pick Elizabeth up from school, and she had a few things she wanted to get done before then. Mary told Karen and Sam to be sure to let her know how her appointment went the next day and thanked her for the coffee and their friendship.

Karen hugged Mary, thanked her for the visit, and reminded her how much she loved her.

Mary knew this. They both did!

While driving back to the cottage, Mary prayed that Karen's appointment the next day would go well and that the baby was strong and healthy. She was excited about them becoming parents and wanted to continue to be a big part of their lives. She knew things would change, but she hoped they would still had time for each other.

The phone rang, and it was Patricia. She was checking on Karen and wanted to ask if they could get together the next day to spend some time planning the baby shower.

Mary agreed but reminded her she had to go to work, and it would need to be after that. "Probably around 4 after I pick Elizabeth up at school. Is that okay?"

Patricia agreed it would be great and that she would bring Faith along so they could play. Patricia had already talked to Victoria, and she would meet them as well. Faith would bring her homework, and she and Elizabeth could do it together.

Mary knew they had better get her shower planned because of the uncertainty about her delivery time; even if they had to have it at Karen's, that would be okay. They were all anxious about the doctor's appointment.

Mary had arrived back at the cottage. JJ met her at the door. She decided they would take a walk on the beach as it wasn't too cold. Winter had come, and she knew she wouldn't have too many days like this one for a while.

JJ was excited as he also loved walking on the beach. She connected his leash, grabbed her keys and phone, and locked the door behind her. As they reached the shore, she began thinking about Michael. She wondered if she would ever walk out here without thinking about him and how he had treated her. She still couldn't get over the fact he'd come back just to tell her he was getting married. Mary thought about their time together when they'd first met and was still unsure of how she could have had it all so wrong. This left Mary with a deep scar that she knew would take years to heal. She knew she had forgiven him, but sometimes, it still hurt.

While she and JJ were walking, a bottle washed out of the water onto the shore in front of her. As she looked down, she stopped to pick it up; she wiped the sand off it and saw a piece of paper that looked like a note inside. She couldn't believe she had it in her hands. I wonder where this came from, she thought. She had a mysterious feeling come over her and wondered if this was meant just for her. She began thinking about what could be inside, how old it was, and where it came from. It excited her but also gave her a sense of uncertainty.

She carried the bottle the rest of the way during their walk and thought about calling Karen. They turned to walk back toward the cottage and, as she looked at the bottle that she held, she wondered if it was a message of love for someone.

"JJ, I guess I won't know until I open it, but I am going to wait until tomorrow when Patricia and Victoria come over. We can all see it together."

Mary spoke, "This way, I won't be alone."

JJ looked up at her and tilted his head as if he could understand her. He was so important to her! God used JJ so often to comfort Mary and, as she cared for him, her heart was filled with love.

Mary and JJ had arrived back at the cottage. She had a little while before having to go to pick up Elizabeth. So she wiped off the bottle she had found with a paper towel and placed it on the counter. She thought about the box and how she would tell Elizabeth about Michael. She opened her closet door and peeked at it. I need to get rid of it, she thought. Why do I still have it tucked in my closet for me to be reminded of his awful ways, she mumbled to herself.

Mary realized she was still angry with Michael and wondered if she would ever be free of her feelings for him. She knew, most importantly, it was the way he left—not just leaving her but Elizabeth, too. She prayed that Elizabeth would never be hurt from all of it but knew one day she probably would. This concerned Mary the most.

Mary was soon sitting in the carpool line to pick up Elizabeth. She always did her best to get there early so the line wasn't so long, but this time, she didn't.

As she sat there, she could see all the kids' faces as their parents picked them up. Most were happy, but some seemed a little sad. She worried about their lives as she began to understand more and more how dependent children were on their parents. She thought about how they were shaped by the thoughts and feelings of adults. She thought about how so many parents struggled just to provide an income to pay the mortgage bills. This is why so many women work now, she thought.

Mary had always desired to be a stay-at-home wife and mom, the one to keep the house in order, the one to show Jesus' love, and the one to be her husband's helper. She had no choice but to work to provide and was grateful for her writing career so she could now be at home with Elizabeth more, as only working part-time allowed her this opportunity. She felt God was going to continue to help her as she shared His message to the world. Mary began to pray for His protection and for the families she saw at the school. Her heart was burdened by so many, and she knew God would restore what was broken in His time.

Mary reached the front of the school and saw Elizabeth walking toward the car. Her smile was one that no one who saw it could forget.

Mary could never have imagined the bond she would have with her daughter until the second she was born.

Everything changed for Mary that day!

When they arrived home, Elizabeth stopped and looked at the bottle on the counter. "Mom, what is this?" she asked.

Mary began to explain how she found it while she and JJ were taking a walk. Elizabeth couldn't believe it!

"Wow! Mom, that's exciting! Why haven't you opened it," she asked.

Mary told Elizabeth that Patricia, Faith, and Victoria were coming over tomorrow after she picked her up from school, and she was planning to open it then.

"Yay," Elizabeth said. She then went into her room, where she saw Sunshine lying on her bed. She plopped down beside her and began to pet her. Sunshine started purring. Elizabeth loved her cat and was happy she enjoyed sleeping on her bed.

The evening went by so fast that before they knew it, it was bedtime. They were both tired from the day. They were looking forward to the next afternoon when they would spend time with their friends and open the bottle that Mary had found.

Mary prayed with Elizabeth, told her she loved her, and kissed her on the forehead before turning out the light and going into her own bedroom.

The sound of the alarm clock startled Mary. It was a new day, and as she sat up and stretched, she could see it was very bright outside. She got up and looked out the window. Snow had covered the ground.

Mary was excited about the snow, but she was also dreading the long, cold winter. When she picked up her phone, she could see she had a message from the school system. The school had been canceled for the day.

Mary wanted to wake up Elizabeth and tell her about the snow but decided to let her sleep in. She walked into the kitchen and turned on her coffeepot. JJ ran in behind her. "Oh, JJ, you need to go out," Mary said. "It snowed last night, and it's going to be very cold." JJ, who was wagging his tail like he could understand every word she was saying, stood there waiting for Mary.

Mary grabbed her boots that sat by the back door, her coat, and his leash and called him over to her. When she opened the door, the wind blew snow into her face. I must start paying closer attention to the weather, Mary thought. They were out and back in very quickly as the snow was getting incredibly deep.

Mary sat down with her coffee in her favorite chair and watched the snowfall. Mary heard Elizabeth coming into the room.

"Why is it so late, Mom? I'm late for school!" Elizabeth said with an anxious tone. She then looked out the window and said, "It snowed! I must not have school today." Elizabeth was very happy it had snowed and was even more happy to be able to stay at home with Mary.

Mary thought about Karen's doctor's appointment and was sad that she may have to miss it. She was so excited about going. She then picked up the phone to call her.

Karen answered and told Mary that the appointment had been canceled, but the doctor called her and asked a lot about how she was feeling. He told her that she could stay up a while today and just be careful not to lift anything heavy but to see how she felt and if anything changed before she could get back in for her new appointment to call. Karen was grateful to at least be able to get out of bed.

Mary told Karen she was grateful for the great news, and she was to let her know if she needed anything. They each said, "I love you," and hung up the call.

The phone rang, and it was Patricia. They were also excited about the snow and wondered if they could organize a video call since they did not wish to venture out on the slippery roads. Mary agreed, and they planned the call for after lunch.

When Mary hung up the phone, she looked over at Elizabeth and said, "Well, I think today should be a pajama day!"

Elizabeth agreed. They both loved pajama days.

Elizabeth asked Mary if she could try making the pancakes by herself for breakfast.

Mary smiled and said, "Yes, of course you can."

Mary loved that Elizabeth enjoyed cooking. "I will help you if you need me, too." Mary saw her pull out the recipe and all the ingredients. Elizabeth reached into the drawer, pulled out Mary's cast iron skillet, and placed it on the stove top.

Elizabeth looked as if she knew what she was doing. She called Mary over after putting the dry ingredients into the bowl and said, "Mom, can you crack this egg for me?"

Mary began to laugh. "Yes, of course, but you must learn how to do this, too."

Elizabeth giggled and said, "I will, but just not today. Another day, maybe."

Elizabeth had done a great job on the pancakes, and they were delicious. They were cooked perfectly with the crispy edges that they loved. She was very surprised but proud of herself. This gave her more confidence and she enjoyed cooking. Just like her mom!

Mary told her how proud of her she was, and Elizabeth said, "I learned from the best, Mom!"

Mary told Elizabeth that she would wash the dishes. She didn't argue. Although she loved helping her mom, washing dishes was not her favorite chore!

After the dishes were sorted, Mary looked at the bottle she had found at the ocean the day before. She wondered if she should open it with Elizabeth since the girls were not coming over. "Let's do it," Mary said. This will be fun!

"I guess it is the Lord's will that we open this one together, Elizabeth," Mary said. JJ came and sat next to Mary.

The cork in the bottle was tight, but Mary pulled it out with a little force. She glanced at Elizabeth. "Are you ready?"

In excitement, Elizabeth answered, "YES!"

Mary turned the bottle upside down, and the slip of paper fell into her lap. She reached for it and could see it was a handwritten note. The note read:

I have spent a week here at the ocean alone and I can't believe you are not here with me. You loved the ocean, and losing you was the hardest lesson I have had to learn. I spoke to you so harshly too many times, and I regret it. I wanted to be honest with you, and I wasn't. I lied to you, and you deserved my trust. Why couldn't I be honest with you? I wanted to give you the life you so deserved, and I didn't know how. I was too proud and selfish. I see it so clearly now and it's too late. I didn't deserve you! You deserved so much more.

I've attempted to find you, but your number isn't working. I fear I will never find you, and I will never be able to tell you how sorry I am. I will never be able to hold you like I did. I will never be able to prove you can trust me. How could I do this to you? You were so good to me.

I prayed to Jesus that he would forgive me, and I hope He has forgiven me for the way that I treated you. You are the best gift I have ever had in my life, and I took you for granted. I guess I always thought you would be here to forgive me and never leave. Even when you were sick, I couldn't nurture you. I still didn't get it. I could still only think of myself. How can this be? I have asked myself this so many times.

I wish I could hold you and start over again, but it's too late now. I have lost you forever! How will I ever forgive myself?

Maybe it's not too late. I pray that you find this letter somehow, someway, and God brings you back to me.

You always loved me no matter what. You always talked to me about Jesus as you wanted so badly for me to be free of the hurt that I had inside, but I would not let it go.

As I stand here by the water's edge writing this letter, I will throw it into the ocean, and my prayer is that you finally know how sorry I am and how much I love you! I do love you, Cindy!

Thank you for loving me and showing me how to love like Jesus. He took you from me, and my heart is broken. I pray it won't be broken forever.

You were my angel, and I couldn't even see it. I am so sorry, my love.

With all my regrets and love for you, Cindy, I will miss you and love you forever. I will keep you in my heart forever, too!

Johnny – Morehead City, NC – June 2019

Mary, with tears flowing from her eyes, looked over at Elizabeth. She had tears flowing, too. "Wow, Elizabeth. This letter is so very sad. It says so much, doesn't it? Do you think she left him, or did she die? I guess we will never know."

Mary considered putting the letter in the newspaper. "Maybe Cindy will see the note and respond," she said.

Elizabeth agreed this would be a great idea and even a little exciting too!

Mary put the note back in the bottle, replaced the cork, and walked over to the window. The snow was still falling.

As Mary and Elizabeth stood looking out the window, watching the snow fall and the waves rolling onto the shore, Mary thought of the regret so many must face every day, and she had some of her own.

She prayed that John would be set free. She then prayed that God would heal the broken and bring hearts back to Him so all could be set free. After all, Jesus is love. She then thought of *1 Corinthians 13: 4-7,* *"Love is patient, love is kind. It does not envy, it does not boast, it is not proud. It does not dishonor others, it is not self-seeking, it is not easily angered, it keeps no record of wrongs. Love does not delight in evil but rejoices with the truth. It always protects, always trusts, always hopes, always perseveres."*

After reading the letter, Mary and Elizabeth's day changed. Their emotions felt vulnerable, and they both could feel the regret and pain he had in his heart. Mary shared her feelings with Elizabeth, "Is it really too late for him and Cindy? Only God knows, I guess."

Mary, with Elizabeth sitting beside her listening to the call, called the newspaper office. When the newsroom picked up the call, she told them about the message in the bottle that she had found.

A lady with a sweet voice seemed excited about the story and promised to post the letter in the paper in the next few days. They asked Mary to fax them a copy and gave her the number to send it to.

Elizabeth, with a mysterious look on her face, smiled while Mary faxed the note to the newspaper office.

Mary and Elizabeth both agreed that it would be a miracle if someone called in.

They prayed that Cindy would find the note that was sent to her years ago.

The sweet lady on the line agreed that if they called in, they would give her Mary's number so she could talk with her herself. Mary agreed that would be perfect.

At that moment, Mary wondered why she had found the bottle. But she was confident that God had a plan for her life, and whatever it was, by His grace, she would follow it.

16

A CHRISTMAS SURPRISE

The snow had stopped, leaving four inches on the ground. The Christmas tree was lit, and a few gifts had been bought. The gifts were sitting on Mary's special Christmas tree skirt that her mom had given her years ago. She had great memories from her childhood that always seemed to come back to her during the Christmas season. Mary still missed her mom every day. She went to be with Jesus many years ago. Mary was hoping to be able to see her family for Christmas but plans had not been confirmed yet. She prayed they could be together.

Mary was looking forward to her call with the girls to discuss Karen's baby shower. She prayed that everything would go well for her as the baby wasn't due until mid-January.

As Mary stood in the kitchen emptying her dishwasher, she saw Elizabeth standing by the bottle that had been found by the ocean. Mary walked over to her and said, "Are you okay, Elizabeth? What are you thinking about?"

Elizabeth began telling her how sad she felt for John, the man who had put the note in the bottle, and she wondered why he had taken the woman it was written to for granted. "I wonder who she was, Mom. I wonder if she is alive. I wonder as he mentioned that he had not cared for her when she was sick. Maybe she just left him."

Mary, replying to Elizabeth, said, "Elizabeth, I guess we will never really know, will we? Maybe someone will answer the letter in the newspaper. We will pray that it happens. I have thought about the letter a lot too. I even thought about why I found it."

Mary went on sharing with Elizabeth. "I don't believe in coincidences, but I can only think about my first husband, Edward. After we divorced, he felt the same way as John for many years. Maybe he still does; I don't know. I do know this, Elizabeth; we should never take anything for granted. Life is short, and when God brings two people together, it should be a bond that is never broken by deception or neglect. Trust and building each other up is a must in a marriage that thrives, Elizabeth. Keeping God first and allowing Him to lead has to be a priority.

"There will be times that we fail, but we must repent quickly and ask for forgiveness. Forgiving someone relieves the person who is forgiving of bitterness and pain. Repenting isn't just turning away from our sins; it is a conscious choice never to do it again. We should always strive to love as Jesus loves us! It can't be done, though, unless Jesus lives in our hearts, and so many people only think of themselves. That will not go well for them in the end, and Jesus sees everything!"

Elizabeth stood there and listened to Mary intently. Mary believed this was a lesson for everyone.

Mary hugged Elizabeth, and she began to pray. *"Father, thank you for the bottle that I found. Thank you for showing us just how fragile life could be for us without you being the center of our lives. May this note be a lesson for all of us that we keep in our hearts forever. In Jesus' name, we pray, Amen."*

Mary was getting ready for her call with the girls. Elizabeth sat down by the Christmas tree, JJ sitting next to her.

The phone rang, and as she answered it, she could see Victoria and Patricia. Mary loved video calls, especially when they couldn't be together in person. Everyone said hello and began talking about the snow. They had not yet attempted to get out, and they were all still in their pajamas. "Snow days are the best," Mary said. Everyone agreed.

Patricia and Victoria had also written some notes.

Mary had memorized everything but decided she had better go grab a scrap piece of paper to write on.

Patricia talked about the cake and Karen's favorite color of lavender, but they all agreed that instead of a cake, they would make cupcakes just like they had at Patricia's and Mary's shower. They had planned to use the same bakery; everything they had bought from them was always so good, and they were always great at delivery.

The baby shower planning was finally done!

The call went well, and all the plans were finalized. Mary would order the cupcakes and make a vegetable tray, Patricia would make her homemade cookies and a fruit tray, and Victoria would make Karen's favorite Petit Fours decorated in white icing with a lavender baby boot.

The girls laughed as they saw Elizabeth in the background of the screen, filming Mary with an old video camera that she had. Mary was happy she had it, but it was so old that it didn't work most of the time. There were times she wished she didn't have it, though, especially when she filmed moments of her not dressed and while her hair was still a mess from sleeping. Elizabeth loved moments like this the most. I may get her a new one for Christmas, Mary thought.

After hanging up the call, Elizabeth wanted Mary and JJ to go out and make snow angels. "JJ can go out with us."

Mary agreed they could, but they needed to dress in warm clothes. "It's freezing out there!" The fireplace in the living room had been on since they got up, and it was toasty warm inside.

Mary and Elizabeth ran to their bedrooms to find warm clothes to put on; they then met back in the living room.

Elizabeth had her waterproof boots on, a heavy coat, and mittens. Mary slipped her feet into her boots that sat by the back door. She called JJ to come with them but without a leash this time. "He will stay with us," Mary said.

As they began walking out the door, Mary remembered she had yet to shovel the steps. She asked Elizabeth if she would wait a minute for her to shovel. Elizabeth agreed she would stay with JJ inside. It didn't take long; soon, they were all lying in the snow making snow angels. JJ loved the snow, dancing around, snow flying everywhere.

They laughed so much, and they knew the memories they were making were priceless.

Mary got up off the ground and, while looking around, giggled, "There are snow angels everywhere. You can see which ones are who's, and Elizabeth, you have made a lot more than I have!"

They both laughed at the same time. They were laughing hysterically, and their toes felt frozen. "It's so cold; let's go back in!"

They began running back to the cottage, and as they walked inside, Mary said, "We need to leave our boots at the door. I'll go grab an old towel to rest them on."

Elizabeth waited for Mary to get back before taking off her boots. After she took them off, she ran to the fireplace to warm her hands and feet. Mary came in behind her. When Mary looked down at Elizabeth's feet, she noticed she had two different-colored socks on, and the designs on each were hilarious. One had stripes of many colors, and the other was pastel with small shapes everywhere.

While looking down at her feet, Mary said, "Elizabeth, where did you get those socks?"

Elizabeth looked down at her feet and then back up at her mom and said, "I don't know, but I love them!"

"Well, I love them too," Mary said.

Elizabeth had the most genuine personality and was always full of surprises.

Mary asked Elizabeth if she wanted a cup of hot chocolate with whipped topping. Elizabeth said with extreme excitement, "YES, PLEASE!" Mary went into the kitchen; there, she pulled out the milk and reached into the pantry for the cocoa and sugar. In no time at all, they were sitting by the Christmas tree, drinking hot chocolate with peppermint sticks and lots of whipped topping. The atmosphere in the cottage was delightful.

Mary, while looking at the lit tree, said, "Today was such a nice surprise. Our plans sure changed, didn't they, Elizabeth?" They were both very joyful as a snow day seemed to be exactly what they needed!

The phone rang, and it was Jimmy. Mary had totally forgotten to tell him about the bottle she had found. He was excited to hear about it and asked if she would show it to him the next time they saw each other.

Mary could tell that Jimmy was hinting to come over, but she wasn't going to invite him this time, as she was enjoying her snow day with Elizabeth. She agreed that he could see the bottle and read the letter. She didn't elaborate too much, and they began talking about the snow. Mary, with excitement, told him they had just come in from making snow angels and were sitting by the tree drinking hot chocolate. He got quiet and he seemed a little envious.

Jimmy began telling Mary how he had been out clearing some of the neighbors' driveways and how he had used the tractor with the blade to clear the parking lot at the Mercy Center. He then said, "It looks like this snow will be here at least until tomorrow as the temperatures haven't risen above freezing all day and they're not expected to."

They talked about Karen and how she was. He seemed excited for her that the doctor had given her the advice to stay up a little to see how she did. "I haven't talked to her today," said Mary. "I need to call her for sure."

Jimmy told Mary he would call her back later in the day, and they hung up the call.

Mary picked up the phone to call Karen. Sam answered.

"Hi, Mary. Karen is lying down right now. I think she is sleeping. She was up a while this morning and started having pains. It scared her, so she has been in bed ever since."

This concerned Mary as she still had a few weeks before the baby was due.

Mary asked Sam to have Karen call her when she got up if she felt up to it.

"Thanks, Mary," Sam said. They both hung up.

Mary was concerned about her friend. She wanted so badly for everything to go well for her and Sam.

The phone rang again, and the caller ID said, Daddy. Mary answered the phone. "Hi, Daddy!"

"Mary, how are you and Elizabeth doing? I saw you got some snow," Daddy said.

Mary began telling him that they had gotten four inches and how they had just come in from making snow angels. "It's freezing out there. We weren't out there very long, Daddy."

Mary's Daddy told her that he had some great news!

"What?" Mary asked.

"Well, I know we are not going to be able to be together on Christmas Day, so I wanted to ask if we can come next week to stay a few days with you and Elizabeth. We will have an early Christmas together, Mary. Is that okay?"

Mary almost dropped the phone. "Daddy, I am so happy. Yes, yes, yes!" she said. "The Inn is decorated so beautifully for Christmas, and I will make sure you each have a room booked. What day is it again, Daddy?"

"I was thinking about next Thursday through Sunday. Is that okay?" Daddy said.

"It's perfect," Mary exclaimed.

"Okay, we will all see you then, Mary. Give Elizabeth a hug for me! We can't wait to see you!"

When they hung up, Elizabeth wanted to know who was on the phone. "You are extremely happy!"

Mary excitedly told her that Grandpa, Sarah, and Beth were coming next week so we could have an early Christmas together.

Elizabeth understood then why Mary was so excited. She was too!

"We have a lot of work added to our schedule the next few days, Elizabeth," Mary said. She explained with excitement that it would be fun, like shopping for gifts, and how they could make Christmas desserts and snacks, too! Mary could feel her energy level rise dramatically. She loved her daddy and sisters, and she was so happy that they had decided to visit for the holidays.

Mary had been enjoying her days off since starting part-time but seemed to still not have enough time to get done what she needed to. She thought about her week ahead and Elizabeth's Christmas break from school coming up and wished she could take off a few weeks. She knew she couldn't because of all the Christmas parties coming up at the Inn, but she was confident that she would figure it out.

Mary asked Elizabeth if she wanted to sit down and do some planning with her. She came and sat by Mary. "Okay, let's think! What would you like for desserts and snacks, Elizabeth? We will write your choices down first."

Elizabeth smiled at Mary with a sweet smile of approval. She began listing all her favorite cookies - Snickerdoodle, Peanut Butter Fudge, and Peanut Butter Delight.

Mary already knew what they would be as Elizabeth always wanted exactly the same ones every year.

Elizabeth then said, "Oh, and let's make a pumpkin roll, too! We usually make it for Thanksgiving, and we didn't this year."

Mary agreed they would make all of them. "That is, of course, if you're going to help me."

Elizabeth giggled and said, "I will help, promise."

Mary thought of some things her daddy loved and wrote down pigs in a blanket, homemade chicken salad, and her mom's homemade pecan pie. The list was growing, and she hoped they could eat all of it.

Elizabeth chimed in with a laugh and said, "Oh, we will!"

Mary had attempted to make a chocolate pie like her mom had made for years but had not been successful until she made one for Thanksgiving that was close to perfect. She thought she would try it again. "Hey, Elizabeth, let's make some of the Puppy Chow and Christmas Bark, too."

Elizabeth, while listening to her tummy growl, said, "Sounds yummy, mom!"

Mary said, "Well, we better make Jimmy's favorite Oatmeal Raisin cookies, too. He would love that."

Mary knew they would also be having dinner at the Inn on Saturday night, so she made a list of reminders to book the hotel rooms and dinner reservations. "Oh, maybe we will get a massage, too, while they are here. Daddy loved it last time," Mary said with joy as she reflected on the memory.

They both realized they had not had any lunch and got up to make a sandwich. Mary pulled out the fresh bread she had just baked, sliced turkey, mayonnaise, and a tomato.

Elizabeth grabbed her favorite chips out of the pantry and her favorite pickles out of the refrigerator.

As Mary reached for a couple of plates in the cabinet, she started thinking about Jimmy. She realized that she was missing him more and more, and it surprised her. She was fighting her feelings for him and realized it was fear. She was fearful of being hurt, but she also knew what God had said and that whatever happened would be His will. I need to spend more time with Him, she thought.

Mary was sure school would also be closed tomorrow, and she needed to work but didn't think she would be able to. "Not early, anyway," said Mary. "I may go in later and just take Elizabeth with me. We will see in the morning, and I will look at the weather for tomorrow to get an idea of the temperatures." Snow doesn't usually stay around very long here, she thought. "It is so pretty, though."

Elizabeth had made each of them a sandwich and placed their plates on the table. Mary poured two glasses of water with a slice of fresh lemon. They sat down to eat.

The cottage was beautifully decorated for Christmas. As Mary looked over at the tree, she could see the ornament that Jimmy had bought her. She remembered the day they met so well, and the memory of what God showed her that day would be etched in her heart forever. She just prayed that what happened between that date and the end would be beautiful. She had to trust God and know that His plans for her were better than her own. She thought once more of the scripture in *John 11:40*, Jesus said, *"Did I not tell you that if you believed, you would see the glory of God?"* Mary was seeking God's peace that she needed so desperately. She thought about asking Jimmy to come over on Saturday. "Maybe we can drive and look at the Christmas decorations at the ballpark," Mary said.

Elizabeth said, "That sounds fun! Let's do it!"

After their lunch, Mary picked up the phone to call Jimmy to invite him over on Saturday afternoon. But he didn't answer the call.

Mary went back into the kitchen to put the dishes in the dishwasher and wipe the counters and table off. Elizabeth had gone to her room to get a movie that she hoped they could watch together. Mary thought that was a great idea, so they both grabbed snuggly blankets, got on the couch, and turned the TV on.

They enjoyed their snuggle time. Elizabeth had great taste in movies as she was very much like Mary and enjoyed wholesome movies about family. Mary was happy about that and hoped it would never change. I guess it could when she gets older, she thought.

Mary got up from the couch and looked at her phone. Jimmy had called back a couple of times, and she had missed his calls while watching the movie with Elizabeth.

She picked up the phone to call him back. He answered on the first ring.

"Tag, you're it," Mary said.

Jimmy laughed and apologized for missing her call, but he had been clearing some snow. Mary loved that he was helping others, which made her feel more positive about him.

Mary told Jimmy what they had been doing all afternoon. "We snuggled and watched a movie by the fireplace, and it was very relaxing."

"What else do you do on snow days, right?" said Jimmy. "Or I guess clearing snow is another one, huh. I wish I had some of your hot chocolate, Mary."

Mary invited Jimmy to come over on Saturday afternoon. She mentioned that they might go and do some Christmas shopping, go out to dinner, and go to the ballpark to see the Christmas lights. Jimmy thought all of this sounded great and agreed to be there a little after lunch. She was excited to tell him the news about her daddy and sisters coming the following Thursday. She hoped that he could also spend some time with them as well. "You can go with us to dinner at the Inn on Saturday night. Can you?"

Jimmy was excited to see her family as he enjoyed them so much at Thanksgiving.

"Hey, Jimmy, could you grill some steaks on Friday night at the cottage?" Mary asked.

Jimmy was very grateful that Mary enjoyed his steaks and said, "Of course I can, Mary."

Mary could feel the excitement in their conversation, and she was looking forward to spending time with him. Mary told Jimmy that she also needed to go to the grocery store on Saturday. "Maybe you should just come over late morning, and we can get a lot of shopping done, Jimmy," Mary said.

Jimmy agreed as he was happy to spend as much time as he could with Mary.

For Jimmy, it didn't really matter what they were doing as long as they were together. They ended the call with the excitement of being together in only two days, as tomorrow was Friday, and they were all excited about the weekend.

Elizabeth had school until Wednesday and then would be out for Christmas break until after the New Year. Elizabeth was looking forward to the break. Pamela agreed to take care of her the three days Mary had to work the next week and then Elizabeth could just go in with Mary when she had to work. Her daughter enjoyed going to work with Mary, and everyone there always spoiled her and made a big deal of her. She loved the attention from everyone, especially all the cupcakes and the food. The Inn had the best mac n cheese on Earth, according to Elizabeth.

Mary opened her laptop and began looking online for some Christmas gifts for her daddy and sisters. She didn't have a lot of luck looking for him, as he always preferred cash. He would always say, "Thank you. It's the right size and the right color." They would always laugh. He was easy to buy for, as cards were always easy to find for someone as loved as Mary loved her daddy.

Sarah and Beth would be easy to buy for, too. Mary always enjoyed buying them things they could use. She was very careful about her gift purchases. She always thought them through and hoped that each one would be special.

Mary enjoyed buying gifts for others. Christmas was her favorite holiday. It wasn't about the gifts for her but about the birth of Jesus, the Savior of the world. Celebrating this with family and friends made it very special for her.

Mary had learned over the period of her lifetime the importance of keeping Jesus close to her heart and not allowing anything to be a priority over Him. She was still learning. Jesus was Mary's best friend and everyone that knew her knew that.

Finally, it was Saturday morning. The snow was still on the ground but had melted quite a bit during the day on Friday. Mary had not ventured out since before the snow and was looking forward to Jimmy coming over and their day together. She was looking forward to the arrival of the gifts she had ordered so they could wrap them and put them under the tree.

It was early, six a.m. She had woken up at 5, tossing and turning before finally getting up. She turned on her coffee and sat and read her bible for a while. She loved how silent the world was early in the morning.

Before she knew it, the sun was coming up and she could see the bright sky through her window. She grabbed her jacket, slipped on her boots and walked out onto the deck. Wow, she thought. The sunrise was stunning. She grabbed her phone to snap a few pictures and was mesmerized. She absolutely loved watching the sunrises at the cottage and the artwork that the Lord painted in the sky were always such a gift to her. She felt they were always a blessing to see.

It was still very cold, but the temperatures were supposed to be in the high 40s with full sun. Mary loved the snow, but she was also happy to see it leave. After all, they had big plans for today and they needed dry roads to get around and enjoy it.

Mary walked back inside and poured herself another cup of coffee when she heard JJ jump off the bed. He always wanted to be close to Mary and when she was busy, he would stay close to Elizabeth if she was home. Sunshine was also up. She had been playing but had jumped up on the couch and was now sitting on a blanket that Mary had been wrapped up in while reading.

Getting hungry, Mary decided on pancakes. Maybe the smell of them will wake Elizabeth up early, she thought. As she pulled out all the ingredients, mixed them, and poured the batter onto the skillet, she glanced over at the bottle, with the note inside, that still sat on the counter. She thought, 2019. "That was five years ago," she said. She wondered why she had found it and if there was any way she would ever know who John was. Mary knew it wasn't possible as it could be anyone, but she prayed once more that whoever it may be was finally happy, and walking with Jesus.

Before the second pancake was done, Mary could hear Elizabeth coming through the living room.

With sleepy eyes, and walking gingerly, she looked up at Mary and said, "Good morning, mom."

Mary, while holding a measuring cup filled with pancake batter, looked over at Elizabeth and said, "Good morning, sweet girl. I thought the smell of these pancakes would wake you."

Elizabeth smiled and said, "You were right! I rolled over and thought, is that my mom's pancakes?" She began to laugh. "I thought I was dreaming, but I am happy I wasn't!"

Mary was happy she was up, and they were both looking forward to their day together with Jimmy.

As soon as the breakfast dishes were put away and the kitchen was clean, she had a phone call that she would soon not forget. As the phone rang and she picked it up, it was Sam.

"Mary, Karen, and I are at the hospital. The baby is coming, and we can't stop it. The doctors are monitoring her and the baby very closely. Please pray!"

"Oh, NO!" Mary exclaimed out loud. "What can I do, Sam?"

Sam replied, "Nothing now, Mary, just pray!"

Mary replied, "We will, right now. Please keep me posted."

Elizabeth heard Mary and ran to her side. "What's wrong?" she asked.

Mary immediately walked into the living room holding Elizabeth's hand and explained that Karen was in labor, and it was too early. "Let's pray right now for our friend, Elizabeth," Mary said. They both got on their knees and began to pray. *"Father, we come to you today in need of your Mercy. We pray that you comfort Sam and Karen. Give them peace that surpasses understanding. Only you know why the baby is coming early, and we ask that you protect the baby and be with the doctors and nurses there at that hospital and bring your healing touch to the baby and Karen." We know you are in full control, and we pray that in these concerning times, you bring your Spirit into that hospital room where they are and take full control of the situation, and may you be glorified. In Jesus' name, we pray, Amen."*

Mary knew it was way too early but picked up her phone to call Pamela and Victoria to give them the news. They were both very concerned and also began to pray.

Before she realized it, the morning had slipped away. Mary had not heard any updated news about Karen and wanted to call Sam so badly, but knew she had to be patient.

The doorbell rang, and Mary could see Jimmy through the window. He was carrying a wrapped box in his hand. Mary opened the door and welcomed him in. Elizabeth came to the door to greet him as well. He seemed very happy to see them. He handed Elizabeth the wrapped box.

Mary looked at him as if to say, "Oh, I thought that was mine."

Jimmy said, "Not this time, Mary." They both chuckled.

Elizabeth thanked him for the gift and began walking over to the tree to put the gift under it.

Jimmy said, "Oh, Elizabeth, that is for you to open now. An early Christmas present, I guess you could say."

Elizabeth was thrilled about that, and she sat on the couch with the gift in her lap.

Jimmy and Mary both walked over to where she was sitting. "Well, open it," Mary said with a giggle.

Elizabeth began opening the gift, and while pulling it out of the box, she had a big smile on her face. It was a small video camera that Jimmy knew she wanted so badly. Elizabeth got up and hugged him, saying, "Thank you!"

Jimmy told her that he knew it was a gift she could use now, and he wanted her to be able to make a video of Christmas.

Mary was delighted with the gift, and was surprised that Jimmy understood Elizabeth so well and knew what she wanted. Mary thanked Jimmy and said, "Now we must watch her closely, as with this new one, it will work all the time, I'm sure! We can't be hopeful that the camera isn't working." They all laughed. Elizabeth grinned with excitement.

"She is going to be an amazing photographer one day," Jimmy said. "Maybe it will be her career."

"I think you're right," Mary said.

Elizabeth had already taken it out of the box and was trying to figure out how it worked. She loved her video camera, and she was beginning to love Jimmy, too.

Although carrying a burden in her heart for her friend, Karen, Mary forced herself to be patient with the updated news about the baby.

Jimmy, Mary, and Elizabeth were doing some Christmas shopping when the phone rang. It was Sam. The sound of his voice on the other end of the line startled Mary.

"Hey, I wanted to give you an update on Karen and the baby," Sam said.

Mary could feel her heart begin to race as she said, "Hi, Sam."

He proceeded to share the news. "Mary, as you know, Karen went into full-blown labor, and there was nothing the doctors could do to stop it. But although the baby was born prematurely and weighed only 5 lbs., Hope is doing well. Karen is doing well, too." He began to cry.

"Mary almost dropped the phone, and with her heart racing and Jimmy and Elizabeth listening in the hope of hearing what was going on, she began to cry too. "Sam, did I hear you just say, Hope? A girl? She's born? Karen is doing well?"

Sam confirmed all the questions she had, and as Mary could see the smile on his face as well as relief from the sound of his voice, she said, "Praise God!"

Mary was delighted to hear the great news. Although Hope would need to stay in the NICU for an extra few days, Karen and Hope were going to be okay. She would survive, and everyone was so happy with the news.

The shopping trip changed a little after Sam's call.

As soon as Mary told them what Sam had shared, Elizabeth said, "Well, it looks like we need to add another gift to our Christmas list," with a sweet, child-like giggle.

Mary caught a glimpse of a carousel in the corner of her eye and people standing around it. Jimmy also saw it and excitedly said, "Let's go girls!" He began running, and while laughing, Mary and Elizabeth followed him.

It had just stopped when they reached the carousel, and an attendant stood in the front selling tickets.

Jimmy pulled the money out of his pocket and said, "This one is on me, girls. This will be fun!"

Mary exclaimed, "I haven't ridden on one of these since you were a baby, Elizabeth."

Elizabeth didn't remember ever riding one, and as she chose the horse she would ride on, Jimmy helped her up. It was a beautiful gold horse with a red ribbon with bells that had been tied around its neck. Just beside it was a double chair that both Jimmy and Mary could ride in together, so they climbed in. Jimmy looked at Mary with a child-like smile and put his arm around her. Mary felt a warm feeling in her heart, and as she looked over at Elizabeth, she could see her watching them.

As the Carousel went around and around and the Christmas music played in the background, the smiles on the three faces were priceless!

The afternoon was filled with laughter, great food, lots of gifts were bought, and many great memories were made.

Jimmy was grateful, and Mary and Elizabeth were too!

Sam and Karen were now parents and had received a beautiful gift.

Baby Hope was a gift from the Lord and a special Christmas surprise. Hope would change their hearts forever!

17

BAKING WITH JIMMY

Finally, Wednesday had come, and Mary's Daddy and sisters were arriving on Thursday.

Mary and Elizabeth had been baking everything on their list and had a few more to make. The list was getting shorter, and Jimmy was coming over around noon to help with any last-minute preparations before they arrived.

While most of the gifts had been wrapped, there were a couple that needed ribbons and bows.

The cottage was beautiful, and the white lights from the tree reflected off the window. Mary stopped to look out at the ocean. Once more, she thought about how blessed she was.

Elizabeth came into the room with the video camera that Jimmy had bought her. She understood how to use it more now and loved it so much. As Mary turned around, she saw the camera pointing at her. Elizabeth had caught a sincere memory of her mom, and as she filmed her, she could see the reflection of the Christmas tree from the window.

Mary exclaimed, "Are you videoing me, Elizabeth?"

"Yes, I am just practicing, but this one is going to be good," she said.

Elizabeth forgot that the video was still recording and began to laugh. "Well, it would have been, anyway."

Mary, with a look that only Elizabeth knew, said, "Don't take videos of me all day." She smiled and then said, "You're still learning. But you will be a pro in no time."

Elizabeth walked back into her bedroom with her hand on her hip while saying, "I hope I will be, Mom."

Mary then said, "Practice makes perfect, Elizabeth. Just practice on someone else, will you?" They both laughed.

Mary was dressed in gray sweatpants and a red sweatshirt. She wore tennis shoes and her favorite cotton socks. She enjoyed her time at home so much. The smell and feel of the cottage were perfect, as she could sense the Christmas season all around her.

Mary realized that she had not talked to Patricia and Victoria the day before because she had been busy shopping to get ready for the visit from her family. Mary, Jimmy, and Elizabeth were so relieved to hear that both Karen and the baby were doing well. She picked up the phone to text them and ask if they had heard about Karen and baby Hope. They had also talked to Sam and were very excited, sharing that they were still praying. They all agreed that they would have the baby shower at her and Sam's house after she got settled in and felt like the company. Mary was grateful that Karen had everything she needed - for the time being anyway.

Mary couldn't wait to see her Daddy and sisters and, as she thought about them, she prayed that they enjoyed their time with her and Elizabeth as well as Jimmy.

As she walked into the kitchen, the doorbell rang. It must be Jimmy. Mary ran to the door to open it for him. She saw he had a wrapped box in his hand.

"Oh, is this one for me, Jimmy?" Mary asked.

"Yes, but you have to wait until Christmas." Jimmy sternly told her.

Mary, with a pouting look, said, "Why do I have to wait?"

Jimmy responded, saying, "Because this one is very important, and it's just for you!"

Jimmy's comment brought a lot of questions to Mary's mind. "Okay, that's not funny. You're going to have me guessing for two more weeks?"

Jimmy thought it was funny that Mary was so curious as to what was in the box and thought he would enjoy this one. "You will see what's inside soon enough, Mary," Jimmy said.

Elizabeth sat and watched them and, with a giggle, said, "Mom, you will not be able to deal with this very well."

Mary agreed.

Mary walked away and, with a laugh, said, "Let's get to baking!"

They all walked into the kitchen and resting on the table was her checklist. She glimpsed at it and said, "Well, we have a lot to get done today." The counter was full of beautiful and exciting sweets.

Jimmy looked over at the oatmeal cookies and, with a grateful look, smiled at Mary. "Can I have just one?"

Mary instantly answered, "No, you have to wait until tomorrow."

Jimmy looked at her and laughed.

Mary then said, "Well, if I can open my gift, you can have at least two."

Jimmy laughed again and said, "That's not going to happen!"

Mary then replied, "Okay, you can have one."

Jimmy opened the container, pulled out a cookie, and said, "Yummy, these are delicious. You even iced them for me."

Mary smiled and said, "Thank you. You can be such a brat, Jimmy!"

They all laughed, but Mary then said, "Well, it's true!"

Mary looked over at the Chocolate pie, her mom's favorite recipe, and was so grateful that she had finally learned to make it after all these years. The memories of her mom at Christmas continued to come to her mind.

When Mary turned around, looking back at the center of the island, Jimmy was standing there. He looked her in the eyes, and before she knew it, he kissed her.

"Thanks again for the cookies, Mary." Jimmy said with a genuine tone of gratefulness.

Mary was startled and saw that Elizabeth had seen him kiss her.

Elizabeth, with rosy cheeks, said nothing. She pretended not to see it.

Christmas music was playing in the background.

Jimmy, looking at the list, said, "It looks like everything has been checked off." As he looked around the kitchen, he felt so grateful that God had brought Mary and Elizabeth into his life. He needed them, and he thought they needed him, too!

The doorbell rang again, and as Mary looked over at Elizabeth, wondering who it was, she started walking toward the door. Through the window, she could see a large box sitting there. The mail service driver was walking back to the truck. She opened the door and walked out onto the deck. As she looked at the box, she could see it was from the publishing company. Her heart began to race, and she could feel her emotions rising up inside of her. Mary reached down to pick up the box, but it was very heavy.

Jimmy saw her and came outside, saying, "Mary, I'll take this in for you." He could see something different in her but had no idea what it was. She asked him to leave the box on the table in the living room while she went to get something to open it.

Elizabeth walked in to also see what was so important in the box.

Mary opened the box and, as she picked up her book, she screamed. "What perfect timing! My books are here just in time to give a copy to my family."

Elizabeth picked up a book, looked at Mary, and said, "Mom, I am so proud of you! This is beautiful!"

Mary handed Jimmy a copy, and not knowing what to say, she said, "Jimmy, I will sign a copy for you, too."

Jimmy thanked her and said, "I am not much of a reader, but I will definitely read your book, Mary." He was also very proud of Mary.

God had blessed Mary with her writing skills, and it was now becoming her career; Mary just knew it.

The items on Mary's baking list were all checked off, but the kitchen was a disaster. Flour was everywhere, along with the chocolate fudge still sitting on the counter that needed to be put into a container. They all worked together to get it all cleaned up.

After they had finished, Mary thought about going to dinner at their local Italian restaurant. Although the Inn had the best Italian food, she wanted something a little more casual. They realized that with all the baking they had done, they had not eaten. The taste of a few sweets was all they'd had. It was only four in the afternoon, so they decided to have an early dinner.

Jimmy's old truck sat in the driveway next to Mary's car. She wanted to ask him to drive, but she was still a little embarrassed for him, so she asked if he would drive them to the restaurant in her car.

Jimmy happily agreed to drive as it gave him a feeling of being needed. Mary knew this too, which was why she had asked him.

Mary had high hopes for Jimmy and prayed that he would continue to do well. He was very talented and knew that his life was headed in the right direction. She felt good about that, for sure.

The drive to the restaurant was peaceful as the sound of Christmas music filled the car. Everyone was tired from all the baking during the day.

While driving, Jimmy heard a song that he loved so much, it brought a tear to his eye. The song was called I'll Be Home for Christmas. Jimmy missed his family's Christmas but was grateful for the visit they had had. He looked over at Mary and said, "Maybe next year, we can also see my family at Christmas."

Mary agreed that that would be nice.

Jimmy missed James and Maddie and wanted so badly to spend more time with them. "I will, Mary! I just know God will make it happen!"

After ordering their entrée at the Italian Restaurant, Jimmy asked if he could lead the prayer. Mary loved that as she wanted nothing more than to one day have a husband who loved her like Jesus. Everyone bowed their heads, and he began to pray. *"Father, thank you for my time with Mary and Elizabeth today. Baking in the kitchen with them and enjoying the decorations at the cottage gave me the warmth that my heart needed. You have blessed me, and I am grateful. Father, please help me to bring reconciliation back to my family. I miss them so much! Please use this food to nourish us and help us, Lord, to grow as we know you have great plans for us. In Jesus' name, we pray, Amen."*

The waitress, with a patient smile, waited to serve their beverages and appetizers. Mary looked up and smiled back, feeling the waitress's genuine respect and patience.

The conversations between each of them were very enjoyable, and as they finished their meal, Mary realized she was enjoying her time with Jimmy and thought Elizabeth was as well.

Mary wanted everything to be perfect and hoped that it would be. She also knew that it wouldn't be. This was what she dreaded, as she wanted nothing more than a peaceful, fulfilled life with Jesus.

When they arrived back at the cottage, Mary asked if they wanted to do something fun. "Let's string some popcorn for the tree!"

Elizabeth thought that would be a lot of fun, and Jimmy, who didn't seem too excited about it, agreed anyway.

Mary went into her sewing kit and got out three sewing needles and thread. She then went into the pantry and pulled out a bag of popcorn she had. Jimmy loved popcorn and offered to make it on the stove.

"This may be fun after all," Jimmy said.

Elizabeth loved the way they interacted with each other.

When the popcorn was ready, Jimmy left the pot out just in case he needed to make more.

Jimmy handed Mary the bowl and said, "Here you go, Mary. Jimmy Pop, it is!"

Mary laughed hysterically, and Elizabeth did, too. They all realized they had a new name for popcorn: Jimmy Pop!

They all agreed to sit on the floor by the tree to string the popcorn. Mary gave each one a sewing needle and a long piece of thread and demonstrated how to make it. Elizabeth and Jimmy paid close attention.

Mary then said, "Ouch! I just poked myself with the point."

Jimmy then said, "Thanks for also showing us what not to do, Mary." They all laughed out loud.

As they sat on the floor stringing popcorn, they talked about how they were looking forward to the family coming and how enjoyable it would be.

Jimmy was excited about seeing them as well. Elizabeth talked about what she wished for in gifts. They were having a lot of fun!

Jimmy talked about his family and how they always celebrated. He missed his family so much but was confident that God was restoring everything for all of them.

The popcorn was all strung and ready to go on the tree.

Jimmy picked up the end of his string and, from the top, began wrapping it around the tree. He then took Mary's string, connected it to his, and continued wrapping it around. Elizabeth stood up and handed hers to Jimmy. He connected hers to Mary's and finished wrapping the tree. The way this was done spoke to both Jimmy and Mary.

Jimmy began to explain what he was feeling. "Remember the scriptures about how we must stay connected to the vine in John? Also, the one about the order of the home in Ephesians? For some reason, I thought about each of those. God showed me this while stringing the popcorn. Okay, stay with me here, lol," Jimmy said. "When I connected each of our strings of popcorn, I realized if they were broken, it wouldn't be the same. If we were not connected spiritually, we would not be the same couple, would we? If we don't stay connected to Jesus, it doesn't go well for us, does it? Wow," Jimmy said. "That's good!"

Mary then said, "You're right! That's profound, Jimmy."

Elizabeth not knowing what to say, then said, "You guys are funny."

They all started laughing out loud and began cleaning up the mess. They all had a lot of fun together, but everyone was tired from the long day of baking.

Mary thanked Jimmy for coming over and for all his help and making the Jimmy Pop. She asked him if he could come back tomorrow around 1 p.m.

Jimmy agreed on the time. They discussed their plans for dinner Thursday night.

Jimmy would bring the steaks from the local butcher shop and marinate them for them.

Mary was tired and was looking forward to seeing her Daddy and sisters the next day.

Jimmy was also looking forward to spending more time with Mary's family.

Mary knew her family would be arriving late in the afternoon and would be tired from the hours of driving.

Elizabeth hugged Jimmy and ran into the house. She wanted to take JJ on a walk around the cottage.

Mary thanked Jimmy for all his help and turned to go inside.

Jimmy pulled her to him and said, "Mary, thank you for today!"

Mary said, "Thank you, Jimmy." She hugged him and they both said goodnight.

As soon as Mary got back into the cottage, she walked over to her box of books. She sat down and looked through it again. She was so happy to be holding it in her hand and couldn't believe the sequel to her first book was published and waiting for readers to also hold it in their hands.

Mary thought about signing three of them with a special message to include. As she pulled them out of the box, she laid them down on the coffee table to get her favorite pen. "Daddy, Beth, and Sarah will be so surprised, she thought." She began writing a sweet message that she knew they would all love.

Mary and Elizabeth were tired from the day, and both decided to get in bed early and watch a Christmas movie. "Tomorrow is a big day, Elizabeth," Mary said. They were so happy and excited to have their family home for the holidays.

Elizabeth had a soft blanket over her and Mary was in her favorite cotton pajamas. JJ was resting beside each of them, and you could hear him snoring occasionally. Mary and Elizabeth would always giggle when they heard it.

The movie had only been playing for about an hour when Mary looked at Elizabeth and saw she was fast asleep. Rather than wake her, Mary got up, turned the TV off, crawled back into bed, and reached for her bible. She read a while, and as she meditated on God's word, she felt so grateful. She thought of her new book and prayed that God would use it to bring readers closer to Him. Her heart was burdened by so many, and she hoped that, in some small way, she could make a difference in the lives of others.

Mary reached up to turn her lamp off, snuggled next to JJ and Elizabeth, closed her eyes, said her prayers, and fell asleep.

18

AN EARLY CHRISTMAS
WITH FAMILY

The light was shining through the window as Mary remembered her family would be there in the afternoon. She smiled, looked over at Elizabeth, stretched, and stood up. Trying not to wake her daughter, she tip-toed out of the bedroom and then went into the kitchen to turn on her coffeepot. JJ didn't get up. He was happy to stay in bed with Elizabeth. Mary looked forward to her coffee every morning and was happy to have some time to enjoy reading her bible and being with the Lord.

Mary poured her coffee and walked over to her writing chair by the window. The cottage felt cool, so she turned on the gas fireplace. As she sat there looking out the window at the ocean, a thought came to her mind that surprised her. She thought of Jimmy and how much she was enjoying his company. She thought about his life and how grateful she was that God had called her to love him. She knew she had to follow God's will for her life, and she was happy that she was beginning to enjoy it. Jimmy was grateful for the change in Mary's attitude. She could feel it.

Mary sat reading her bible. When she read the scripture in *Luke 15:7, "I tell you that in the same way, there will be more rejoicing in heaven over one sinner who repents than over ninety-nine righteous persons who do not need to repent.*" Mary thought, Heaven must be rejoicing over Jimmy's life right now.

Mary closed her bible and stared out the window. The sun was shining, but the temperature was in the low 40s. Winter was not her favorite season, but Christmas was one of her favorite holidays, and being able to be with her family was a gift all by itself. Although she knew it wasn't Christmas yet, she was happy that they could share an early one together.

Mary walked over to the coffee table where her books were lying and decided to wrap them. As she began her task, she felt so joyful and happy that her books had arrived.

As she was wrapping, Elizabeth walked into the room. "Mom, I slept with you last night!"

Mary told her that she had fallen asleep before the movie was over, and she didn't want to move her. Elizabeth smiled at her mom; then she put on her coat so she could take JJ out for a walk.

The morning had gone by slowly as the excitement of seeing Jimmy and their family filled their hearts. Jimmy had called to tell Mary he had already marinated the steaks for dinner. Mary was happy he was coming and realized she had missed him since he left the day before.

Mary wanted to take a walk on the beach as she had missed it so much since it had gotten so cold out. She did still take walks, but not as often as she liked to.

As she stood in the kitchen doing some tidying up, the phone rang. "Daddy, is everything okay?" Mary asked when she picked up the phone.

"Hi, Mary. We were so excited to see you, we left early. We are only an hour away," her daddy said.

Mary was delighted and called Elizabeth over to tell her. Elizabeth was filled with joy and couldn't wait until they arrived. Mary said, "That's great, daddy. We can't wait to see y'all. Be careful; we'll see you in just a bit. Hurry!"

When they hung up the phone, Mary called Jimmy. When he answered, he asked if everything was okay. Mary began telling him that her family had left early and would be there in an hour. She asked him if he could come early, too.

Jimmy agreed that he would grab the steaks and come over now. Mary said, "Okay, Jimmy, we will see you soon."

It didn't take long until the doorbell rang. Jimmy was standing at the door. As she opened it to let him in, she could see he had the steaks in his left hand and a very full-looking bag in his right.

Mary asked what was in it.

With a flirtatious look, Jimmy said, "Mary, you are a little nosey." Then, with a smile, he added, "I picked up another couple of gifts to go under the tree."

Mary smiled at him to show she was pleased with his generosity. "Are they for me?" she asked.

Jimmy laughed. "Mary, you're kind of a brat too."

"No, I'm not a brat at all, but you sure are!" They both laughed, and Mary could see Elizabeth trying to hold back the laughter as well.

Jimmy walked over to the tree. He placed the gifts to the left of it, so he knew exactly where to find them.

Just a few seconds later, the doorbell rang. Mary and Elizabeth ran to the door.

Daddy was standing at the door with a huge grin on his face. He grabbed Mary and then Elizabeth and said, "I have missed you two so much!"

Mary began to cry and said, "Daddy, we have missed you more, I promise!"

She could see Sarah and Beth getting some things out of the car. As they walked toward the door, Beth and Sarah sat the boxes down and hugged Mary and Elizabeth.

They were all together at last.

Mary asked if she could help carry something, and Sarah handed her a box. The box was filled with wrapped Christmas gifts. Mary loved getting gifts and was excited to see what was inside the box. Beth was very crafty, and she always included something handmade. She had once given Mary an Afghan that she had crocheted, and Mary still treasured it.

When they were all inside the cottage, Mary could see her daddy standing in the kitchen talking to Jimmy. Her daddy had a smile on his face, and she could see he was enjoying the conversation. This made Mary smile.

Christmas had come early, and the love that filled the cottage was beautiful!

Mary had planned to spend some time with the family at the cottage but also wanted to take them over to the Inn to get their luggage placed in their rooms before dinner.

Mary made sandwiches for everyone, and while they sat around and ate, they had a great conversation. She was so happy that her family was there with them and was so grateful for their time together. Her daddy looked great for his age, and he seemed to be happier about Jimmy being around. She thought it must have been because they had spent Thanksgiving together, and he enjoyed spending time with him. Sarah and Beth looked great as usual, and Elizabeth, with her video recorder in her hand filming everyone, looked happy about seeing her family, too.

Mary asked if everyone wanted to go to the Inn and drop off their luggage before dinner. Everyone agreed.

Mary's daddy asked how Mr. Henry was doing, and he hoped that he would be at the Inn so they could see him. Mary began sharing how well he was doing, and she also expressed that she hoped that they could meet Pamela while they were there.

Jimmy drove Mary and Elizabeth to the Inn, and her daddy followed them. When they arrived at the front door, the bellman came out to greet them. He remembered her family from their last visit and told them how happy he was to see them all. He began getting their luggage out of the car and carrying it to their assigned rooms.

As soon as they walked over the Inn, Mr. Henry greeted them at the door. Mary's daddy smiled, shook his hand, and told him how nice it was to see him. They loved the Inn, and since there wasn't enough room for them to spend the night at the cottage, they could not think of a better place to stay.

Mary could not see Pamela and she wanted the family to meet her, so she walked over to her office. But Mary discovered she had a client sitting in front of her. Mary slipped silently away and met the family back in the lobby. She was overjoyed that Pamela was doing such a great job, and although she would miss her time there full-time, she was even more grateful that she was only working part-time now.

Mr. Henry invited them to the restaurant for a cup of coffee. Everybody agreed, and Mary particularly was happy. The waitress greeted each of them as Mr. Henry sat down. He asked her to please to bring coffee and not to forget the maple syrup.

The waitress smiled at Mr. Henry and said, "Oh, and should I bring the dessert you and I talked about?"

Mr. Henry smiled and nodded.

Mary looked over at Mr. Henry and said, "You are too much, Mr. Henry."

Mr. Henry looked back at her with a smile and answered, "You deserve nothing less than the best, Mary."

The atmosphere at the Inn was incredible. Everyone was so nice, and the service was first class.

The waitress came to the table and served everyone a cup of freshly brewed coffee and a chocolate cupcake. Mr. Henry had added sparklers and, as each one was lit, he stood up and congratulated Mary on her new book and for all the outstanding service she had provided to so many guests at the Inn. He then said, "Mary, you deserve this chocolate cupcake, and I am grateful that now you have earned more time at home with Elizabeth."

Mary's daddy sat there with an impressed look on his face. He was proud of Mary and her accomplishments; in fact, he was proud of all his girls!

Mary hugged Mr. Henry and thanked him for always being such an amazing boss. She loved Mr. Henry so much, and his love for her was more like that of a daughter than a friend.

Mary sat back down and, to help alleviate the tears, said, "Let's eat our cupcakes."

They all began to eat while sipping on their coffee; they could not be happier that they were together.

Mary looked up and saw Pamela was walking toward them. She got up to hug her and introduced her to her family. Pamela seemed to be so thrilled to meet all of them, and they were as well. She stayed and talked for a few minutes and then excused herself as she had another client coming in.

Mary got up and said to Pamela, "Thank you for all that you are doing. I knew this job was perfect for you the second I met you."

Pamela smiled at Mary and said, "Mary, you and I know that God had this all planned long before we ever knew it."

Mary agreed and while smiling, turned to walk back to the table. Jimmy was talking to Mr. Henry, who also had begun to enjoy his company.

Jimmy was fitting in with Mary's family very well and everyone could not have been more pleased.

The afternoon had been delightful. Everyone was enjoying themselves, and the dessert and coffee that Mr. Henry had provided hit the spot.

When arriving back at the cottage, Daddy found a cozy chair next to the fireplace. The Christmas tree was lit, and Elizabeth was recording everyone with her new video recorder that Jimmy had bought her.

Presents surrounded the tree, and everybody couldn't wait to open them. They had planned a nice Christmas dinner on Saturday evening and thought they would open them after that. Mary had bought a ham to bake, and they would put together some of their favorite sides. The desserts were already made, and Mary's chocolate pie would be one they would all love.

Mary stood in the doorway between the kitchen and living room and enjoyed watching her daddy sleeping in the chair. He loved late afternoon naps by the fireplace. Everyone else stayed in the kitchen talking softly to avoid waking him. It was difficult as there was so much to catch up on, and sometimes, the laughter could be heard outside.

Mary turned to join the others in the kitchen with a grateful heart. She saw Sarah preparing a salad and Beth was getting the fresh bread out that she had prepared at home to bring with her. Jimmy had the steaks out of the refrigerator and Mary went into the pantry to get the potatoes to roast. Everyone loved Mary's roasted potatoes with onions, garlic, and peppers.

Mary asked Elizabeth if she could set the table. She sat her video camera down and realized it needed to be charged. She grabbed the charger out of her room and began charging it before getting the dishes out of the cabinet. Elizabeth then began counting everyone in the room and was happy to pull out six plate settings for the table. It was usually only her and Mary for meals, and it was refreshing to see her family there joining them.

Mary and Elizabeth were not able to see their family as often as they wanted, but they felt sure now that with Mary only having to work part-time, this was going to change.

Jimmy tip-toed through the living room, hoping not to wake Daddy up. But when he opened the door to go out on the deck to light the grill, it startled him.

Daddy sat up in the chair, looked over at Jimmy, and said, "Well, did I sleep through dinner?"

Jimmy told him no, that he was just about to grill the steaks, and he woke up just in time.

Daddy smiled a sleepy smile, stretched, and walked into the kitchen.

Everyone was happy to see him, and they were also happy that he had rested a little, as they knew he was tired from the trip.

Elizabeth had completed setting the table with Mary's Christmas china, and Mary had placed a red Christmas arrangement on it with two lit candles inside. The table was beautiful!

Dinner was ready and everyone was just waiting for Jimmy to bring the steaks in from the grill.

Mary took a platter out to him and asked how much longer it would be. Jimmy had just turned them for the last time. Mary had come out just in time. As she stood by him, shivering, Jimmy put his arms around her, looked around to see if anyone was there, hugged her, and kissed her on the cheek. Mary loved the attention that she received from him, and it was very hard for Jimmy to hold back the kisses as he was in love with Mary. He hoped that she would follow the Lord in her decision and marry him. He was trying hard to be patient with her, though, as he understood her concerns.

When Mary and Jimmy walked back inside with the platter of steaks, everyone was sitting at the table. The food looked fantastic, as everything was very fresh, including the lemon garlic butter sauce that Jimmy poured over the steaks. Mary had made a homemade lemon and ginger salad dressing that was wonderful.

Elizabeth had also filled each of their glasses with Mary's homemade sweet tea and placed an extra pitcher on the table for refills.

Dinner with the family and Jimmy couldn't have been any better. Mary and Elizabeth were so happy that everyone was together again.

After the kitchen was cleaned, they all met in the living room. Jimmy had something he wanted to share, and everyone was very curious as to what it was.

When everyone was seated, Jimmy stood up by the Christmas tree and said, "I wanted to do this tomorrow night, but I couldn't wait any longer."

Elizabeth ran to get her video recorder, feeling this one would be a memory that she wanted to have forever.

Jimmy waited for Elizabeth to return, and as she sat down, he began to speak again. "I want to begin by saying, thank you all for being so kind to me and not judging me. I have always felt the sincerity in each of you, and your love for me is from Jesus. I can feel Him through each of you."

Mary sat there wondering what in the world Jimmy was up to! Her heart began to race as she had no idea what was happening. Is that an engagement ring in the box, she thought to herself.

Jimmy then walked over to the tree, picked up a small box, and, while holding it in his hand, said, "Mary, you know how much I love you, don't you. I know how important your family is to you, and I wanted them to be here when I did this." He handed her the box and asked her to open it.

Mary sat with her hands shaking; then, slowly, she began to unwrap it. Everyone was watching, and no one spoke. The room was totally silent.

Finally, the package was unwrapped, and as she opened the box inside, she took a deep breath. It was a cross necklace with diamonds shaped into a heart in the center. "Oh, this is so beautiful, Jimmy," Mary said. Everyone got up to see it, and Elizabeth was still standing there filming.

Elizabeth loved the look on Mary's face and enjoyed seeing her happy smile. She wanted her mom to be happy.

Mary loved the cross necklace and, most importantly, was happy it wasn't an engagement ring.

Jimmy shared that he knew that God had brought them together and wanted the necklace that he had given her to be a reminder for them both that Jesus was the only way, and that even when things didn't make sense, if it was His will, then it was the right path to take.

Everyone loved Mary's new necklace. Jimmy's thoughts behind it were special, and Mary understood his words to be true. She just had to walk in it. This was where she was struggling.

It was time for the evening to end and for the family to return to the Inn for bed. Their day had been filled with so many emotions, and everyone was pleased.

Mary and Elizabeth sat on the couch together, looked around the room, and felt joy. It was time for bed, and although they didn't want a perfect day to end, it had to.

Friday morning had come, and the anticipation of being back with their family was exciting.

They spent the entire day together, and Mary quickly thought of them having to leave on Sunday. They had spent the day having breakfast at the Inn, shopping in town, and looking at some of the historic homes that Mary's daddy had wanted to see. They took a carriage ride in the evening just before dark and had dinner by the water. Everyone had a great time, and Elizabeth had pictures and videos to share of their time together.

Before they all left, Mary remembered that she had forgotten to mention to her daddy that they had scheduled massages on Saturday, so she said, "Oh, Daddy, I forgot to tell you that we will meet you, Sarah, and Beth, for breakfast in the morning at 9, and we are all having massages."

He beamed with excitement as he remembered the last one was fantastic and wondered why he had waited so long to have another. Beth and Sarah began to laugh as they all remembered the look on their daddy's face when he came out of the room before.

They all hugged and said goodnight.

Before going to bed, Mary told Elizabeth, "We must enjoy every minute we have together. The weekend will go very fast, and I am already dreading Sunday when they must leave."

Saturday morning came quickly, and they were leaving to meet Mary's dad and sisters at the Inn. They were all having a massage after breakfast. Jimmy had called to tell Mary that he was on his way and would meet them there.

When Mary and Elizabeth pulled up at the Inn, Jimmy had just arrived.

As they walked in together, they could see Mary's daddy, Beth, and Sarah coming out of the elevator. "Perfect timing," Mary said. Her daddy looked rested, and they all agreed they had a great night's sleep. Mary was tired as she hadn't slept as well as she had hoped to.

They walked into the restaurant together and were greeted by a cheerful hostess. "Hi, Mary," she said. She motioned for them to follow her to the table that was assigned to them.

They each had a light breakfast and coffee. Mary's Danish was light but tasty. The food at the Inn was always wonderful!

They had all finished their breakfast when they realized they were almost late for their appointments to have their massages.

Mary quickly stood up and said, "Well, let's go get a wonderful massage."

Jimmy was excited, too, as it had been a very long time since he had had a massage.

Elizabeth wasn't interested, so she stayed in the restaurant and helped the hostess. She felt all grown up and felt like an employee. Mary knew this was a great experience for her at such a young age.

The Inn had organized everything as usual, and Mary felt blessed that Mr. Henry always took care of the bill.

They each went into their separate rooms and agreed they would relax and enjoy their massages. Mary was emotionally exhausted and knew that she would enjoy the quiet time. She was happy that her daddy had not put up a fuss and was also eager to have his second massage in his lifetime. She loved it that he was excited.

The time they were separated went by quickly, and as they were all finished, they met back in the foyer. One by one, you could tell they were all very relaxed as they greeted each other. Mary went into the restaurant to get Elizabeth. She was happy to see her mom but enjoyed her time working.

When they arrived back at the cottage, the temperature had warmed up a bit. Although it was still very chilly, her daddy asked if they could take a walk on the beach. Everyone agreed, and with coats on to stay warm, they headed out to the ocean. Jimmy took Mary's hand, and JJ's leash and Elizabeth walked beside them.

The time at the beach was enjoyable, but the breeze coming off the ocean was cold. They all looked for seashells, which were everywhere. Most had broken edges, but each found one that they loved to keep for memories.

When they returned from the beach, the girls had spent the afternoon preparing some casseroles and homemade rolls for their Christmas dinner. Jimmy and Daddy sat in the living room and watched football. Jimmy loved Mary's daddy, and as they watched the game, you could hear him call a play occasionally. Jimmy laughed as if he was right every time. He had not realized how much Mary's daddy loved football.

The cottage was filled with love, and everyone felt the peace of Jesus. While listening to the sound of the football game and her sisters laughing at the stories they were telling, Mary's heart was filled with love. Family is everything, she thought.

Elizabeth had spent the afternoon recording everything that happened. She really put her heart and soul into it as if it was a real movie she was making. Mary loved it and knew that she was having a great time pretending.

The day went by quickly, and with all the baking, football, and a nice walk on the beach, it was soon time for dinner.

Elizabeth had set the table again with Mary's Christmas dishes.

Except for a few snacks, everyone had skipped lunch and was ready to eat.

Everyone was finally seated at the table, and Mary's daddy asked if he could lead the prayer.

Mary, of course, agreed.

He began to pray. *"Father, thank you for the time here with my daughters and granddaughter. Thank you for also allowing Jimmy to be a part of our Christmas celebration with us. You have blessed our family, and we thank you. Please use this food to nourish our bodies and we ask that you protect us, carry us, and continue to help us to be more like you each day. In Jesus' name, we pray! Amen."*

Mary looked at her daddy and said, "Thank you, daddy!" She loved hearing her daddy pray and having him there with her and Elizabeth.

Mary thought of the scripture in *Colossians 3:20,* *"Children, obey your parents in everything, for this pleases the Lord."* Mary loved her daddy and always wanted to honor him as he was a wonderful father and role model. She knew she was blessed to have him.

Everyone helped themselves and ate until they couldn't eat anymore. The chocolate pie was a great surprise, and as they talked about their mom, the memories of her made it feel as if she were in the room with them.

Mary thought it was time to open gifts. With excitement, Elizabeth agreed. She was the only child in the room, so everyone let her open the first gift. As she sat next to Mary, and began pulling off the wrapping, she was reminded to stop and look at who it was from so she could thank them. This gift was from her grandpa. He looked at Elizabeth with a heart filled with so much love for her. As she pulled off the last of the wrappings, she looked at her gift in amazement. Then she stood up, hugged her grandpa very tightly, and said, "How did you know, Grandpa?" He had bought her a very nice camera that she could use for years. Elizabeth was so happy!

As the Christmas music played softly in the background, one by one, the gifts were opened, and everyone loved them. Beth had made lots of homemade gifts that they could each keep forever, and Sarah had bought all the things they most needed. Jimmy had bought each of them a small gift as it was all that he could afford, but they all loved them anyway.

Mary's book was a great surprise to everyone, and they were all so proud of her!

The laughter and joy in the room were priceless, and although it was a sad time to know the evening was ending, it was filled with memories that would last forever. Elizabeth made sure she had it all recorded, too!

After everyone left, Elizabeth took her camera out of the box and snapped pictures of JJ and Sunshine. She loved her new camera and all her gifts, but she loved her family the most.

It was Sunday morning, and they all agreed to meet at the cottage for breakfast. Mary had been up very early preparing a French toast casserole and had already had a cup of coffee when the doorbell rang. It was Jimmy. Mary opened the door for him, and realizing they were all alone, Jimmy hugged her and began kissing her as if to say he had missed her so much. Mary was wearing the new necklace that Jimmy had given her, and as Mary kissed him back, she realized she was in love with him. She also realized that Jesus had put that love in her heart for Jimmy, and there was no backing out now.

Minutes later, while Mary and Jimmy were in the kitchen having coffee, Elizabeth came into the room. She had her camera in her hand, and before Mary and Jimmy could realize it, she had already snapped a picture of them. They both smiled at Elizabeth and told her to come here. Together, they hugged Elizabeth with the tightest hug and told her they loved her so much.

Elizabeth accepted the hug with gratitude, looked up at each of them, and said, "I love you both, too."

Everyone's hearts were full.

The timer on the oven went off just as the doorbell rang for the second time; Daddy, Beth, and Sarah were there. They had said thank you and goodbye to everybody at the Inn, and their car was packed with their belongings. Mary was very sad to see them all leave, but they were at least able to have breakfast together before going.

When they walked in, they could see the tree was lit, and the fireplace was on; the cottage felt toasty warm. The table was already set, the coffee freshly brewed, and sitting on the table was a glass of freshly squeezed orange juice and a freshly baked French toast casserole with their favorite maple syrup.

Daddy sat down at the table and said, "Well, there is nothing like this in the world. Here with my family and this amazing breakfast in front of me. I wish I could do this every day."

Mary and Elizabeth wished he could, too!

The casserole was amazing, and there was laughter and smiles in the room, but the smiles were beginning to fade. Everyone knew their time together was coming to an end. The time together was a blessing and such a beautiful gift, but they all wished it could last forever.

After many hugs and tears, Mary, Jimmy, and Elizabeth stood on the deck and watched their family drive away. Their hearts were full but sad. Their Christmas celebration had been perfect. They were all blessed, but Mary and Elizabeth knew how much they would miss all of them. They were also confident that the Lord would bring them back together soon, and they had each other - a gift only Jesus could give!

19

A BABY SHOWER

Christmas had come and gone, and as Mary sat with Elizabeth, thinking about their Christmas together with Jimmy and remembering the early celebration they had had with her family, she felt sad that it was all over.

The time with their family had been a time that would never be forgotten. Mary was grateful for every minute she had with her family and promised herself she would never take them for granted. It could be easy to do, she thought. "We must live every day in the joy that Jesus gives us and only one day at a time," Mary said to Elizabeth. "I have learned that we can never predict our life as we would like to; it changes quickly, as I think we both have learned."

Mary thought about the scripture in *Matthew 6:34, "Therefore do not worry about tomorrow, for tomorrow will worry about itself. Each day has enough trouble of its own."* As she shared this with Elizabeth, she was constantly reminded of how she needed to do this herself. Mary was learning not to have too many expectations because life could change so suddenly.

The phone rang, and it was Karen. Mary had called her, and she was calling her back. Mary was happy to hear from her. Although Mary had called to check on her from time to time, she wanted to help her more if she could. But Mary had been so busy with her own plans and knew that she and her family needed time together to bond. She was thankful for the photos of Hope that Karen had sent her and loved each one. Baby Hope was beautiful!

Mary hadn't spent time with her friends for Christmas and hoped they could spend time together for a New Year's Eve celebration. "We will have to make this happen," Mary said.

Karen sounded happy. She was feeling well, and Hope was growing and thriving. Mary was so pleased to hear the great news. Their prayers had been answered. Mary whispered a prayer, "Thank you, Jesus!"

Mary asked Karen if she was feeling up to finally having her baby shower.

Karen insisted she was and that, more than anything, she needed to see her friends. She apologized for not having the time to spend with them during the holidays, but with the sleepless nights and her family being in town since Hope was born, she had not had any time. Karen had had a lot of help from family, and she was so grateful.

Hope was still trying to get on a schedule that accommodated them because she wanted to stay up all night and sleep all day.

Mary remembered the sleepless nights with Elizabeth and totally understood.

Mary asked if she and Sam were getting out at all, to which Karen answered, "We haven't been anywhere really since Hope was born."

Mary thought it would be nice to have the baby shower early in the afternoon and asked if 1 p.m. the day before New Year's Eve sounded good for her.

Karen felt that that time would be perfect.

As soon as Mary hung up the call, she called Patricia. When Patricia answered, she sounded happy to hear from Mary. They talked about their Christmas visit with family and how much they enjoyed it this year. Patricia told Mary about a few of the gifts that Faith had got and how excited she was.

Mary couldn't believe that she and Elizabeth both had cameras. "Oh, Patricia, the girls are going to have so much fun at the baby shower. Guess what? Jimmy bought Elizabeth a video camera, and Daddy bought her a camera."

Patricia was excited and couldn't wait to tell Faith. Mary suggested that they both take pictures during the baby shower, which Patricia thought was a great idea.

Mary asked Patricia if she could still make her famous homemade cookies and a fruit tray.

Patricia told her she would be happy to. She was a great baker, and her friends all knew it.

Patricia also agreed to order and pick up the cupcakes.

Mary was grateful for her help, and they said they would see each other then and hung up the call.

Mary then called Victoria. Victoria didn't answer, so she left a message for her to call her back.

Mary put down the phone and went into her room to get a notebook to take some notes. Elizabeth was in her room watching a movie with JJ.

Mary sat down in her writing chair and thought of what she could make for the baby shower. Their plans for Karen's shower had changed so drastically with baby Hope being born so soon, that she had forgotten what they had discussed.

As she flipped through her notebook, Mary found her original notes. "This should be fun," Mary said to herself. Looking through her notes, she could see everything they had agreed on and thought that it all still sounded perfect.

Patricia had agreed to get the cupcakes, so she marked them off her list. Her original list read:

Karen's Baby Shower

Mary

Punch, Vegetable platter with dips, cupcakes and decorations

Patricia

Homemade cookies and a fruit tray.

Victoria

Karen's favorite Petit Fours, decorated in white icing with a lavender baby boot.

Mary felt a little overwhelmed and realized that sometimes she was just too organized. She needed to relax and not allow details to take over the joy of a simple get-together. She then said, "Well, Patricia had agreed to pick up the cupcakes, so I could cross that off my list. I need not stress over it and just enjoy my friends. The details will work themselves out. After all, nothing is perfect. We will have a great time!"

The phone rang, and it was Victoria. "Hi, Victoria," Mary exclaimed with excitement.

Victoria was excited to hear from Mary. They talked about their Christmas holiday with family and how enjoyable it was for everybody.

Mary was happy to hear her friend's voice as they hadn't talked during the holidays. She realized this was the first Christmas in a long time that they hadn't been together.

Mary proceeded to share that Karen and baby Hope were doing well, and she had talked to her earlier in the day. "Victoria, we are planning to have Karen's baby shower at 1 p.m. the day before, New Year's Eve, and also wanted to talk to you about possibly having a New Year's Eve celebration if we can all work out the details. How does that sound?"

Mary said. "Are you and John available?

Victoria said, "I don't know of anything that we are doing that day, and that sounds great, Mary. I have missed all of you so much!"

Mary was delighted that it looked like all the plans were working out great!

Mary asked Victoria if she could make and bring the items on the original list for the baby shower: Karen's favorite Petit Fours, decorated in white icing with a lavender baby boot on top. Victoria agreed she would, and they agreed to talk later.

Mary checked everything off the list and remembered she needed to go out and get the decorations for both the baby shower and the New Year's Eve celebration. She thought she would go to the party shop downtown, and maybe she and Elizabeth could grab a pizza.

Mary went into Elizabeth's room and asked if she wanted to go grab a pizza for lunch.

Elizabeth's movie was almost over, and Elizabeth said, "Yes, that sounds great!"

Mary thought pizza sounded great, too, after all the holiday meals that they had had so much of. Mary told Elizabeth that they would leave in about an hour.

Mary wondered if Jimmy would like to go, so she picked up the phone to call.

Jimmy loved pizza. When he answered the call, Mary told him what they were doing and asked if he wanted to meet them for pizza in about an hour. Jimmy agreed to meet them and seemed happy about the plans. She explained about the calls she had made to her friends and that they all agreed to Karen's baby shower for Baby Hope.

Jimmy didn't sound too excited about the baby shower but agreed to meet for pizza in an hour and hung up the call.

Mary realized that there had always been so much planning involved in all the years she had worked full-time at the Inn. Maybe that's why I am feeling so overwhelmed. I think I'm tired and would just like to write for a while. She decided after the New Year that she would do just that: start another manuscript.

The thought of the warmer weather, starting another manuscript, working only part-time, and having more time to visit family made Mary's heart happy again. This season is almost over, she thought.

Mary and Elizabeth had arrived at the Pizza restaurant. Jimmy had not arrived yet, so Mary thought she would sit in the car and wait for him.

Mary couldn't wait for warmer weather. She loved the ocean and missed her walks on the beach. Winter was not her favorite season, and since Christmas had passed, she was ready for winter to be over.

Elizabeth saw Jimmy coming into the parking lot.

Mary looked over as he parked in the space beside them. They all got out and greeted each other.

Mary, Elizabeth, and Jimmy walked in, and everyone there knew Mary. It had been a while since they had seen her, so they asked how she was doing. They looked over at Jimmy with a questionable look as if they had never seen him with her before.

When the waitress came over, they had decided on a pepperoni pizza. Elizabeth quickly spoke up to say, "With extra cheese!" Both Mary and Jimmy looked over at Elizabeth at the same time.

Elizabeth was a little shy, so her speaking up like that had surprised them both.

The pizza was amazing, as always, and it was time to go shopping.

Jimmy had decided not to go because he had some work to do at the Mercy Center before dark. He hugged Mary and Elizabeth and said, "I guess I will see you two on New Year's Eve." They all agreed that it was a great plan and mentioned that they would talk over the phone to finalize the plans. They both said goodbye, and Jimmy drove away.

Mary sat there a minute and thought, "Wow, we only have a few days before New Year's Eve." Elizabeth was surprised, too, as they had been so busy that time had just flown by.

Mary knew having the baby shower the day before the New Year's Eve party would be a lot on her, but she knew she could handle it.

Mary put her car in drive and headed to the party store. She needed to pick up the decorations for Karen's baby shower and the party.

When they arrived at the party store, Mary found a parking space right up front. They ran in and, while looking, found everything they needed. The prices were very reasonable, and Mary was happy about that. She had a budget that she wanted to stay within, and the total came below her budget.

When leaving the party store, Mary decided to go by the grocery store and pick up what she needed for the shower.

This time, the parking lot was packed with cars, and she had to park way away from the store. "It's okay, Elizabeth. We need to walk off some of this food we have been eating," Mary said.

Elizabeth agreed, and she was stuffed from all the extra cheese on the Pizza.

Mary laughed.

As they walked in, Mary saw Tiffany at the register. She was happy that she was there and was sure to try and get in her line so they could talk for a minute or two.

Mary picked up everything they needed and headed to the front. Tiffany just happened to be standing at the end of her register and motioned for them to come over. She gave Mary a hug, looked at Elizabeth, and said, "Look at you; you are all grown up."

Elizabeth, with a shy look, said, "Hi, Tiffany."

Tiffany talked about their wedding coming up in the summer and how excited they both were. Mary mentioned she had not received the invitation but to please be sure to send it.

Tiffany was doing well, and Mary was so grateful!

Mary remembered that they had purchased a Christmas gift for baby Hope but wanted to get her something else, so they decided to go by the department store and see what they had there that she could use.

When they arrived and walked inside, the baby department was just to the right. Mary and Elizabeth walked over, and Mary had thoughts that triggered her emotions. She remembered walking into the department when Elizabeth was a baby and looking at all the cute clothes. She remembered picking up a plush musical lamb for her, and as she had that thought, she looked down, and there was one just like it. The lamb played the song "Jesus Loves Me". Mary looked over at Elizabeth and said, "Do you remember having a lamb like this?"

Elizabeth knew exactly where her plush lamb was and told her mom.

Mary was surprised!

Elizabeth had kept it in her dresser drawer and occasionally went back to it and played it. "Well, that's it," Mary said. This is exactly what we will get for baby Hope. Elizabeth picked one up, turned the music on, and smiled. She hoped that Hope would love hers as much as she had.

Mary had picked up the gift wrap at the party store, so they were all done shopping. "We can go home now and put on our pajamas, Elizabeth," Mary said. Maybe cuddle and watch a movie together."

Elizabeth was happy. They needed to both catch up on their rest the next couple of days so they could enjoy the baby shower and the New Year's Eve celebration that was planned.

Mary had not seen Jimmy since they had pizza together and he had not called. She wondered what he was up to but didn't worry about it. Most importantly, she wanted God to lead, and she sure didn't want to get in His way.

The day for the baby shower had finally arrived, and Mary was looking forward to seeing her friend Karen and her new baby, Hope.

When Elizabeth got up, Mary had already been up for a couple of hours, so breakfast was already made. She wanted to let Mary sleep in because she knew school would be starting again, and she would have to be up early on weekdays.

Elizabeth had enjoyed her Christmas break and was looking forward to warmer weather, too.

It was almost eleven a.m., and Mary and Elizabeth couldn't wait to see their friends.

Mary was putting out the last-minute decorations when the doorbell rang. Patricia, Faith, Karen, and Baby Hope were at the door. Mary and Elizabeth ran to open the door. When they walked in, baby Hope was tucked in her carrier, wrapped in a lightweight cotton blanket.

Karen walked into the living room and sat the carrier on the couch. The smiles in the room filled everyone's hearts with joy. Hugs were given and they all walked over to the couch to finally see Baby Hope. She was still tiny but had the prettiest skin, and her eyes were so beautiful.

Faith and Elizabeth giggled while showing off their cameras to each other and were also happy to be together again.

Mary couldn't believe how much hair Hope had already and commented about it.

Karen had her diaper bag filled with all the items she may need and seemed a little nervous. It was the first time they had been out other than for Hope's check-up at the doctor since she was born. Her check-up had gone well, and they all knew she was an answer to prayer.

Karen and Patricia looked great. Mary had not seen them since their Thanksgiving celebration, and they were all happy to be together again.

Elizabeth couldn't keep her eyes off Baby Hope, and Karen noticed it right away.

Karen asked Elizabeth if she wanted to hold her, and Elizabeth said, "Yes, please." She had Elizabeth sit on the couch while she got her out of her carrier and then gently placed her in her arms.

Elizabeth smiled from ear to ear and already loved her so much.

"You are going to make a great babysitter when Hope gets a little older," Karen said.

Elizabeth loved the thought of helping Karen and babysitting for her.

Mary had gone into the attic to bring down Elizabeth's bassinet, which she had when she was a baby. It was covered in a freshly cleaned, soft, lightweight cotton blanket.

Surprised, Karen saw it sitting there and asked whose it was.

Mary told her she had got it down for Baby Hope, so when they visited, she had a safe place to take a nap. She also hoped that she could keep her some for Karen when she felt up to it. After all, Karen had been there so much when Elizabeth was a baby, and now was the time to repay the favor.

A few minutes later, the doorbell rang again. It was Victoria. They were all together again.

Mary decorated the table so pretty. She had also set up another table for Karen and Hope's gifts. The center island was filled with great food. "This will be a little different baby shower than most as usually the baby isn't invited," Mary said. They all grinned, and Karen replied, "I think I like it better this way." They all agreed.

The Christmas tree was still set up in the living room, and Mary had the lights on. She didn't usually take hers down until after the New Year as she loved it and kept it up as long as she could. Everyone was enjoying it, and the mood in the room was peaceful.

Karen walked into the kitchen with the girls and couldn't stop talking about how pretty everything looked.

Elizabeth and Faith were both videoing and taking lots of pictures.

The punch bowl filled with Mary's homemade punch sat in the center of the island.

One cup at a time, Mary poured the punch into each one, handed them to everyone, and said, "Let's do cheers for Karen and Baby Hope!" As each one picked up their cups, they each looked at Karen and said something that was on their hearts.

Karen, with a tear coming down her cheek, said, "Thank you all so much! The last time we were together was at our Thanksgiving celebration, and we all know what happened after that. Thank you each for praying so hard for us. God answered our prayers, and I couldn't be more grateful. I also couldn't be more grateful for each of your friendships. You all mean so much to me!"

Karen still had memories of fear lying in the hospital bed as Hope was in the NICU. She had wanted a baby for so long, and the thoughts of losing her were unbearable.

Everyone was enjoying the food. The cupcakes turned out amazing, and the Pettit fours were delicious!

It was time for Karen to open her gifts.

Everyone walked into the living room, where Baby Hope was sleeping in the bassinet. She seemed to be such a good baby, and so far, no one had heard a peep from her.

Karen opened her gifts one by one. She loved each one, especially the plush lamb that sang, "Jesus Loves Me."

Mary was happy that Karen and Baby Hope were staying for a few hours after the party and hoped that maybe Karen would lie down and take a short nap while she took care of Hope.

Karen looked tired and Mary enjoyed taking care of Hope so Karen could rest a while.

Mary had missed Elizabeth as a baby so much, and holding Hope brought back many memories for her—memories that Mary knew would never leave her heart.

The afternoon was quiet and peaceful. Mary talked Karen into taking a nap. Elizabeth and Faith played in Elizabeth's room and looked through all the pictures they had taken.

Mary got to spend time with Baby Hope while Karen lay down, and everything in their world seemed perfect!

The baby shower had been a beautiful time for the girls and Karen was grateful for everything.

The friendships that God had given each of them were indescribable, and they each knew that life would be very different without each other.

20

A NEW YEAR'S EVE
CELEBRATION

Mary sat by the window, drinking her coffee with her bible in front of her. She was thinking about Karen's baby shower the day before and how special it was. She was thinking about the year that had passed, of the seasons changing in her life bringing a bittersweet feeling to her heart. She began to think about all that had happened: her second book being published, seeing Michael, and the closure she found at the very place they had met: at the edge of the water near her cottage. She thought about the package he had sent and remembered how long it took her to open it. She thought about meeting Jimmy and how God was doing something amazing in his life. She thought about Karen having baby Hope and how grateful she was for their answered prayers. She thought about her readers and how much they had encouraged her, and most importantly, she thought about how good God had been to her and Elizabeth.

Mary recognized the Lord's blessings, and as they all came back to her at once, she became overwhelmed by the Lord's goodness in her life.

In just a few hours, a new year would begin, she thought.

Jimmy was planning to be at the cottage around 2 p.m. He was making homemade meatballs and pasta for their New Year's Eve celebration. When she initially asked him about making them, he seemed hesitant. Mary suspected it may have been because she had already told everyone he was making them before she had asked him.

Patricia, Paul, Victoria, John, and Faith were planning to arrive at 5 p.m.

Karen, Sam, and Baby Hope were going to be a little later, as Sam had work to do before coming by to pick Karen and Hope up so they could all drive together to meet Mary and Jimmy at the cottage.

Patricia was making her famous homemade bread. Victoria was bringing a vegetable tray with dip and a fruit tray. Karen was making a dessert; but that, she'd insisted, would be a surprise.

Mary thought about how well they had planned the party and was pleased that she and her friends would be together when the New Year rang in.

Mary felt a little irritated about Jimmy's response about making the meatballs. "I can't believe that he wouldn't be excited about it or is it that I made plans for him without asking him first? I guess I was wrong, but he'll get over it." Mary felt something in her spirit that she didn't like. She seemed to have some pride inside of her from the sound of Jimmy's voice on the phone. She prayed that the feeling would leave her. Mary knew she was tired, and she had too much going on. She wanted to do all these things, but really, she just wanted to close the door to her room and write. Writing was what she enjoyed doing the most, and somehow, it took her mind off everything. "That's what I enjoy about it, I guess," Mary whispered to herself.

The doorbell rang, and Mary could see Jimmy standing at the door. Mary welcomed him in. She was happy he was there, and he seemed happy to be there. However, she was still puzzled as to what he had been doing all day. But he didn't seem to want to tell her.

The punch that was left from the shower the day before would be served for the party. Mary had put it away and planned to add ice cream and pineapple juice to it when she put it back out.

Jimmy was working hard in the kitchen, and the cottage smelled like an Italian restaurant. He had made Mary meatballs before, and they were delicious. Mary couldn't wait to try them.

The New Year's Eve celebration had begun, and everyone, especially Jimmy, had a lot to celebrate!

As everyone brought in the food they had all prepared, Mary set it out on the bar. Jimmy was finishing up the meatballs and pasta, as he liked to fry them in the pan before adding them to the sauce. This made them extra tasty, and Jimmy knew it, as all the drippings from the pan went into the sauce, giving the sauce an amazing flavor.

While Mary looked at the bar displaying all of the food, she realized Karen's dessert wasn't out.

Karen was sitting on the couch nursing Hope when Mary walked into the living room and asked her, "Did you make dessert, Karen?" with a smile that Karen knew well.

Karen answered, "I told you it was a surprise, Mary."

"But where is it?" Mary wanted to know.

Karen didn't reply.

Mary shook her head and, with a smile, walked back into the kitchen. Jimmy was sweating from standing over the hot stove and Mary asked him if she could get him a glass of water.

"I thought you would never ask," Jimmy said.

Elizabeth and Faith were playing in Elizabeth's room and, from time to time, would come out to take pictures and film everyone. They loved feeling like photographers and always played the part well.

Jimmy had put the meatballs and spaghetti on the table, the bread was sliced, and Mary had prepared a salad.

It was time for dinner.

The conversation in the cottage was a great sound. Everyone was laughing and talking about different things.

Baby Hope was sleeping peacefully in Elizabeth's old bassinet and the night felt perfect.

Jimmy was a talker, and people enjoyed listening to him. Sometimes, though, he didn't know when to stop, and Mary thought he needed to work on being a better listener.

Mary finally tapped her spoon on the counter, startling JJ who'd been snoozing on the couch. "Let's have dinner," she announced.

Everyone came into the kitchen and sat at the table.

Mary looked over and asked Jimmy if he would bless their food.

Jimmy had not been praying from his heart very long and Mary didn't want to embarrass him, but she loved hearing Jimmy's prayers and thought he would be okay. He began to pray. *"Father, thank you for this special evening with Mary, Elizabeth, and our friends. Thank you for a new year that will be here in just a few hours, if you allow. We pray that you will continue to help us daily to walk in your will and your will alone. Thank you, Lord, for this food. In Jesus' name, we pray."*

Everyone was grateful for his prayer and, at the same time, said, *"Amen."*

The food was incredibly delicious, and everyone was soon stuffed. The talk around the table about Jimmy's meatballs didn't stop until most of them were gone. This made him happy as he enjoyed the confirmation.

Mary looked over at Karen and, with a look of anticipation, Karen asked Sam if he would open the cooler she had left by the front door, and bring in what was in there.

Sam left, soon returning with a beautiful homemade blueberry cheesecake. Everyone said, "Whoa! Karen, you outdid yourself." Karen beamed with pride as she also enjoyed serving her friends.

While Karen sliced the cheesecake, Mary removed everyone's plates, replacing them with dessert plates. Then they all had a slice and it was better than delicious!

With full tummies and happy hearts, the girls cleaned up the kitchen while the guys went outside to sit by the fire pit.

After the kitchen was cleaned, Karen picked up Hope from the bassinet and put her in her baby pack. Then, she, the girls, Elizabeth, and Faith went to join the guys.

The night was filled with laughter, stories, and great food. Occasionally, Jimmy would tell a joke that he thought was funny, and everyone would laugh with him. He wasn't the best joke sharer, but everyone sure loved him.

It was 10:30 p.m., and in no time at all it would be New Year. Mary looked over at Jimmy, who was talking to Sam. He looked a little nervous. Sam had a serious but joyful look on his face.

Mary looked at Karen and said, "What's Jimmy saying to Sam?"

Karen didn't know.

After about an hour or so of sitting by the fire pit and listening to everyone's stories, Mary realized the time, as she wanted to be inside at midnight. Jimmy took Mary's hand and led her back into the house. Everyone followed them.

Seconds later, Jimmy waved his hands, silencing everybody. He then asked Mary if she would stand with him next to the Christmas tree. A little confused, she did as he asked. Jimmy got down on one knee, reached into his pocket, opened the box he had in his hand, and while looking intently into Mary's eyes, said, "Mary, you are the most amazing woman I have ever met. I am so grateful to God that you and Elizabeth are in my life. Mary, I couldn't think of anyone else I would rather spend the rest of my life with. Will you marry me?"

Mary had tears flowing from her eyes.

You couldn't hear a sound in the room. She looked over at Elizabeth, who also had tears in her eyes too. She nodded to her Mom, so Mary answered, "Yes."

Jimmy got to his feet, picked her up, twirled her around and around, kissed her, and said, "I love you, Mary!"

Elizabeth came over and, as he sat Mary back down, Mary reached for them both, hugging them with joyous laughter.

Everyone in the room applauded. Then the countdown to another year began. Three, two, one, and everyone shouted, "HAPPY NEW YEAR!"

The New Year's Eve celebration was a huge success!

But would Jimmy and Mary get married?

21

LETTER OF FORGIVENESS

Mary sat in her writing chair sipping her hot drink. The lighting in the room was dim as the sun had just begun to rise. She had been sitting there for about an hour thinking about her life. She thought about Elizabeth and how much she had grown to love Jimmy. She thought about her friends and how grateful she was for them. She thought about Baby Hope and how much she had grown through the Spring season. She was playing the New Year's Eve celebration over and over in her head and couldn't believe that Jimmy had surprised her the way he had. Although they had not set a date yet, they were both happy, and Pastor Butch would not give up telling them that he had their wedding vows written.

Pastor Butch had been there on many occasions when Jimmy had needed him. He had been their pastor for some time. He was modest man who always had a smile that reminded everyone who knew him of the heart of Jesus.

Pastor Butch loved Jimmy and prayed that God would fill his heart with His love and help him to walk with Jesus.

Mary loved the sound of the birds chirping outside the window.

It was almost summer, and Mary and Elizabeth were happy that school would be out soon. Mary's part-time job was going well, and she enjoyed writing and spending so much more time with Elizabeth.

Mary had decided to spend the entire summer with her daughter. On the days that she had to work, she would take Elizabeth with her - unless, of course, her daughter had the opportunity to spend the day with Faith. They enjoyed sleepovers, and Patricia loved having her stay with them. Mary knew that no matter what, it would work out.

Jimmy had taken on a role in marketing, doing sponsorships for a racing team. He was very good at his job and loved meeting new people. He had a great personality, and everyone loved him.

Jimmy had not seen his family since their trip together to visit them, but he had talked with them on the phone a lot. They had discussed going to the beach during the summer as a family, and they had asked him if he could bring Mary and Elizabeth along. They had enjoyed their visit with Mary and wanted to get to know Elizabeth as well. They talked about bringing James and Maddie, too. Jimmy was excited about it, and Mary was thinking about whether they would take the trip or not. If they did, they were hoping to go as soon as school was out for the summer.

Jimmy's parents were happy to see him doing so well. They were still a bit nervous but grateful.

The sun was finally shining brightly, and as she got up to get another cup of coffee, Mary thought about going for a walk on the beach. She didn't want to leave Elizabeth alone, but she didn't want to wake her either. She decided to go, so she reached into the cabinet to pull out a to-go cup for her drink. She thought she would leave Elizabeth a note so she wouldn't worry. JJ was still asleep, too, but she thought about taking him. She changed her mind as she wanted JJ to be with Elizabeth. She pulled out a notepad and began writing the note. *"Elizabeth, Mom is taking a short walk on the beach. I will be back shortly. I didn't want to wake you. I love you!"*

Mary grabbed her keys and coffee and walked out on the deck, locking the door behind her.

The sun felt great as Mary strolled down the walkway to the beach. She hoped she would find another seashell that spoke to her heart. The waves were crashing onto the shore, and the sound of the ocean was always so breathtaking for Mary. She loved her cottage and hoped she never had to move.

As she reached the shore, she saw two people walking together. It must be tourists, she thought. She continued walking, enjoying being barefoot, as she had left her shoes up on the walkway just before the steps. Mary enjoyed walking right on the edge, so the salt water splashed on her feet as the waves rolled over them. She could see the couple coming closer to her and thought how nice it would have been to have Jimmy with her.

Mary looked down, and what she saw was amazing. Washing up on the shore was another bottle. "Wow," she said. She walked over to it and, as she got closer, she saw the cork was missing. "Oh, this one is empty," she said. Mary had hoped that there would be another mysterious message for her to read, but this time there was nothing. She wondered if there had been a note, and the cork came out somehow. She loved the bottle and thought, well, I'll keep it anyway. Even without a message, maybe it was once important to somebody.

Mary had lived at the cottage for many years now and found it strange that she had never seen a bottle wash up like that. Then, this year, she had found two!

As she picked up the bottle and wiped the sand off it with her hands, the couple she had seen down the beach was walking passed her. As she looked over, they smiled and wished her a good morning.

Mary answered with a "Good Morning" of her own, smiling back at them.

As she went on her way, it suddenly occurred to her that the man looked like Michael. But it couldn't have been, she thought. My mind is playing tricks on me. Why would he be here?

Mary realized she had been walking for a while and needed to turn back. She didn't want Elizabeth at home too long by herself.

As she wandered along, she found a seashell that she knew she had to keep. It was another heart-shaped one, but this time, the fragments that had broken off were what made it heart-shaped. The right edge was worn, and she thought about her life with Edward and then with Michael. Mary thought of the scripture in *Psalm 147:3, "He heals the brokenhearted and binds up their wounds."* She began to pray, *"Father, thank you for loving me and for healing my broken heart. I could have never guessed that my life would have been shaped as it is today with the pain of my past relationships, but You, Lord, are merciful, You are wonderful, and You are my best friend. Thank you, Father. In Jesus' name, I pray."* Mary had peace once again, knowing that everything that had happened in her life, pain or joy, had shaped her into who she was, and she was grateful.

Mary had arrived back at the cottage, and when she opened the door, she could see Elizabeth in the kitchen. She was flipping pancakes on the griddle, and Mary couldn't believe her eyes.

"Elizabeth, wow, you made mom breakfast," Mary said with a tone of gratefulness.

Elizabeth told her she heard her when she went out and saw the note that she had written to her, so she took JJ out for a walk, fed him, and decided to make breakfast. "Mom, I love surprising you," Elizabeth said.

Mary was amazed how mature Elizabeth was becoming. Half of her was happy, the other half was sad to see her growing up so fast.

When Mary looked at the table; Elizabeth had already set it. There were two glasses of orange juice poured. Elizabeth asked her to have a seat, and with a smile so big that it almost hurt, Mary sat down. Elizabeth brought the platter of pancakes over and sat down with her mom.

The pancakes were so good, and Mary and Elizabeth were happy. Elizabeth had learned so much from Mary in the kitchen and knew that scratch-made pancakes were the best.

After breakfast, the phone rang. It was Jimmy. As soon as Mary picked up the phone, Jimmy said in an exciting tone, "Mary, I talked to Mom and Dad this morning, and they have already booked the condo at the beach. They plan to be there in less than two weeks. Mary, they are bringing James and Maddie and would really love for us to go. Can we?"

Mary thought about it for a minute, looked over at Elizabeth, who had heard the conversation, and with a smile on her face, Mary agreed they would go. Everyone was happy that they would finally all be together.

Jimmy had a call and asked Mary if he could talk to her later. Pastor Butch was calling. She agreed they would talk later in the day, and they hung up the call.

The rest of the day was filled with chores and grocery shopping. Mary and Elizabeth had lunch at the pizza restaurant, and it was yummy, as always. They were both looking forward to school letting out for the summer in a week. Everyone was excited about the beach trip, including James and Maddie. They were excited about meeting Elizabeth for the first time too.

"We don't have a lot of time to prepare for the beach trip," Mary said to Elizabeth as they were driving back to the cottage. "It's only a couple of weeks away."

The phone rang, and it was Jimmy. "Mary, Pastor Butch keeps reminding me of our wedding vows, and I told him we didn't have a date planned yet. I told him we were going to the beach in a couple of weeks, and he was welcome to come down to meet my parents. He said he would be down there on Wednesday night."

"Jimmy, he doesn't think we are getting married there, does he?" Mary said.

Jimmy answered that he'd told him they were not.

"Okay, good," Mary said.

Jimmy then said, "It will be nice to see him, though, and I'm happy he will get to meet my parents. He has done a lot for me, you know."

Mary agreed.

When Mary and Elizabeth arrived back at the cottage, they unloaded the car and put away their groceries. Elizabeth went to her room and pulled out her small suitcase and began packing for the beach. Mary walked in and said, "What are you doing, girl?"

Elizabeth laughed and said, "I'm packing for the beach!"

Mary laughed, too, and said, "Well, we aren't leaving tomorrow."

They both began to laugh, and Elizabeth said, "I'm just excited!"

Mary was happy that they were going to a new beach, one that Elizabeth had not been to. After all, they lived in a cottage at the ocean. Something new is always good, I guess, Mary thought.

Mary walked into her own room and into her closet. She saw the box from Michael still sitting on the shelf. She wanted to talk to Elizabeth but just couldn't do it. She did not want to break her heart with anything like that. After all, she's happy. Let's not change it. At least for now, anyway.

Elizabeth had also got her in the mood to think about what she would take to the beach. She thought about her outfits and knew that she wouldn't pack anything dressy, as they would probably make meals at the condo most of the time to save some money. She really didn't know what to expect but figured whatever she brought would be just fine. She closed her closet door and thought, I'll do this next week.

It was Friday, and the week had gone by way too fast. It was Elizabeth's last day of school, and Mary could not believe how fast the school year had gone by.

When they arrived home, the phone rang. Mary didn't recognize the number on the caller ID. Reluctantly, she picked up the call, and a quiet lady said, "Hi, is this Mary?"

Mary with a hesitant tone, said, "Yes, this is Mary." The lady on the other line didn't sound familiar at all, and before Mary could speak, she said, "Hi, I'm Cindy. I was reading the newspaper today and saw a letter, a message that was found in a bottle, that I guess you found."

Mary's mouth dropped open, and Elizabeth could feel the atmosphere in the cottage change. Mary muted the phone and called Elizabeth to come in. Elizabeth came into the room with a look of concern on her face. She thought something must be wrong. Mary looked over at her and whispered, "It's that Cindy." Elizabeth couldn't believe what she was hearing.

Elizabeth sat there listening; she could not believe that God had answered her prayers, and they'd found the person the letter was written to.

Cindy said, "Hi, Mary, are you there?"

Mary began to speak. "Yes, I'm here. Can you hear me?"

Cindy began to share that she had seen Johnny's letter in the newspaper and wanted to know if she could meet her somewhere to get it. "I think that message was to me, Mary."

You could hear her trying to hold back the tears on the phone.

Mary and Elizabeth were shocked. They could not believe that they were going to meet Cindy, for whom the note had been written.

They arranged a meeting the next day at 9 a.m. They planned to meet at the local café for breakfast.

The evening was quiet, and as the fireplace warmed the cottage, Mary and Elizabeth sat and talked about the note, Cindy, and their meeting the next morning. This was not planned, but they knew, regardless, it was important. They had to fit it into their schedule.

They talked about the sound of Cindy's voice and how she must be feeling after reading the note in the newspaper.

Mary was sad for her. Elizabeth felt the same way.

It was getting late, and they had to get to bed. After all, they needed to get up much sooner than expected.

Mary checked on Elizabeth, and she was already asleep. She was tired from her day.

Mary had showered and was in bed, lying next to JJ. She couldn't get the letter off her mind and how God had allowed her to find it. She prayed that in some small way, she could be Jesus' hands and feet and bring two people back together.

She then had a thought that surprised her: unlike Michael and I, that's for sure.

Morning came, and Mary had slept soundly all night. She couldn't believe she had slept until 7 a.m. She instantly remembered her meeting with Cindy at 9 a.m.

Mary walked into the kitchen, and her coffee had already finished brewing. She had the timer set, and she loved that. As she poured her drink, she thought about getting Elizabeth up, but decided to let her sleep a while longer.

The cottage was a little chilly from the night air, so she turned on the fireplace, sat in her favorite chair, and opened her bible. As she sipped on her coffee and read, she thought about Cindy. She couldn't focus on her reading and so began to pray. "Lord, I need you to please guide me with the words to say to Cindy as we meet this morning. *Father, only you know what happened in that relationship. I feel hearts are broken, and I pray that you restore them and they'll have your will in their lives. In Jesus' name, I pray, Amen.*"

Mary returned to her bible and found complete comfort. As she enjoyed reading and spending time with the Lord, she found peace that the Lord would carry her through her day.

As she walked toward her bedroom, she stopped at Elizabeth's room to wake her. But Elizabeth was already up and sitting on her bed. Elizabeth looked over at her mom standing at the door and said, "Mom, I'm excited about today. We will finally know a little more about Johnny and Cindy and I thank God he is giving us this chance to find some closure to this story."

Mary smiled at Elizabeth and said, "Me too, baby. Now, let's get ready so we can go."

Elizabeth and Mary got dressed and met back in the kitchen.

Time had passed quickly, and it was already 8:30, and they still needed to take JJ out. He had slept in, and Mary and Elizabeth were surprised.

Finally, they pulled into the parking space at the café. Neither Mary nor Elizabeth knew what Cindy looked like or how to find her.

As they walked in, they saw a lady sitting by herself. She looked a little sad. She was wearing a blue sweater and jeans. Her long blonde hair was put up in a ponytail, and she wore glasses. Her glasses were a light color and looked a little too big for her face.

Mary walked over to the table and asked, "Are you Cindy?"

"Yes, I'm Cindy. Are you Mary?"

Mary said, "Yes, I am Mary, and this is my daughter Elizabeth." They said hello, and Mary and Elizabeth took a seat at the booth.

Cindy began to speak. "I tried so hard to show him Jesus. I wanted so bad for him to change. He never would. And now I see this letter from him."

Mary could see that Cindy was still very hurt and broken over their relationship.

It had been years!

Mary pulled out the original note, and as she held the bottle in her hand, Cindy began to cry.

"I don't even know where to find him. When I left, I was sure I would never see him again. Truthfully, I never wanted to. I had given up on him totally, but I never could forget him. I knew he had more in him than that, and he just wouldn't let go of his selfishness! Now, all these years later, this message comes back to me. What does this mean, Mary?" She began to sob at the table.

Elizabeth just sat there. She had no idea what to say, but what was in her heart was real, and she could feel it.

Mary reached for Cindy's hand and asked if she could pray with her.

Cindy said, "Yes, please!"

Mary began to pray. *"Father, I was taking my daily walk on the beach when this bottle came to the shore. I was there when it brushed my foot as I was walking. Father, I wasn't sure until now why you sent it to me, and I'm grateful. Thank you for bringing Cindy into my life, and Lord, may we find Johnny so they can reunite if this is your will. In Jesus' name, we pray, Amen."*

When she looked up, Cindy had pulled a phone number out of her pocket. It was Johnny's.

Mary asked her to dial the number. Cindy's hands were shaking, so she could barely press the buttons on the phone, but she finally dialed the number. She had the call on speaker.

On the 2nd ring, someone answered, "Hello."

Cindy spoke, "Johnny, is this you?"

"Yes, this is Johnny," the man answered.

"This is Cindy."

There was silence. The only thing they could hear on the other end was someone who sounded like they were crying and couldn't speak.

Finally, Cindy heard. "Cindy, is this you? It can't be! Where are you?"

Cindy shared that she was with a friend at the café downtown, and they were going to have breakfast together. Mary found your note in the bottle that you threw into the ocean. "I have it now, Johnny!"

Johnny confirmed their location and, before hanging up the call, said, "I will be there in twenty minutes."

The phone disconnected.

Cindy couldn't believe what was happening.

Mary and Elizabeth sat there in disbelief but gratefulness.

Neither felt like breakfast and while sipping a cup of coffee, Mary looked at Cindy, who was facing the door. Her face turned almost white, and tears began to flow.

Johnny was walking through the door. Cindy jumped up from the table and ran to him. They grabbed each other with a hug that looked as if they couldn't be separated.

Mary looked over at Elizabeth, and they both had tears in their eyes.

Mary motioned for Elizabeth to get up. As they walked toward the door, Mary and Elizabeth both saw God restore two broken hearts and prayed that he would never take her for granted in the future.

Johnny and Cindy had found each other, and both were different people now. The note had found its way home.

22

ANOTHER SURPRISE

The beach trip was only a few days away. Mary had not talked to Jimmy's Mom or Dad, but he had. He had all the information that they needed, such as the location address, and everyone was excited about being together.

Jimmy was arriving to pick Mary and Elizabeth up at 6 p.m. for dinner. It was almost 5:30, and they were ready and waiting for him.

Before he arrived, Elizabeth sat down on the couch next to Mary. Mary scooted up to the edge of the couch, looked over at Elizabeth, and said, "Elizabeth, are you excited about the beach trip?"

Elizabeth, looking down, and in a shy voice, said, "Yes, I think so. I hope I love his family, and we all get along."

Mary then asked her if she was looking forward to meeting Jimmy's children: James and Maddie.

Elizabeth looked a little shy and answered, "I guess so."

Mary knew this was all new for her daughter and felt sad in some ways that she had to experience anything in life that was hard. Mary wanted her life to be perfect. She also knew that she was fooling herself into thinking that it would be.

The doorbell rang, and it was Jimmy. When Mary went to the door to open it for him, she saw a shiny truck in the driveway.

"Jimmy, did you get a new truck?" Mary said.

Elizabeth came running to the door also. Jimmy modestly answered, "Well, it's not new, but it's new to me,"

Mary always wanted Jimmy to feel great and, with a very happy tone, said, "It's very nice, Jimmy. We'd love for you to drive us to dinner tonight. Will you?"

Jimmy, with a humble look, agreed.

After gathering up everything they needed, they locked up the house and walked over to Jimmy's truck.

Jimmy walked over to the back passenger door and opened it. He then had Elizabeth climb in first. He then opened the front passenger door for Mary. "And you, my darling." She smiled and got in, too, glancing around the inside and admiring how new it all looked. Jimmy got in last. He could tell they were happy for him, and he felt grateful.

This gave Jimmy a feeling of confidence.

Jimmy desired to rebuild his life and wanted everyone to be proud of him. Mary was proud of Jimmy, but she'd always been a tiny bit embarrassed about the first truck that the Mercy Center had given him. This one was a lot better! However, Jimmy was grateful for both.

Dinner was great, but the waitress staff was different from what they remembered. The food wasn't the same either.

"Something was different tonight," Mary said.

"Yes, it was," Jimmy agreed.

They hoped it was just an unusual time or that they were short-staffed because they loved the pizza place and didn't want anything to change.

The next few days were busy packing and planning for their trip.

Mary was nervous, and she thought Jimmy may have been, too. He hadn't spent any time with his parents since the trip Mary had taken with him, and he hadn't had a chance to really spend any time with Maddie when he was there. She was in middle school and had a busy schedule with after-school activities. He had talked to both James and Maddie on the phone quite a bit and was very excited about spending some quality time with them.

Mary and Elizabeth had packed everything they thought they needed for the trip. Jimmy was going to pack when he got off work.

Jimmy planned to be at the cottage at 7 a.m. the next morning for the trip to the beach. Mary had more room in her car for all their luggage, so they decided that Jimmy could drive her car.

It was close to bedtime, and Mary wanted to read her bible for a while before bed. Elizabeth had already had her shower and was in her pajamas, watching a movie in her room. Mary walked in and sat next to her.

Elizabeth looked up at her and, after pausing the movie, she said, "Hi, Mom."

Mary told her how much she loved her and asked her for a second time if she was nervous about meeting James and Maddie. Elizabeth said, "Not really. I'm excited about it."

Mary was happy that she was excited; she told her she was going to her room to read her bible for a while and asked if she could pray for her.

Elizabeth said, "Of course, mom."

Mary prayed, kissed her on the forehead, told her to be sure to turn off her TV before going to sleep, and said, "Goodnight, baby."

Elizabeth hugged Mary, wished her goodnight and told her she loved her too.

As Mary walked out of Elizabeth's room, her daughter switched the TV back on. Mary didn't want to smother Elizabeth but wanted her to never forget how much she loved her.

Mary felt sad again. She knew that Elizabeth was about to experience some changes in her life, and she wanted so badly for them to be perfect for her. After all, it had only been Mary and Elizabeth for so long.

Mary then thought every mother desires for their children to have a perfect life.

Mary went into her room, and with JJ lying next to her, she opened her bible. As she read, the words on the pages seemed to magnify off the page. She had to take a second look, and while feeling a little overwhelmed, she read the scripture in *Ecclesiastes 3:11: "He has made everything beautiful in its time. He has also set eternity in the human heart; yet no one can fathom what God has done from the beginning to end."*

"Okay, Lord, I trust you," Mary prayed.

Mary closed her bible, turned off her light, pulled the covers over her, and went to sleep.

Mary had set her clock for 5 a.m. She was sure that would give her and Elizabeth plenty of time to be ready before Jimmy arrived at 7 a.m.

Mary had already discussed with Patricia to bring JJ by on their way, and she was fine with it. Patricia got up early every morning, so it wasn't a big deal. Faith had promised to take care of JJ while they were gone, and Mary had agreed to pay her for the help. JJ loved them, and Mary knew he would be okay there, but she and Elizabeth would miss him. Patricia also agreed to come by the cottage every day to pick up the mail and take care of Sunshine.

Startled by the sound of the clock going off, Mary couldn't believe it was already time to get up. She had slept well.

While walking into the kitchen to turn her coffee on to brew, she began asking God to give her peace. She had no idea what the week ahead would be like, but she hoped it would be peaceful and enjoyable.

As she waited for her coffee, she sat down at the table and prayed. *"Father, you have been so good to me, thank you! You have given me so much more than I deserve, and I am coming to you once again to ask for peace. I am trying to trust You, and I ask that you forgive me for the times that I haven't. Thank you for loving me and Elizabeth. I pray for Your protection, guidance, wisdom, and discernment. Keep us safe as we travel today. In Jesus' name, I pray, Amen."*

Mary's coffee was ready, and she was happy. She wondered how anyone had ever made it through a day without it. Mary thought she would read her bible for a few minutes, shower, and then wake Elizabeth up. Jimmy would be here before she knew it, she thought. She sat for a minute. Then, with a little anxiety about the trip, she got up, and carrying her coffee with her, returned to her room.

Mary picked a simple, blue cotton dress and her sandals for the drive to the beach. She also clipped her hair up to keep it out of her eyes.

After Mary had dressed and had put away all her cosmetics in her luggage, she brought everything out into the living room by the door.

Mary walked into Elizabeth's room to wake her. She was still asleep. Mary leaned over her bed and whispered, "Elizabeth, it's time to wake up, baby. We are going on our trip today."

Elizabeth sat up slowly and sleepily said, "Okay, I'm getting up." She had already laid out the clothes that she wanted to wear, and surprisingly, she had also picked out a simple cotton dress - but Elizabeth's was red. And instead of sandals, she had decided on a pair of white tennis shoes.

Elizabeth crawled out of bed and walked over to the bathroom. As she brushed her teeth, she thought about meeting James and Maddie. She hoped they would like her, and she would like them. "I'm not sure I want my mom to get married," she whispered as she looked at herself in the mirror.

Elizabeth prayed that God would bring her a brother and a sister that she loved and hoped that they would love her just as strongly back.

This was all going to be new to Elizabeth and she knew that. Elizabeth liked her life just like it was. With just her and her mom.

Elizabeth began feeling sad. Her thoughts were more than she could handle.

Mary walked back into the kitchen to feed JJ and to make sure she had packed everything he needed at Patricia's. She had forgotten his favorite toys, as he had been playing with them the night before. She went over and got them and placed them in the bag; now JJ had everything he needed.

Elizabeth walked into the kitchen with her suitcase. As she walked in, Mary asked her to place it by the door.

"Do you have everything, Elizabeth?" Mary asked.

"I think so," Elizabeth said. Then she frowned. "Hold on!" She then ran back to her room, opened her drawer, and got out her stuffed baby lamb. She wanted to take it with her as she loved it, and it brought her some form of security.

Mary loved that she was still fond of something she had when she was a baby. As she opened her suitcase to put it inside, Mary asked if she could just peek through the contents to check to be sure everything was there. Elizabeth didn't seem to mind. When Mary was happy nothing had been forgotten, they closed it up.

Mary had packed snacks for them to eat on the road.

Elizabeth looked through the snack bag and asked if she could bring her favorite cookies, too.

Mary agreed, so Elizabeth ran off to get them. When she returned, she put them in the bag, too.

"This should be a fun day, Elizabeth," Mary said.

Elizabeth agreed. Now she was finally starting to wake up, she looked over at the freshly baked cinnamon rolls Mary had made to also bring along.

"Can I have one of these, Mom?"

Mary said, "Of course, baby, that's why I made them. I already had one, and I also have one out for Jimmy."

After the first bite, Elizabeth, licking her lips, said, "Yum, Mom! These are so good."

Mary smiled. "I think Jimmy will enjoy them too."

As soon as she said Jimmy's name, the doorbell rang. He was standing at the door.

When he walked in, he seemed happy. "Hello, how are my two favorite girls this morning?" he asked them.

Mary handed Jimmy a cinnamon roll, and he was delighted.

Jimmy finished his cinnamon roll and told Mary how good they were. "That hit the spot," Jimmy said.

Mary was glad he enjoyed it. "Now, let's get going."

They packed up the car. Then, soon after, they were driving to Patricia's to drop off JJ. Patricia was waiting for them when they arrived. They hugged; Mary told JJ goodbye with a sad look on her face, wishing she could take him with her.

While walking back toward the car, Mary told Patricia that she promised to call every day.

Patricia, shouted, "You don't have to, Mary."

Mary shouted back, "Yes, I do, Patricia." The two women laughed.

They were on their way to the beach. Jimmy was driving.

The trip went quickly, and the traffic was light. They were all grateful for that.

When the GPS informed them they were only three miles away, Jimmy's phone rang. It was his dad. They had already arrived and wanted to know when they could expect them. James and Maddie were anxious but excited. Jimmy told them they would be there in no time at all.

Minutes later, they were pulling into the parking lot of the rented condo. Jimmy saw his family standing there waiting for them. Elizabeth, peaking through the seats while looking out of the front window, seemed a little nervous. They were finally there, and Mary thought Jimmy looked nervous, too.

It only took a few minutes before everyone was talking. Elizabeth had met Jimmy's parents, James and Maddie, and they all seemed to be comfortable although Elizabeth had become a little shy.

Mary looked over at Elizabeth and whispered, "It's going to all be okay, baby."

Elizabeth nodded her head back to her as if saying, okay, mom.

Mary hugged James and said hello to Maddie and his parents.

Jimmy, with a tear in his eye, looked around at everyone, realizing that he was back with his family at last and he felt very blessed.

Jimmy, Mary, and Elizabeth took their luggage to their rooms.

Jimmy's mom made a tray of ham, turkey, and cheese sandwiches for everyone and put chips and pickles on the bar. They had lunch together, chatting away happily. After a while, everyone wanted to go for a swim, so they put on their swimsuits and met at the pool. Mary was sitting in one of the lounge chairs next to Jimmy and was watching the children play. James, Maddie and Elizabeth seemed to be having a great time together.

This made Mary very happy as she was concerned about how they would get along.

Mary wanted more than anything for Elizabeth to be happy. It looked as if she was.

Mary could never imagine Elizabeth ever hurting, being sad, or anything but joyful. She knew she was fooling herself as she knew life wasn't perfect for anyone.

They all had a great time together and the week was going too fast. It was filled with laughter, walks on the beach to see the sunrise and sand between their toes. Jimmy rode waves on boards with the kids while Mary watched from the shore. Jimmy's Dad didn't like being in the sun for too long; he always seemed to get sunburned, so he was always the one at the condo making lunch for everyone. The bonding time had been incredible for all of them.

Jimmy's Dad and Mom were so happy to be spending time with Jimmy, and Jimmy loved every second with them and his children, as well as Elizabeth and Mary.

The phone rang, and it was Pastor Butch. He was on his way. Jimmy's Mom and Dad were unsure of why he was coming, but Jimmy reassured them that the pastor wanted to meet them and get to know them. It was already Wednesday.

When Jimmy answered the call, he asked Mary if she wanted to walk over to the condo. She agreed that it would be fine and told Elizabeth she would be right back. Very confused, as she didn't know what was going on, they left the pool and began walking to the condo.

Back at the condo, Jimmy said, "Pastor Butch is on the way, Mary. He thinks we are getting married tomorrow." He then asked, "Are we getting married?"

Mary then said, "I don't know, do you?" They went around and around a few times with the same questions until Mary finally said, "Well, I do, if you do."

They realized they didn't have a marriage license, and Mary didn't bring anything to wear to get married in.

Jimmy called his mom on her cell phone and asked if they would mind watching the kids for a while. He told them they were driving an hour away to do some shopping and would be back soon. She agreed that she would watch them, and it wasn't a problem.

Jimmy and Mary drove over to the county office, and with only fifteen minutes left before it closed, they walked out with their marriage license. They realized on the way back that they didn't have wedding rings, but it was too late for that now. Pastor Butch was there waiting for them.

When they arrived back at the condo, everyone seemed a little confused. Jimmy and Mary announced that they were getting married the next morning on the beach. Everyone seemed excited for them - but were they?

Elizabeth looked a little unsure of how this would change their lives, and Mary was very concerned, mostly for Elizabeth, but she had to trust that the Lord knew exactly what He was doing, and she had to walk in His will. After all, Pastor Butch had written their wedding vows at 3 a.m., and he was just waiting for the right time to marry them. This was that time!

Mary was sad that her family was not there too and knew they would be totally surprised when they heard the news.

That evening Jimmy and Mary met with Pastor Butch for a couple of hours while he counseled them. The kids were inside, watching a movie together. He talked about many things and Mary was tired and ready for it to all be over with. She knew this decision would change her and Elizabeth's life forever.

The next morning, at 4 a.m., Jimmy woke Mary up and said, "We must go somewhere and find a couple of wedding bands."

Mary got up, dressed, brushed her teeth, and they left. They found a popular retail store that was open 24 hours, parked, walked in, and went straight to the jewelry counter.

The jewelry counter was closed until 8 am. Jimmy went to the manager and shared that they were getting married at 7 a.m. and needed to buy a couple of wedding bands. He graciously opened the counter, and before Jimmy and Mary knew it, they were holding their wedding rings in their hands. They were beautiful with three engraved crosses on the front. Although they only cost $700 in total, they were pleased.

They then thought about some other things they needed. They needed flowers. They found the artificial flower department and picked out flowers for Jimmy's mom and a couple of flowers for Mary to hold. Although they were artificial, Mary was grateful that they looked real - from a distance anyway.

The bakery had fresh doughnuts, so they grabbed a box on their way to the check-out line. Jimmy and Mary both laughed as they thought about doughnuts being their wedding cake.

Jimmy and Mary had what they needed. They guessed they were getting married, after all.

When they arrived back at the condo, Jimmy's mom came out in a beautiful white flowing dress. She looked like the bride. "Mary, I bought this dress with me because I didn't know if there would be a wedding this week," she said.

Mary looked so confused and said, "Well, I am the bride, and I sure didn't expect to be getting married this week. Why is it that everyone knew this but me."

Everyone laughed.

It was very early in the morning. Everyone was ready for a wedding.

Pastor Butch led everyone down to the water. With sand between their toes, Jimmy and Mary stood looking at each other. The sunrise was magnificent, and the breeze from the ocean was incredible.

With the warmth of the sun shining on her face, Mary still had some fear and felt a heavy burden for Elizabeth. She had spent many years as a single mom and in some ways felt, if she controlled her daughter's life with her protection, Elizabeth would have a perfect life.

Mary had developed distrust in her heart that had created fear of her own choices as her sincerity and love had been taken advantage of so often. Her heart was still hurting, and she was afraid.

As Mary glanced over at Elizabeth, Maddie and James, she saw looks of concern but also joy.

Mary knew the scripture in *1 Corinthians 14:33*, *"For God is not a God of disorder but of peace – as in all the congregations of the Lord's people."* She whispered a prayer, *"Lord, is this confusion coming from my broken heart or from you?"*

Standing by the water's edge, Jimmy looked at Mary with a smile that showed confidence and humility.

Jimmy's mom, dressed in her beautiful white flowing dress, looked more like the bride than Mary. After all, a wedding had not been planned, and Mary did not feel ready. But was she?

Jimmy's dad stood by his wife of over 40 years with a humble look on his face. He had no idea why a marriage ceremony was being performed, but he approved.

Pastor Butch stood with the family and, while sharing the message that God had put in his heart at 3 a.m. months ago, Mary submitted to the will of God for her life and remembered the words He often reminded her of in *Matthew 8:26*; he answered, *"You of little faith, why are you so afraid?" Then he got up and rebuked the winds and the waves, and it was completely calm."*

Pastor Butch asked Jimmy to place the ring on Mary's finger, and as he did, while looking over at Elizabeth for approval, she said, "I do." Mary could feel a sense of peace. She knew immediately that only God could calm the storm of fear she had going on in her heart as she relinquished the feeling of control over her own life and submitted to His will and His alone.

Pastor Butch then asked Mary to put the ring on Jimmy's finger, and he said, "I do." Mary knew there was no backing out now.

Jimmy was smiling from ear to ear. He was happier than Mary had ever seen him.

As Pastor Butch said the words, "I pronounce you husband and wife," the bond of Holy Matrimony was sealed.

Having no idea what the future had in store for her and Elizabeth, Mary's faith became more real that day than it ever had. She knew her life was God's. She realized that loving Him with all her heart, soul, and mind and walking in complete faith in His will for her life was her only choice.

She also knew that God makes everything beautiful in His time and seeing Jimmy's life being transformed was a blessing. Mary's life was being transformed too.

Although not at all what Mary had expected and certainly not the dream wedding she had imagined, Jimmy and Mary were now husband and wife.

The memory of this day would be etched into the hearts of everyone forever. Will the anointing moment of Pastor Butch writing Jimmy and Mary's wedding vows at 3 a.m., as asked, be revealed as a testament to God's sovereignty, and will Jimmy be the man of God that Mary had prayed for?

Mary had no choice but to follow God's will for her life and by His grace, she did. She knew He would lead the way as Matthew *7: 13-14 is clear, "Enter through the narrow gate. For wide is the gate and broad is the road that leads to destruction, and many enter through it. But small is the gate and narrow the road that leads to life, and only a few find it."*

Will their marriage be what Mary had always desired?

Mary was confident that she would allow Jesus to lead and that whatever happened after this day would be for His glory!

AFTERWORD

Thank you for reading *When Jesus Leads*, the sequel to *When Jesus Calls*, and a venue for Martha to share her heart with you.

All scriptures used in this story are there to remind us of how amazing God's love is. He loves us and can use our failures for our good. Genesis 50:20 says, *"You intended to harm me, but God intended it for good to accomplish what is now being done, the saving of many lives."* When we repent of our sins and trust Him, we can believe that we will see the glory of God in our lives. Faith is believing in what we can't see. He is waiting for you right now. He loves you deeply.

God bless you and my prayer is for everyone reading this story to come to know Jesus in a personal way. It will be the most important decision you will ever make in this lifetime. Do not believe the lie of the enemy. You are worthy, in Jesus' name.

Martha Gayle used Mary as the main character in her When Jesus Calls series as she desires to be more like Mary in God's word and a little less like Martha. They currently live in the Smokey Mountains of Tennessee with their two Shih Tzu's, Mumford and Biscuit. Remington and Jake are two more of their favorites. They live outside in the pasture.

Sadly, JJ has passed away, and we still miss him every day.

Elizabeth is happily married and lives in N.C. with her husband. James and Maddie are happy; they are all grown up and living in the Mid-West.

Jimmy and Martha are still waiting for grandkids.

Look for my next book as this story continues.

Visit my website at marthagayle.com

John 11:40 says, *"Did I not tell you that if you believed, you would see the glory of God?"*

Always Believe! Never Give Up!
Martha Gayle

INTERNATIONAL BIBLE SCRIPTURES FOR REFERENCE

John 3:8

Matthew 8:26

Ecclesiastes 3: 1-2

Psalm 17:8

Psalm 16:11

Ephesians 4:2-3

Matthew 6: 14-15

John 4:18

Philippians 4:7

Psalm 56: 3-4

Ecclesiastes 3:11

1 Peter 5:7

Proverbs 4:23

Psalm 23

Exodus 14:14

Romans 12:10

Ecclesiastes 8:6

Like 15:32

1 Corinthians 1:27

Acts 4:13

Matthew 6: 25-34

John 4:18

Romans 12:10

Colossians 3:13

1 John 4:12

Hebrews 12:14

Genesis 50:20

Colossians 3:13

Ephesians 5:25-27

Psalm 31:3

Matthew 11: 28-30

Philippians 4: 6-7

Luke 15

Proverbs 19:21

Romans 8:28

Daniel 9:9

Proverbs 3: 5-6

Matthew 19:26

Matthew 8:26

John 12:24

Matthew 17:20

1 Corinthians 13: 4-7

John 11:40

James 1:17

Luke 15:7

Colossians 3:20

Matthew 6:34

Psalm 147:3

Ecclesiastes 3:11

Matthew 7: 13-14

STUDY NOTES

STUDY NOTES

STUDY NOTES

STUDY NOTES